FLOODGATES
Mary Calmes

Dreamspinner Press

Published by
Dreamspinner Press
5032 Capital Circle SW
Suite 2, PMB# 279
Tallahassee, FL 32305-7886
USA
http://www.dreamspinnerpress.com/

Floodgates
© 2014 Mary Calmes.

Cover Art
© 2014 Reese Dante.
http://www.reesedante.com
Cover content is for illustrative purposes only and any person depicted on the cover is a model.

ISBN: 978-1-62798-737-0
Digital ISBN: 978-1-62798-738-7

Printed in the United States of America
First Edition
March 2014

Readers Love Mary Calmes's

Old Loyalty, New Love

"I thought this one was lots of fun and really liked it. *Definitely* recommended."

—Joyfully Jay

"FANTASTIC! Miss Calmes did it again! What an amazing shifting story and so much promise there for more.... I want to express my delight about this new story and that I sincerely hope that Mary Calmes will be continuing this as a series."

—The Blog of Sid Love

"This story had passion, suspense, humor and action The combination of passion and chemistry, want and needing were just the right mix to send my romantic heart a flutter. Overall a winner of a story and I will be waiting and hoping for more of this series."

—Sinfully Sexy Book Reviews

"It's pretty much got the whole package. You will walk away feeling like a part of the story and wanting to know what happens next and for me that's what makes a great book."

—Guilty Indulgence

"This book was picked for me for a challenge and it is an absolute gem. As my 3rd book of 2014 it has gone straight into my favourite pile and will definitely be re-read."

—Prism Book Alliance

"Mary Calmes has done it again with *Old Loyalty, New Love*. As usual, her characters have exceptional depth and make you feel as if you know them personally."

—The Novel Approach

"Beautiful and captivating story about friendship and loyalty told within the world of shifters."

—The Romance Reviews

By MARY CALMES

NOVELS

CHANGE OF HEART SERIES
Change of Heart • Trusted Bond • Honored Vow
Crucible of Fate

A Matter of Time Vol. 1 & 2
Bulletproof • But For You
Parting Shot

Acrobat
Floodgates
The Guardian
Mine
Old Loyalty, New Love
Three Fates (anthology)
Timing
Warders Vol. 1 & 2

NOVELLAS
After the Sunset
Again
Any Closer
Frog
Heart of the Race
Romanus
The Servant
Steamroller
Still
What Can Be
Where you Lead

THE WARDER SERIES
His Hearth • Tooth & Nail • Heart in Hand
Sinnerman • Nexus • Cherish Your Name

Published by DREAMSPINNER PRESS
http://www.dreamspinnerpress.com

To Cardeno C., thank you for all your tremendous support, and Lisa Horan, I always feel better after we talk, and finally to Lynn West, without whom nothing of mine would ever have a title.

CHAPTER
One

THE SHOT went off over my head, exploding the horrible framed picture of dogs playing poker. I had always hated it, had complained that it didn't belong in our upscale office close to Jackson Square, but shot into a million pieces was a fate I had never imagined it having.

I dove under the desk and crouched there, hearing men going from room to room, yelling out that there was no one there to whoever was still in the room with me. I knew they were waiting, hesitating, because they weren't sure if I had a gun or not. If they'd known where they were, the answer would have been self-explanatory. But if they had checked, they would have never been there to begin with.

They were in the wrong place on an early Wednesday morning in October because someone hadn't done their homework. They didn't know at this point that they'd made a mistake. They would, and there would be hell to pay on their end, and there was some consolation in that for me, but it didn't help at the moment. I was still about to be dead at thirty-three because someone had, again, confused one brother for another.

Weighing my options, I considered going out the window or out the back. I had seconds to decide. The window would be faster, but it had a frame, and since the building was a historical one, chances were good that it was sturdier than it appeared. There was no guarantee it would give under my weight. Plus, I didn't have much space to build up momentum, and there was the glass to consider. The back door was safer all the way around… if I didn't get shot. The "if" was kind of funny since, when we moved to our office from the old one close to the Embarcadero, and I had brought up his infamous brother to him, Dimah Mashir had assured me that, honest to God, nothing exciting was ever going to happen. His brother, Kirill, was the one involved in nefarious pursuits; he, Dimah, was the legitimate one. As I ran around the office, a lamp exploding beside me, papers blowing up off my desk, chunks of bookcase whizzing through the air, the whole room blasting apart, my only thought was that if I lived through the attempt on my life, I was going to rip my partner a new one.

Flying into the hall, I hit the wall hard, bounced off, turned, and saw a guy running in with what looked like a semiautomatic pistol in his hands. I wheeled around and took off in the opposite direction, toward the back. The only advantage I had was that I knew where I was going and they didn't.

I skidded around the corner, went right, then left, through the small staff kitchen/breakroom, into the conference area, out the other side, and down the stairs to the door with the panic bar. What didn't help was that the door had an alarm—it was a fire exit—so the bells went off the second I hurled it open. At least I had a little head start.

Up and over the chain-link fence, and then I came down on the hood of a car on the other side. I lost my footing and banged hard, bounced, and then slid off into gravel. Normally, I was a bit more coordinated than that, but as I had been in the process of making coffee since the cup I'd had on the way in wasn't enough, I was not at the top of my game.

Hearing sirens in the distance, I covered my head with my arms as I ran, completely missing the calf-high chain sectioning off the parking lot. I tripped forward down onto the hood of a parked black Mercedes Benz. It was lucky I fell, though, so that the bullet hit my left bicep and not the back of my head. Sometimes it just didn't feel like luck until the end.

THE COPS came, and, of course, the second I gave my name—

"Tracy Brandt."

—the question came.

"Brandt?" And then, "Any relation to Inspector Alexander Brandt, now Agent Brandt?"

What was I going to do, lie? "Yes," I groaned. "He's my brother."

They wouldn't have known—no one knew every Drug Enforcement Agency agent off the top of their head—but Alex had started out as a cop here in San Francisco, so a lot of guys knew of or remembered him. So the officer nodded slowly before turning away and yelling over his shoulder, "Call Brandt over at DEA!"

The whole time I sat in the back of the ambulance getting checked out, answering questions fired at me, I was hoping and praying that my brother would come alone. I wasn't up to seeing his old partner. The fact that they didn't work together anymore improved my chances.

"You're bleeding," the EMT noted.

Checking my left bicep, I looked where she was pointing. "Bullet must have grazed me."

"We need to get you to the hospital."

"Oh yes," I said happily. "Let's do that."

The look she gave me was funny. Apparently most people weren't excited to go to the hospital. But it was a quick trip, and by the time we were on our way and I thought about whom I could possibly see, as opposed to whom I was hoping to avoid, it was too late.

The day was going from bad to worse.

I WAS sitting on the little bed in the ER, waiting to be bandaged up, having had the lavage already—fancy word for "rinse"—when my phone rang. I answered without checking the caller ID because I was bored.

"Tracy."

Just the sound of the man's voice, his accent, told me who it was. "Dimah."

"Are you hurt?"

"I was grazed by a bullet, nothing serious."

Silence.

"It's okay."

"No."

"Yes, it is," I assured him. "I'm just glad Marta is out on maternity leave so she wasn't in the office with me. I think—"

"I will come there."

"No, don't. I'm fine, I promise."

"I want to see for myself."

"It'll be a whole thing," I warned him. "Agent Brandt, right?"

"Your brother is no concern of mine."

I sighed deeply. "I'll come by around five."

"It is ten in the morning now. Do you expect me to wait hours to see you?"

"I—"

"No," he said gruffly. "When you are done, wherever you are, I will be there."

"You really—"

But he'd hung up, and calling him back would be useless.

"Tracy?"

Looking up, I saw Katie Crenshaw, one of my ex's best friends. They had come to the program at County together. I had thought we were also better friends, but when he and I separated, she had disappeared from my life.

"Hello," I greeted her.

She rushed across the floor, but when she reached for my face, I tipped away from her touch.

"I don't deserve that," she said flatly, and I saw how wounded her eyes looked.

"I have a doctor," I informed her.

She took a quick breath and thrust a cordless phone at me, probably the one from the nurse's station that I had seen my ex use. I didn't take it. There was no reason for me to do anything she asked. "Please, Tracy, just talk to him."

I took the phone and put it to my ear. "Yes?"

"Are you all right?" Breckin Alcott, my ex, sounded scared. "What happened?"

I cleared my throat. "Bullet grazed me. It's no big deal."

He caught his breath. "No big deal?"

"Really. Dr. Lin says I'll be perfectly fine, with a nice scar to tell the tale."

"You should see Amir Kattan in plastic—"

"I think a scar sounds romantic."

"You—"

"I'm fine. Thanks for calling. I'll talk to you—"

"Wait."

So I did. It was still a habit, listening to him. You didn't stop doing something after two years even with a four-month moratorium.

"I want to come home."

I cleared my throat, and when I did Katie drifted away from me across the room, giving me space. "I heard you've got a nice place in Pacific Heights with your new salary bump. Why would you want to come back to Noe Valley with me?" I sounded petulant I was sure, but my arm hurt.

"You know why."

And I almost got sucked in; I was that close to tumbling into the trap of the same old argument, the familiar back and forth, all over again. But I stopped myself before it escalated. "I don't think—"

"Are you sure you're okay?"

He diverted me, and I let him because it was the polite thing to do and I was my father's child. "I'm fine," I soothed him, lying, my voice cracking a little with how scared I still was. The adrenaline had left by the time the police arrived, and I couldn't seem to stop shaking. "No worries."

He huffed out a breath. "But I do worry. I'll leave for the airport now and—"

"Where are you?"

"I'm in Chicago; I'm supposed to be here until Friday, but—"

"Are you there on business?"

"Of course I'm here on business!" he snapped defensively, and that was new. It had never happened before I came home early from my five-day family reunion in June and found him fucking his friend Sean Granger on our couch. I had left my dad and my brothers in Tahoe because I had missed my boyfriend. He hadn't been able to get the time off—an ER doctor's schedule was not his own. But it turned out he had the weekend off. My fairy tale had ended right that second, and now all I could think about was how beautifully it had begun.

People were forever looking at us, the gorgeous hot blond doctor and his... assistant? No one ever looked at us and thought, *Oh yeah they fit, they're a couple*. On some couples it was easy to spot the connection, but not us. And I loved that. I loved the way eyebrows would raise when the most breathtaking man in the room passed everyone else up to reach me. I got a charge out of it every time. Sometimes after a few drinks—bravery by bottle—we would get asked. How? What made Breckin Alcott ever stop and look at a plain guy like Tracy Brandt?

"He had to stop," I always said. "I was bleeding, after all."

"No." Breckin would grin—the one that made his eyes sparkle—and then run his fingers through my hair. "It was his sense of humor. I'm a slave to his laugh."

My sense of humor runs to the absurd, and it was that, above all else, that drew him to me. I had never stopped traffic; I did, however, stop Breckin Alcott in his tracks.

I was on my way to work, late, as usual, with the four other people I carpooled with, when we were hit by another car. It was one of those accidents where the person at fault is easily recognizable, as well as the victim. In our case there were five of us. The car rolled over what felt like seventy-five times but I guess was actually only once. We ended up on a hill.

Now the "hill" part is relative when you're talking about San Francisco. People call them hills, but they go straight up and straight down, so the angle can be more precarious than the word "hill" implies. Everyone got out but me and my friend Matt. That was okay with me as he was, and is, one of my favorite people in the world. The two of us were on the crushed side, so we were pinned in there pretty good. I heard him start to breathe a little weird, so I asked him if this little fix we were presently in was going to keep him from his hot date later on.

"Oh shit," he swore from the front seat. "I do have a date tonight, don't I?"

"Yes," I reminded him, putting the leer in my voice, "with the hot sportscaster."

"Tracy, honey, that man is so fine." He sighed, turning his head around to look at me. "And the package was lookin'—oh, Jesus, your eye's bleeding!"

I shook my head at him slowly, wanting him to be less screechy—small area and all that. "It's, like, my eyebrow or something. Don't worry about it. Just tell me about this guy. Hell, we're gonna be here awhile."

"You're sure you're okay?" His voice was rising again, sounding worried.

"Absolutely," I assured him even though my right wrist was going numb. Better numb, though, than the shooting pain that had been happening before. "Hurry up and talk, though, so I don't fret back here."

He nodded. "Okay, so, we met at Spin and he just walks up and—"

"Morning, folks," came the interruption as a man poked his head in the broken-out window.

We both looked at the man at the same time, and he started laughing. Breckin told me later he had never seen two people who were trapped inside a crushed car look so annoyed. It was completely unexpected and refreshing. I suppose most people would panic even after they had been assured by several firemen that they would not be blowing up or rolling anymore. We knew we would get out; it was simply a matter of when. I trusted firemen. They weren't like policemen, who had a difficult reputation. Firemen were always there to help; they didn't hand out parking or speeding tickets or scare you. So when one of them came to the door over and over and told you that they were working on it, I just figured, yeah, they were working on it.

"Our understanding is that it's tricky," I told the stranger in our midst. "If you pull Matt out it puts some strain on where I am and I get crushed, and if you pull me out, the same scenario plays itself out for him. Is that the gist of it?"

"Yes," he said cheerfully.

"Okay, then," I sighed, then took a deep breath. "So what's the plan?"

"I'm not sure; I'm not with the fire department."

"Who are you, then?" I asked. "And what are you good for?"

"I'm a doctor. I'm on my monthly ride-along, and so, here we all are," he finished with a smile.

"Where are you from?" Matt inquired, really looking at him.

"Why do you ask?"

"Because you've got an accent," I said, trying not to laugh. "Where are you from?"

"Why, I'm from Georgia, sir," he informed me.

Maybe because I was losing blood, maybe because I had a concussion, possibly because his eyes were so blue and crinkled in half when he smiled—I didn't know. All I did know then was that he was making me feel better.

"I have never been to Georgia," I said and then looked over at Matt. "But I'm thinking perhaps we should plan a trip soon."

"Oh yes, definitely," Matt agreed. "Let us be off to the state with the peaches."

"You two still having a good time in there?" a voice asked from the other side.

I turned and found Kevin Baylor, our fireman. "Kevin!" I yelled out.

"Kev!" Matt echoed me. "Kevin, my man, give us the good news!"

"Kevin, my love!" I laughed because he was shaking his head like he couldn't believe us. "Get us the hell out of here!"

"What's goin' on, baby?" Matt asked quickly. "Gonna be out in a sec, right?"

He laughed before saying, "Not yet, guys, but we're working on it. We might have to get a crane out here."

"Fabulous," I said cheerfully, looking at Matt. "A crane. Maybe we'll make the evening news."

"TV?" Matt asked. "Am I gonna be on TV?"

"If he's gonna be on TV, we need some stylists in here first."

"Damn right," Matt agreed wholeheartedly.

"Did you call his boss like he asked you to?" I asked my new friend.

"What did the bitch, I mean my boss, say?" Matt asked after a deep intake of breath. "Am I in trouble?"

"She said that you were excused from work today."

"Oh hallelujah," Matt ranted. "Praise the Lord and pass the biscuits, I get a goddamn day off because I'm trapped inside a fuckin' upside-down car."

"C'mon, Kev," I teased the fireman, "you were surprised his boss wasn't more concerned, weren't you? C'mon, you can tell him. You were kinda shocked, kinda taken aback."

Kevin nodded, scowling. "I was a little, if I'm being honest."

Matt laughed out loud. "She's such a bitch," he shouted, reaching out for my good left hand. "I finally have the perfect excuse to get out of work, and there's nothing she can do about it!"

I was chuckling. Matt was giddy and cackling.

"What do you two do?" the doctor asked us.

"I'm an event coordinator," Matt told him. "At Grant Chessman."

"And you?" the doctor asked me, his voice like velvet.

"I'm a bookkeeper at an import-export company," I answered, and I realized suddenly that I was really thirsty. "Hey, Kev, can I have some water?"

"You could have some ice chips."

"Why can't I have water?"

"Why can't he have water?" Matt asked, furrowing his eyebrows.

They exchanged looks then, the doctor and the fireman, and for the first time I felt a twinge of worry.

"Guys?"

"It's in case we have to operate on ya," the doctor answered me softly, his tone designed to comfort me, which it did.

"That's direct and to the point," Matt said matter-of-factly, trying to sound braver than he felt. I could hear the fear in his voice. "Now you two need to go away so I can finish telling my friend about my hot date tonight."

The fireman smiled and rose from his crouching position next to the window, but the doctor didn't move.

"He's serious now," I assured him. "He can get a bit graphic. Might make ya blush."

"Can I take a quick look at you first?"

"Go ahead," I said, trying to shift in my seat so I could get my wrist free to show him. "Look at me."

He leaned into the car then, and it was only at that moment that I realized the door lock was upside down. I was not in my seat; I was sitting on the roof of the car. The dome light was in the crack of my ass, my head was next to a hanging seatbelt, and the reason I couldn't get out was because most of the trunk was beside me.

"Is our friend Sara okay?" I asked. "She was sitting right here beside me."

"It's truly a miracle, but she is indeed all right. Only you and your friend here are looking to have sustained some serious injuries."

"How serious?" I heard the edge in my voice.

"Well." He grinned at me, and for the second time I noticed his warm eyes that were a gorgeous dark indigo, almost violet. They sparkled when he smiled. "I think you probably have a concussion," he answered gently, "and you—" He indicted Matt with a jerk of his head. "—I think you've got a concussion as well. You're both obviously experiencing some shock."

"We're so not in shock," I choked out, "this is us all the time."

Matt laughed then, and I dissolved into a fit of giggling.

The doctor smiled at us and left.

"Oh, he's a dish," Matt said as soon as the doctor was out of earshot.

"He's from Georgia," I told him. "He's a peach."

Matt rolled his eyes and resumed telling me all the intimate details of the sportscaster's anatomy that he had discovered thus far. The first date had been good; the second was sure to be better.

We were not alone long before the doctor reappeared at my door.

"Let's talk a little," he said to me.

"Okay," I agreed. "What would you like to know, Doc?"

"Names would be good for starters," he said warmly, really looking at me, into my eyes.

"Well, my name's Tracy." I yawned. "Tracy Brandt, and this is my dear friend Matthew Sato."

"Pleased to meet both of y'all," he said, and I noticed how his gaze never left mine. "My name's Breck Alcott."

"Breck?" Matt asked. "Is that short for something?"

"Breckin."

"Breckin? Are you kidding? What kinda name is that?"

"Manners," I scolded him.

Matt groaned loudly.

"Listen," the doctor began. "I—"

"For the record," I informed him, "I think Breckin's a fabulous name."

"Oh dear God, stop this shameful display of flirtation," Matt teased me.

"That's good," Breck said, and I saw that he was really, *really* looking at me. "Now, I want to tell you both what's going on out here."

The upshot was that the doors were holding up the car. If they moved the doors to get us out, the car would basically cave in on itself with us inside.

"That's a bummer," I said to Matt, who nodded his agreement.

Breckin shook his head at us. "Here's what we're going to do. We're going to raise the car up off the ground and pull Matt out first. You, Tracy, are wedged in pretty tight, but Matt we think will come out easy."

"Groovy," I told him. I was getting really tired all of a sudden. "Go ahead and get him out. I'm not pissed about being last or anything."

"No, no," Breckin barked at me suddenly, and my eyes snapped open. "You don't get to fall asleep. Not even for a minute."

I hadn't realized my eyes had closed until I jerked back awake. I didn't usually fall asleep so fast. Looking around, though, I realized that it really wasn't so fast. Matt was gone. There was only the doctor and me.

"Is he okay?"

"Matthew will be fine."

"You're sure?" I prodded, looking him square in the eye.

"I am," he said gently, and his eyes softened as he looked at me. "What import-export company?"

"What?"

"You said earlier that you worked for an import-export company. Which one?"

"Zhabin Daher."

He squinted at me.

"Yes," I teased him. "I work for Dimah Mashir."

"Didn't he go to prison?"

"In fact, he did not," I informed him haughtily. "All charges were dropped."

"Didn't he put some guy through a wood chipper and use him for chum?"

"Oh dear God," I groaned as he started laughing.

"Wasn't there some informant that they found with a Columbian Necktie?"

I gave him the most pained look I could manage.

"What?" He chuckled at my irritation. "I heard he's a very bad man."

"You heard wrong." I was adamant.

"Okay," he allowed, putting a hand on my cheek. "I really don't like how dilated your pupils are, so I'm going to go talk to—"

"Wait."

"What?"

I coughed. "Since I'll never see you again after today, I'm gonna tell you something that I wouldn't otherwise."

"Go ahead and talk, but you must open your eyes and look at me."

Again, I hadn't realized my eyes were closed until I opened them back up to look at him.

"Perfect," he said all soft and lazy, the drawl clear in his voice. I just loved the sound of it, all slow and gentle and warm.

"I bet you get this all the time, but you're gorgeous."

"I do," he agreed, grinning at me crazily. "I hear that a lot."

"And you smell really... good, and well, I'm really a smell kinda guy, so that's all good, and your voice is like...." I trailed off, not because I was embarrassed but because I could no longer collect my thoughts. I wasn't sure if it was him being so close to me or if I was losing blood somewhere.

"I hear that all a lot," he teased me, tilting my chin with his hand so I had to look into the dancing blue again. "Tell me some more."

"Whatever," I groaned, lifting out of his gentle hold. "I'm over it now."

When he reached for me, I let him take my hand.

"I think it's the accent that does it," he said, raising my hand to his face and then placing my palm flat against his cheek. "Men—and woman—dig the whole southern-gentleman thing."

I was having trouble breathing. "Are you doing this to keep me awake?"

"Why? Is it working?"

"It is," I confessed, nodding and trying to pull my hand away.

He held tighter, and I asked him to call my brother if I died. Not my dad, but my brother. Better Alex told Dad than the other way around. My father had been the one to have to make the calls when my mother died. Let him be second this time around.

"You're not going to die," Breckin promised me. "I won't let you."

"Hardly fair of you to use all your charm on unsuspecting men," I said, pulling my hand free with a good hard yank.

"Yes, sir," he said slowly, his eyes twinkling as he gazed at me. "I promise to refrain from doing so in the future."

"I don't think it's possible." I was miserable all of a sudden. "I bet you're married or about to be married, aren't you? I bet you're not even gay."

He shook his head. "No on both counts, and I'm bi, actually."

"Yeah?"

"I swear."

"So that's a real thing? Bi?"

He started laughing.

"I just—all the guys I know who swear they're bi are just plain old gay."

"Oh yeah?"

"It's not funny." I was indignant.

"Well, honey, I promise you that bi is a real thing."

I considered that.

"Now, what were you going to ask me?"

"Not sure I want to after the bi thing."

He snorted out a laugh. "Please."

"Fine. Would you go...," I started, but then I trailed off, suddenly remembering who I was. I was not as beautiful as the man. We were not a matching set.

"Would I go...," he repeated, waiting.

"Forget it." I shifted in my seat uncomfortably.

"I will go anywhere with you."

"Ha! You're just saying that because you don't expect me to live."

"You'll live," he assured me. "And we'll go dancing."

"Dancing," I sighed and then heard him talking to me from far away. He was telling me to open my eyes, but I just couldn't, no matter how much I wanted to see him.

The waking up hurt, and when I finally did my dad and my brother were there in the hospital room with me. My brother Alex was asleep with his feet on the edge of my bed, and my dad was asleep in a chair by the window. The doctor was standing beside my bed, looking down at me.

"Hey, Doc," I croaked up at him.

"You've got an awfully concerned family here," he said, smiling. "I couldn't get either of them to go home."

"There's one more brother too," I told him, just to be saying something. "And when he hears about this he'll be flying out from New York to make sure I'm really alive."

"Well, you can tell him from me that you are very much alive."

His smile was contagious—I had to return it. "Am I okay? Or are you getting ready to give them bad news?"

He ran it down for me: the mild concussion, broken right wrist, broken ribs, two in all, the cut above my left eyebrow, and a gaping one in my left wrist that had needed fourteen stitches to close.

"But your feet are okay, so I can count on the dancing."

"Awww, Doc, now that I'm okay, don't sweat it. You're off the hook for the dancing."

He leaned down on the bed then, put one hand on either side of my head, and looked at me hard. "I don't want to be off the hook."

"Why not?" I asked him seriously.

"I don't know, really, I just feel that we should go dancing."

"It'll be awhile before I can," I said, suddenly aware that he was looming above me, waiting, not moving.

"I'll just hang around your place until you're up to it."

"Oh yeah? You gonna come by and sit around with me?"

"I think I have to."

"Why?"

"I don't know. There's something, I'm just not sure what."

I reached up then, and with one hand in a cast and the other taped up with tubes coming out of it, put both around the back of his neck. It was so strange to be touching him so intimately, to be thinking of kissing a man I hardly knew. Normally there were steps to a seduction, but my rulebook had gone right out the window.

"You're going to follow me home?"

"I'd like to."

"Why?"

"I just have to." He looked perplexed, almost annoyed. "I can't promise I will feel like this tomorrow," he said honestly, "because this has never happened to me before, and I'm not really sure what it is."

"Like, maybe it might wear off in a while, and you'll want to get the hell away from me?" I teased him, as was my way, at the same time holding my breath.

"Yeah," he said softly, his voice husky. "Maybe."

There was a long silence before I spoke again. "I feel like I've known you a long time."

He nodded. "I feel the same."

Like old love, not new love. Not love at first sight, more like love rediscovered. An "oh it's you" love. Comfortable even before it began. I pulled him down to me and breathed him in before I kissed him. No awkward moment, no jerky movement of uncertainty, no inhibitions. We fit. I felt it, he felt it. I relaxed; I sighed in his arms and held him tight. He would not get away from me. Not that he seemed to want to go anywhere.

But he was right; it could wear off, the feeling of homecoming, and it finally did two years later, the day I walked into my house and my life changed. As days went, it had been one of my worst. The relationship ended as it began: surprisingly.

"Tracy!" Breckin's sharp tone jarred me back to the present.

"Sorry, my mind wandered."

"No, I'm sorry, forgive me," he pleaded.

"It's fine, but I was just making conversation," I explained. "I wasn't accusing you of anything."

"No, I know you, I overreacted and… I just don't want you to think that there's been anyone at all since we've been apart."

"Okay."

"You don't believe me."

"It's not really any of my business," I reminded him.

He coughed softly. "I'll get on the first plane out and—"

"Don't, there's no need. I'm really all right. Just come home on Friday like you planned."

"I won't be in until late, or I'd come by and see you."

"Don't worry about it."

"Could I see you Saturday night?"

"Actually, I'm supposed to go out with Matt, Ira, and Eric on Saturday. We're meeting some of Ira's new girlfriend's friends at Mabon."

"Oh?"

"Did you follow that?" I teased him.

"I did. I speak Tracy. Can I come?"

"Sure," I replied after a minute. "But you have to remember that Matt's still Matt, right?"

"Meaning he's still pissed at me," he stated.

"Yes."

"And will probably always be."

"Probably," I agreed. "I told you to tell him we were just taking a break. He didn't need to know the why. No one but you and I needed to know what was up."

"No, he didn't, and that's my mistake. I thought he would appreciate my honesty and we'd still be friends."

"I think in any kind of breakup, people take sides. I haven't seen any of your friends either."

"Yes, but we're just taking some time, we're not breaking up. We're not done."

He kept saying that, but I didn't believe him, and I wasn't sure he believed it himself anymore. When he had first moved out, there had still been hope, but now, after four months, both of us settling into our separate lives, it was time to use the word "over" because that's what we truly were.

"Okay," I said quickly, not wanting to reiterate, again, that we were through. I had told him that day, that week, when I moved in with Matt and Eric until all his stuff was out of my house, and again when he'd come by once for his mail before the change of address kicked in. We were finished. I had always figured myself for the type to forgive an infidelity, but it turned out that trust was the bitch, not the actual act. I could forgive him fucking his friend on our couch, but wondering if he was going to do it again, that was where the problem lay. Out of sight, I always wondered what, or who, he was doing. So whereas he was talking about us getting back together, I was simply working on remaining friends. I hoped he'd get on board soon before even that wasn't possible. "I gotta go. Do you want to talk to Katie again?"

"Please," he answered, and I was going to pass her the phone, but he stopped me.

"Hey, real quick."

"Yeah?"

"You know we're going to talk about Dimah Mashir when I get home, right?"

Something else that he had no say in—where I worked and with who—that I didn't have the energy to deal with. "Sure."

"No, Tracy, really."

"Okay."

"Good. I'll see you Saturday."

What was I supposed to say? Thanks? I couldn't say I loved him, because it wasn't true anymore. "Great."

Apparently that was enough because he hung up, leaving me to sit there and wonder if trying to be his friend was really in my best interest. Maybe just cutting him out of my life altogether would be, as Matt said constantly, the smartest thing. Hard to know what the best answer was: cut your losses and run or stay and try to build something new on what had been. Everything would have been clearer if I just had some coffee.

CHAPTER
Two

A NURSE came in and dressed my wound, then gave me a tetanus shot that hurt more than getting grazed by the bullet, and when she was done, she told me to hold on for the doctor. Translation: sit tight for the ice age. When my phone rang again, I was relieved it was my buddy Ira Kohn and not my brother.

"Hey, my mom just called me. She was watching the midday news and said that your office was shot up? Is that right?"

"Yeah," I muttered.

"What the hell is going on?"

"You know what's going on," I answered, my voice dropping. "Think about it."

He was quiet a second and then came a long sigh. "Oh, I get it. Wrong office."

I grunted.

"You guys should move down to the diamond district or something. People have to be buzzed in if they even want to look at a stone. Or Chinatown—you can work over a dim sum place."

"How would that be helpful?"

"You like dim sum."

"So clever today, when I almost fuckin' died," I growled at him.

"Did you really, or are you screwing with me?"

I had to lie, or he'd be really pissed. He'd wanted me to quit since he found out who I worked with. Ira and I had been friends since a chance meeting four years ago at the gym. When he'd found out about Dimah

Mashir, that we were partners, he nearly had a seizure. He, like Alex, never let it go. "It was just noisy."

"You're sure?"

"Yeah."

"You're not being brave, are you?"

"Me?"

He chuckled warmly. "Okay, fine. But I think I should come pick you up anyway."

Ira was being so nice, worrying more than usual, and that was so… out of character. Why was he…? "Oh hell no," I flared irritably. "You do not get to use me as an excuse to bail on dinner."

"What dinner?"

"Fuck you, Ira."

"Oh? Wait. Is that tonight?" He sounded so innocent.

"Worst. Actor. Ever," I pronounced. "You know it's tonight."

"What?" he said with way too much squeak in his voice. He was looking for any reason not to go. He was like a wolf ready to gnaw off its own foot to get out of seeing his mother.

"I'm fine; you're the guy taking the shiksa goddess home to his very nice, very kind, but extremely volatile Jewish mother." I snorted. "Lemme know how it goes. You can stay with me if you need to hide after."

"You could come," he said brightly.

"No."

"But my mother loves you. And you're hurt," he said, obviously deep in thought. "She would feel sorry for you and—"

"And if you were engaged to me, she might let you live." I laughed evilly.

He groaned loudly. "She really does like you."

"All parents like me; I'm an accountant, for crissakes. I'm the poster child for dependability."

"Are you really okay?"

"I'm fine, the bullet only grazed me. It's like a deep scrape, that's it. You and I both know if I was really dying, I'd be working it to my advantage."

"True," he admitted.

"Yeah, see? So it's fine. Call me later if your mother doesn't kill you."

"You're so funny," he said sarcastically.

"And by the way, I told Breckin he could come with us on Saturday."

"What?" His voice started rising. "What did you say?"

"Bye."

"No, you—"

"Hang up the phone!" came the sharply yelled order.

I was done anyway, so I ended the call, not even having to look up to know my brother had just stormed into the room.

"What the fuck, Trace?" he snarled at me.

And, of course, because my luck was never that good, I was not only looking at Alex Brandt, my older brother, but also at his ex-partner, Cordell Nolan—Cord, for short.

I was going to have a monster of a headache, I was just certain.

Both men charged across the room, and as they were both big—my brother at six foot three, Cord two inches taller—I felt crowded and smothered, even though at five foot eleven, I wasn't tiny myself.

"How many times have I told you that working with Dimah Mashir is gonna get you fuckin' killed?" Alex barked at me.

I shook my head.

"Yes," he insisted. "Yes, it will. And you can talk that fuckin' bullshit about how Dimah's the good brother and his brother Kirill is the monster, but so you know, there is no record of a Kirill Mashir ever even coming into this country. He died in some Russian prison when he was eighteen, and that was the end of him."

Dimah Mashir and I had met when I was fresh out of college looking for my first job as an accountant. My degree was in management accounting, but I had no great desire to be a CPA. He'd offered me a bookkeeping position at his company, but said there would be a lot to the job.

"I'll get bored if there's not more to it than just crunching numbers."

"You won't be bored; I want you to run office as well," he said in his gorgeous thick Russian accent that made my dick hard.

"How do you know I can do that?"

"I am looking at you, am I not?"

It was one of the nicest things anyone had ever said to me.

Six years ago, after I'd worked for him for four years, Dimah asked me to be his partner, and I had quickly accepted. I had bought shares with my savings, we had signed paperwork, and simple as that, we went into business together. So after ten years of first employment and then friendship, I knew my partner. He was not a liar, and even if he were, he definitely wouldn't ever lie to me. His business—our business—was completely legitimate. I set up things like 401(k)s and retirement packages, I was the bookkeeper, I paid personnel, vendors, and Dimah was in charge of logistics. He did the legwork, went to the wharf, watched goods come in, and shipped others out. Ours was an easy distribution of responsibilities. His brother, Kirill, had his own endeavors and those, from what Dimah told me, walked a thin line between clean and criminal. Being in business with Kirill might get you used for chum if loyalty was not high on your priority list. I didn't know the whole story of why the two brothers weren't partners, and I honestly didn't care. They were completely separate, and since I saw our books on a daily basis, I knew where every penny came from and where it flowed out to. I could say with great certainty that if Dimah said he did, in fact, have a brother, then he did, for certain, have one. A living, breathing one, even if no one else I knew had ever seen him.

"Your partner is a criminal," my brother told me for the billionth time.

"My partner is a businessman," I corrected. Again.

Cord grunted and flicked his moss-green gaze to me. "What's under the bandage?"

"Just a scratch."

Alex growled. "We both know a scratch doesn't get you taken to the hospital in a fuckin' ambu—"

"That's it," I cut my brother off, picking up my phone. "I'm telling. I'm calling Dad right now, so you better watch out."

He grabbed the phone out of my hand, slammed it down on the bed beside me, and then took my face in his hands, forcing me to look up at him. "You scared the fuck outta me. I lost Mom. I ain't losing you."

God, he had to play the mom card? "You realize I'm thirty-three years old, right?"

"I will always be older than you."

Yes, he would. "You can see I'm fine."

He was squinting so he wouldn't cry, but his eyes were red-rimmed anyway.

"Really," I said, yanking free and then putting out my arms for him. "I'm good."

Leaning in fast, he clutched me tight, burying his face down in my shoulder. Underneath the outer persona of prickly, volatile, alpha DEA agent lay his great heart that couldn't take losing one more member of his family. I had to be more sensitive to that fact.

Glancing over at Cord, I saw him shaking his head, the condescension just dripping off of him. He was such an asshole, and he had no right to judge me. When I flipped him off, I saw him clench his jaw in irritation.

"He's fine, Al," Cord growled. "Now ask him why someone would shoot up his office first thing this morning?"

Alex pulled back to look at me. "Trace?"

"I have no idea."

"Hazard a guess," Cord said snidely.

"I don't have one."

"Maybe somebody thought shooting up the office and killing you would send Dimah Mashir a message."

"Like what? Like 'I'm going to shoot the bookkeeper so nobody gets paid'?"

Before Cord could tear into me, Alex excused himself to take a call. We both watched him walk to the opposite end of the room before Cord moved up close to me.

"He was a wreck on the way over here," he said, leaning close.

"Which I'm sorry for, but—"

"Not enough to get another job, though, right?"

"I like my job," I said, defending myself. "And I own half that business."

"You're putting your brother through the wringer for no good reason. Way to be a dick."

"You didn't even listen to me," I sighed. "And I don't tell him not to go undercover for months on end and miss Christmas with his family, so why should I worry what—"

"You could get another job." He was relentless.

"It's not a job," I repeated. "It's my business as much as Dimah's. Should I say it again so you hear me this time?"

"It's selfish," he berated me. "Your brother's in law enforcement; you should show some fuckin' respect."

"How so?"

"By not working with a member of the Russian mob, for starters!"

Russian mob. Was he kidding? "You have no idea what you're talking about."

"You should think about someone besides yourself."

I smiled slowly.

"Tracy," he warned me.

There was no way to stifle my snort of laughter.

"Listen to me—"

"Did you really just say that to me? Think about someone besides yourself? Did that actually come out of your mouth?"

"You—"

"You're giving me life advice? You? The man who doesn't even get first names when he fucks?"

"Tracy—"

"The man who once had a quickie in a men's room when he was on a date with somebody else?"

"I'm gonna kill your brother. Why does he tell you that shit?"

"The man who once washed off a condom with soap and water so he could reuse it?"

"That's not exac—"

"Disgusting is what that is," I apprised Cord, talking over him, shaking my head in revulsion. "Think about someone besides yourself.... Gimme a fuckin' break."

"If you weren't hurt—"

"I wouldn't even be seeing you right now, Cord, so what the hell? Why are you even here? You guys aren't even partners anymore. What'd he do, call you to come give me shit with him?"

He opened his mouth to really give it to me with both barrels, but Alex saw him.

"Cord, lay off," Alex directed from the other side of the room.

I arched an eyebrow, baiting him. "Better listen to your buddy."

"You're a real piece of work, you know that?"

I took a breath. "You know what, Cord, I—"

"Stop," he ordered calmly, surprising me with his tone but even more with sliding his hand around the side of my neck. I went mute as he stroked up and down my throat with his thumb, and I stilled under the surprisingly tender touch. "We were both concerned, not just Alex."

I was stunned. "You were?"

"Of course."

He was worried? He cared?

"We were having breakfast when he got the call, so that's why I'm here. I wanted to come see you. I had to."

Had to?

Staring up at him, caught in the surprisingly warm gaze, I was amazed at my own reaction, at the tingly feeling in the pit of my stomach. Why did being the focus of all Cord Nolan's attention make my chest tighten?

We had a history that was both sporadic and temperamental. We had been dancing around each other for years, almost close and then abruptly apart. The first time I had met Cord, five years ago, was at a party to celebrate him and Alex being promoted. They were both going to be inspectors with the San Francisco Police Department. I had been walking into my brother's loft; Cord had been on his way out on a beer run. The collision wasn't hard, but he'd had to grab me so I wouldn't fall down since he was so much bigger and stronger. It had been like getting sideswiped by a train.

"I'm so...." I couldn't remember what I was saying when I looked up at him. I gave a sharp intake of breath that there was no way he missed.

"You're his little brother, right? Tracy?"

"Yeah," I'd said, all I could manage gazing up into his beautiful olive-green eyes. Combined with the short sable-brown hair, broad shoulders, and thick muscular frame, the man was easily the most beautiful thing I'd ever seen in my life.

"He says you're smart."

It was better that than the alternative.

He smiled slightly, just a trace of softness around his mouth, a crinkle of laugh lines, and my breath caught again.

Fuck.

"He didn't say you were mute."

I had seen beautiful men before, but nothing like him. And it wasn't as though he was movie-star handsome, but there was strength in his face, and between the sharp angled features, the smirking curl to his mouth, and the bored look in his eyes, I was utterly transfixed. Any man who dared me to be brilliant, to dazzle him? Of course I was all over that.

He went on speaking even though I was obviously afflicted in some way. "I'm Cord. Cord Nolan. Your brother's new partner," he finished and extended a hand to me.

I was supposed to touch him and retain higher brain function? There was no way.

He grunted after a minute, dropping his hand. "Okay, so I guess you didn't like whatever Alex told you about me."

There was disappointment on his face, like maybe he'd been expecting more from his new partner's supposedly smart brother. Before he could turn, I grabbed his hand and held it tight. "Sorry."

His eyes widened, and he squeezed my hand automatically.

"I just—" I raked my fingers through my hair roughly. "Sorry."

He ran his gaze all over me, head to toe. "No, it's okay."

"Good," I said, realizing he still hadn't let my hand go and that I hardly cared. Just the slight touch was sending jolts of electric current running up and down my spine.

"I'm going on a beer run. You wanna come?"

And I did, but my brain kicked on. What would prompt him, out of the blue, to invite me? He didn't even know me.

"Come on," he offered seductively, his voice low and full of heat.

Being the focus of all his attention made my cock thicken in my jeans. He was dangerous, it was easy to see, and I wanted to taste him, but…. "Maybe not," I whispered, easing free, taking a step back.

He took one closer. "Why not? You've got bottom written all over you."

Oh... lovely.

"You can ride my cock in the car, and we'll be back here before the party even gets going."

I understood. The man was a big-time player. He saw me as a quick diversion, a meaningless notch in his bedpost, utterly forgettable. Obviously he had an itch that needed a scratch, and there I was, looking up at him with hungry, needy, puppy-dog eyes. I would have offered to fuck me over the hood of a car on the side of the road too.

"What's the matter?"

I was such an idiot, still susceptible to his breed of bad boy at twenty-eight. "Alex."

"Your brother doesn't need to know, does he?"

"No, of course not."

"Then come on, just—Where ya goin'?"

I didn't realize I had been walking backward, inching away, as I spoke to him. "Nowhere. I... I just don't fuck like that."

"Like what?"

"Like it doesn't mean anything."

"So to you it has to mean everything?" he asked dryly.

"No, just more than nothing."

He scoffed. "No one-night stands for you, huh, princess? Don't you think you're a little old to be saying no?"

"And you don't think you're a little old to still be fucking in your car?"

"I'm only seven years older than you." He winked at me. "That's not ancient."

And he was right; thirty-five wasn't a fossil. He was a year younger than Alex, both of them having joined the police force right out of college. They had started as patrolmen and were then on the inspector track—a job Cord would keep and my brother would leave to join the DEA—but at the time, the way he sounded, defensive, made me wonder who Cord was trying to convince of his maturity.

"I have years before I even think about settling down."

"Sure," I said, walking by him.

He caught my arm. "You're sure you only do serious?"

"I do."

"Your loss," he assured me and left.

It had been the beginning of a mess. Every time we saw each other from then on, there was teasing and flirting, irritation, near misses, and endless, annoying banter. There had not, however, ever been Cord reaching out to touch me with tender warmth. That was brand new.

"Trace?"

"Sorry," I said quickly, leaning back, away from him, away from his touch, not wanting to let my guard down, ever, with Cord Nolan.

"No, you're fine, I just—"

"I was grazed by a bullet," I explained quickly as my doctor walked into the room. "But I'm fine now. Please be sure to put that in your report, Inspector Nolan."

He glowered at me, and that was good. I liked us smack dab in the middle of familiar territory. At least some things never changed.

SINCE MY brother and his charming ex-partner had to leave, I figured that meant my office getting shot up was not, in fact, the most interesting thing to happen in all of San Francisco on a Wednesday morning. But that did not stop Alex from sending two police officers to escort me down to the Mission Station to answer questions, write up a statement, wait while it was typed up, read it again, sign it, and then tell the story all over again to another pair of inspectors on the organized crime task force. I was hungry, sore, and cranky by the time I finally got out of there hours later. The only thing that sounded good was my bed.

What was nice was that as soon as I limped out the front door of the police station, a huge Hummer pulled up beside the curb. The window rolled down, and I found myself looking at Pavel Babić, one of the guys who worked for me.

"Hey." I smiled at him as I limped over to the vehicle.

He squinted at me.

"What?" I asked as I reached the door of the car and leaned my elbow on the open window.

"When you set up my retirement plan, you put Slavic and not Russian on the paperwork."

"Yeah? So?"

"That is correct."

"You think I don't check that stuff?"

His smile made his ordinary face quite handsome. "No, I should know better."

I groaned and bent over, trying to stretch out my back. He touched my shoulder. "What happened?"

"A bullet grazed me, that's all."

"Get in."

I groaned as I straightened up. "Food and bed, and that's it."

The back opened, and a man got out and held the door open for me. I didn't know him, which was weird. I knew almost everyone who worked for me, even the guys on the docks. "I'm going," I started to tell him but then thought better of it and leaned forward so I could look inside. Dimah was in the back seat.

"Food," I whimpered.

"*Da*," he agreed sharply, his hand gesture just as cutting. "Come now."

"Dimah," I whined, pushing him like I always did. The man was normally malleable. We were good friends, after all. "I just—"

"Tracy," he snapped, "come here!"

He was acting odd; he was normally much more lenient with me, had been from the start, let me do basically whatever I wanted, but not at present. Something was different.

I didn't want him ranting like a maniac, so I took a deep breath, climbed up into the car, and moved toward the back. I wasn't prepared for the car to move suddenly, and I lost my balance and fell forward against him.

"Shit, I'm sorry," I groaned, trying to squirm out of the man's lap, only succeeding in tangling my legs with his more, my right leg over his left thigh and under his right knee, more on my back than my ass.

"Sit still," he ordered sharply, one hand on my upper thigh, the other on my knee.

I froze, and when I did, I realized how warm his hands were and the strength in them as he maneuvered me off him back up to a sitting position.

When he bent close I caught a whiff of cloves and citrus and something woodsy. I inhaled deeply, and he turned his head and caught me.

"Sorry," I said fast, biting the corner of my lip.

"No," he said gruffly, his ice-blue eyes lifting to mine. "You have nothing to be sorry for."

That close, all I could do was stare.

Dimah Mashir had sharp, sculpted features from his high cheekbones to a strong angled jaw. His long straight nose was gorgeous, and he had a full bottom lip and a thinner top one. The scar under his right eye and the small missing section of eyebrow over it gave me the idea that at some point he'd been in a knife fight. I imagined a battle to the death over some woman who had, of course, rewarded him when his opponent lay dead.

I had a pretty active imagination.

"You will tell me from the start as we drive to Menshinstvo for dinner."

Menshinstvo was his bar off of Sixth Street, close to Market and Folsom. It was kind of local and divey, small, with a kitchen that one of his uncles cooked in only when he felt like it or if Dimah was going to be there. There were always big guys in suits sitting out front, and no one who didn't speak fluent Russian had any business even loitering anywhere near the place.

Slouched in the back of the car, I explained what happened, the abbreviated version, and Dimah didn't grill me or try and make me remember more than I did.

"I have already spoken to Kirill."

I knew he hated to do that. Ever. Dimah had spent his life separating himself from his brother and his brother's world. "You didn't have to."

"I did," he contradicted me. "He had to let those who wanted his attention know that they have mine instead."

"I'm fine."

"Yes, and everyone is fortunate that you are."

"It's not your job to take care of me."

"You are my partner. If not mine, then whose?"

Once we got to the bar, the five of us poured out of the Hummer and walked in the front door.

The strong aroma of garlic and pepper hit me as soon as I walked in, and when we all filled up a table in the back, the first thing I got was a half-full tumbler of vodka.

"I need a soda, or I'm gonna fall asleep."

"Drink," Dimah commanded.

I threw it back, and he poured me another, but a woman brought a pitcher of ice water and several glasses, so I at least got to hydrate.

Dimah made everyone speak English, which was nice of him, and when the pickle plate was brought to the table, I started in on the cucumbers and mushrooms.

"Do you want soup?" he asked me.

Since I got stuck eating borscht the last time I was there, I said no as strongly as I could without offending him. I had barely choked it down.

"No soup this time."

Thank God. "Okay."

He went back to talking with the others and sitting there, drinking, while everyone smoked around me. I started to get really sleepy. When I put my head down on the table, no one said a word to me.

The conversation changed. I heard the English give way to Russian, and after a while, someone's voice was in my ear.

"Are you going to pass out?"

"Hopefully not," I answered Iosif Bazin, one of the guys who worked with Dimah on the logistics end.

"You have so much trust in him, in Dimah. Why?"

"Because he's trustworthy," I answered softly. "We're partners."

"You are strange man not to listen to others, only yourself."

I had no idea why that was odd. "He's a good man."

"You are what keeps him so." He bumped me gently in the shoulder as the table dissolved into laughter that was cut short by a sharp command.

"*Ataide*."

When I sat up, I found Dimah hovering over me, staring down at Iosif, who had taken his spot. He must have gone to wash his hands before dinner, because his coat, suit jacket, and tie were off, and his sleeves were rolled up.

Iosif said something under his breath in Russian without meeting Dimah's eyes and then moved quickly to walk the few feet to the bar.

It was weird; you could feel the tension in the room.

"The bathroom is yours, *dorogoi*," Dimah whispered.

I was being excused, so I didn't argue, just got up, a little unsteadily, and walked back to the bathroom. It was nicer than I expected, so I washed up, even ran cold water on my face, before trudging back to the table.

"*Nye-zaboyteya*," Dimah was saying as I flopped back down beside him.

There were two new guys sitting across from me who I had seen around the office, coming and going, but whom I had never met.

One of the strangers addressed me. "You look tired."

I nodded.

"I am Vassi Leshev," he said, tipping his head at the man beside him. "And this is Danya Kudrin."

Immediately I offered him my hand.

His eyes flicked to Dimah, who gave him the slightest nod. Vassi then took my hand in his, covering it with his other in the two-handed shake I always found so warm and genuine. Danya did the same thing, his gaze locked on mine as he did.

"Pleasure to meet you both," I assured them, smiling.

"And you," Vassi returned hoarsely. "It is not everyone Dimah lets meet his partner."

"Tracy."

I gave Dimah my attention.

"You know I would have never left you alone in the office if I thought for a moment it was not safe."

"No, I know," I replied, bumping him with my shoulder.

He grunted. "Eat now."

I was about to point out that there wasn't any food on the table when everything arrived, hot and steaming and smelling amazing.

"I think he's drooling," another man said, teasing me, and Dimah chuckled.

"Here, you will like this."

And I did. The dish was called pelmeni. It was like ravioli filled with minced pork, and I could eat a million of them if no one stopped me.

There were also crepes filled with cottage cheese that Dimah slathered with apricot jam for me, and more vodka, but I got to take a pass after two more glasses and had tea instead.

Afterward, sated and exhausted, I was afraid I was going to fall into a coma if I didn't get home.

"Get up," Dimah ordered, and I followed his direction.

I shook hands with all the men I had sat with, and then walked with Dimah, Vassi, and Danya back to the Hummer.

Inside, Dimah and I again sat in the back as he gave the driver my address in Noe Valley. I sprawled over the seat, head rolled sideways, looking at him as he gently put a hand on my knee.

"Are you afraid to return to the office on Friday?"

"No, why? Should I be?"

"No," he insisted quietly. "You have nothing to concern yourself with. Those men will not come again, I have made certain."

"Well, no, of course not, they were obviously in the wrong place."

"*Da*," Dimah agreed softly, "in wrong place."

"Wait," I said, my brain fuzzy with vodka and the need to sleep. "Tomorrow's Thursday? How come I'm not working tomorrow?"

"You take the day for rest. You sleep, you eat, and that's all. I will have the office cleaned up tomorrow while you are not there. Friday, you come back. It will be nice again."

"Do me a favor," I said with a yawn. "Don't replace the picture of the dogs playing cards, all right? I saw some nice paintings at that new gallery down the street from us. Let's get some actual art in there."

"Whatever you want, *dorogoi*. You take the checkbook, get what you think."

"Yeah?"

"Yes. Whatever you want."

"Can I do that tomorrow if I want? Shop for the office?"

"*Da*. I will have Vassi bring by the checkbook in the morning, and he can drive. What time do you plan to get up?"

"I dunno. Noon?"

"You're funny man."

"That's what I hear," I said sarcastically.

It didn't take long for me to fall asleep again in the car, and when we arrived at my house, Dimah gently shook me and put me out on the sidewalk. I was confused because he had been so concerned all night, and then to sort of dump me outside my little A-frame with the wood-planked porch seemed cold. But when I swiveled around, almost taking a header over my little white picket fence, I saw Cord sitting on my front steps.

"Why are you here?" I called over to him.

"I came to check on you."

"Why?" I whined without meaning to.

"Because I should."

"That makes no sense," I mumbled as I opened and closed the front gate and started toward him.

"Don't mutter," he scolded me. "If you have something to say, speak up."

"Does Alex know you're here?" I asked, noticing the gold shield on his belt. Normally whatever jacket he was wearing covered it, but he only had a sweater on over a T-shirt, and it was hung up on his holster. I could admit to finding the badge and gun ridiculously sexy; I was as susceptible to the whole danger thing as the next person.

"No."

"Then why are you?"

He changed the subject. "You noticed that your thug partner saw me, right?"

I scoffed at the implication. "My partner is not a criminal."

"Just—"

"Cord," I said softly, reaching him, then crossing my arms as I hovered. "He's not. I would not work with a criminal. Can we give this a rest?"

"Yes, you would, if you thought underneath he was a good guy."

I threw up my hands. "You've got the—"

He grabbed my right wrist and yanked me down beside him on the porch.

"For crissakes, Nolan," I groused at him, straightening up, bracing myself with a hand on his muscular thigh.

"I thought you were going to get married."

"What?" I asked, turning to look at him.

"Breckin Alcott."

"Yeah?"

"Your brother said you were going to marry him."

"I was," I said, sniffling, able to slide over, put some distance between his big, hard, warm body and mine. "I still might. We're taking some time."

"What the fuck does that even mean?"

"Why are we talking about this?" I asked defensively. "Since when do you even care?"

"You smell like smoke and sweat," he snapped disdainfully. "And alcohol."

"Cigarettes and sweat I'll give you, but what does vodka smell like? Nothing. It smells like nothing, so—"

"You're hammered," he accused me.

"I am not." I defended myself, shivering in the chill air.

"Go in if you're cold."

"I am," I snapped at him, irritated. "Why do you always have to bark out orders at everyone?"

"Maybe it's just you," he said gruffly. "You ever considered that?"

And I hadn't, really.

"You don't think about me at all," he mumbled.

It was an odd thing to say, just out of the blue. "That's not true," I said too quickly.

"No?"

"No," I answered, my voice much too breathy, but unable to get any louder. He was just so *there,* in my space, always too close. His height, his presence, the broad shoulders, and the burly chest, all of him made me want to touch, just once, to see what the muscles felt like that rippled under his clothes. I heard from other people that he intimidated them, but I had never gotten that. All I registered was heat. As he leaned close, my shiver was involuntary; there was no way to hide my reaction.

"Go inside," he husked. "I'm just waiting for the patrol car to show up. They got pulled off because someone thought they heard a prowler."

I cleared my throat. "Did it ever occur to you or Alex that if my partner was a criminal, having the brother of a DEA agent working for him wouldn't be too smart?"

His gaze stayed locked on mine.

"So maybe, just maybe, he's a legitimate businessman."

"No, that never crossed my mind."

"And maybe seeing you out here he thought I was your late-night booty call and that's why he left."

"What?"

"Or maybe," I said cheekily, "you're mine."

"I'm your what?" he asked indignantly.

"The man I call to come fuck me at"—I checked my dive watch—"twelve thirty on a weeknight."

He got to his feet, as did I, and only because I'd stepped up to the porch, two up, was I taller than him. On equal ground, he could rest his chin on the top of my head as he was six five to my five eleven. He was bulkier too, covered in thick, heavy muscle. "No one in their right mind thinks you call me and I come running. You're deluded if you think so."

My eyes fluttered at how full of himself he was.

"Trace."

"What?" I asked as he joined me on the porch.

He took hold of my chin and tilted my head back so he was gazing down into my eyes. "Please don't give your brother any more heart palpitations."

"I'll try."

Taking a step forward, into my space, he leaned close, and under the porch lights, I could see the sepia flecks in his moss-green eyes.

"Thank you for waiting for the changing of the guard."

"You're welcome."

His hand was warm, and whether he realized it or not, his thumb was rubbing over my jaw.

"Do you want to come in?" I swallowed so I wouldn't make any telltale whimpering sound of desire. I was hurt, and I wanted someone to lie in bed beside me and watch TV while I slept. Even more, I wanted to be fucked through the mattress. There had been no one since Breckin, and that had been four months ago. I wanted, *needed*, a man. It took everything in me not to yell at him to get his ass in my bed. It was the alcohol, and I knew that, but it didn't help the hunger for him. My inhibitions were nonexistent. I wanted more than anything to be naked under him, under his hands.

"I better not," he said, dragging his thumb along my bottom lip before he let me go. "You're a little too defenseless tonight."

I was going to ask what the hell that meant, but he turned and left me on my front step watching him do what he always did—walk away.

CHAPTER
Three

ORIGINALLY MY agenda for Saturday night had been for Matt, Eric, and me to meet Ira and his new girlfriend, Courtney Abernathy, out at a club they would enjoy. But then Courtney had asked to bring along her two best girlfriends, and I had added Breckin because I was a gutless coward. So what had started out small had gotten bigger than I had wanted, and that was before Alex called earlier in the evening and interrogated me about where I was going. He never questioned—he demanded. In the dictionary under "overprotective" there should have been a picture of my brother the DEA agent.

The only part of my plan that remained was the place I chose. Mabon was a mixed club, which was good for our mixed group, and I'd already had a couple of mojitos by the time everyone started showing up.

"Does the bartender make a good cosmo here?" Eric asked me.

"Yeah, really good. Order one."

"Get me one too," Matt chimed in.

"Yes, dear," he said, leaving the high table near the dance floor that I'd commandeered.

Matt leaned in close to me. "I love it when he calls me dear, even when he's being sarcastic."

"Yes, I know." I chuckled. It was nice to see a relationship that worked. All those years ago, Matt had decided after his second date with the sportscaster that he was going to keep the man, and it had been smooth sailing for them from the start. My sometimes obnoxious, decidedly jaded best friend had fallen hard and fast. What was perfect was that Eric Harmon felt the same way about him.

"Why are we here again?" he whined at me. "I wanted to go to Castaway and have the white-peach sangria. Why aren't we there?"

"Because that's a gay club," I reminded him.

He made a circle with his index finger to indicate us both. "We're gay, in case you haven't noticed."

"But Courtney's not," I reminded him, "and neither is Ira."

"Why do I care?"

"C'mon, Matt."

"What? Ira never cared."

"Which makes him a really good sport and us a bunch of selfish pricks."

"How's that?"

"We're shitty wingmen. None of us helped him get laid."

Matt's face crumpled in disgust. "He never wanted to get laid; he was shopping for a wife. Do you not remember going through those online profiles with him?"

"We're still crappy friends."

"Who are crappy friends?" Eric asked as he returned, passing Matt his cosmo and me my third mojito.

"Thank you, sir." I beamed at him.

"Anytime, Trace," he said, flashing me a smile back.

"And we're crappy friends," I informed him. "To Ira."

"Oh, yeah, because we never went out with him to a straight club to pick up women," Eric stated, nodding. "I know."

"You've thought about this too?"

"Sure," Eric answered his boyfriend. "He was always so great about going out with us when we used to do that. That's why we have to make sure to get Courtney to like us."

"It's so nice that we're on the same page." I grinned at him.

"Why do I care about Courtney?" Matt asked Eric and me.

"Because we want her to like us," I explained to him. "Courtney's bringing her girlfriends with her tonight, and we're trying to make a good impression and make them comfortable, so that's why we're here. If Courtney's friends don't like us, then they will take Courtney and Ira away, and we will never see them again. Do you understand?"

"What part of that do you think I don't understand?" he snapped flippantly.

"Well, then, be nice," Eric instructed him. "Those girls have to have a good time. They have to want to hang out with us."

"Everyone wants to hang out with us—we're fabulous."

I groaned, and Eric smacked Matt in the back of the head.

"What was that for?"

"We're really not fabulous," I reminded him. "We're all kinds of boring, and our circle is only five people counting Ira and Courtney."

"Can that be right?"

"We all have other acquaintances we see once in a blue moon, but on a regular every Sunday for brunch, every Wednesday for dinner, and every Friday for drinks basis, when was the last time we were out in a big group?"

Matt opened his mouth.

I cut him off. "Since college."

He went quiet.

"There, you see? Our normal is you, me, Eric, and Ira having dinner, playing cards, and putting in a movie we never finish because we talk through it."

"Which I hate, by the way," Eric chimed in. "I still don't know what happened at the end of *Life of Pi*."

Matt rolled his eyes.

"But really," I pressed, "we've all been friends so long we forget sometimes how to be social."

"And now that Ira's found someone, if we want to keep him around, we have to get her to like us too."

"And it's good practice for when you get a new guy," Eric said, and then he took another sip of his drink. "I mean, I like Ira a lot, but I love you. Matt and me, and you and your new guy, will be bonded at the hip for life."

I looked at him and so did Matt.

"What?" Eric seemed confused at the attention.

"New guy?" I questioned him.

He scowled. "Of course. You're not going to be celibate for the rest of your life, Trace. That's ridiculous. There'll be someone new in our group eventually."

"Not by inviting the ex along there won't," Matt commented.

"What?"

He nodded at his boyfriend. "Yeah. You get to see *him* tonight if he shows."

The *him* could not have been uttered with any more revulsion if he tried.

"Matt—"

"For fuck's sake, Tracy, you don't hold on to a guy who lies to you." Eric's gaze was back on me, and I saw the disappointment and concern in his bright-blue eyes.

"Eric—"

"No," he snapped at me. "He slept with that guy and—"

"I didn't say we were ever going to be more than friends," I pointed out.

"Why would you even be friends with someone who fucked you over?"

"Eric—"

"And you never really loved him anyway."

This was new. "I'm sorry?" I said defensively.

"Guys," Matt began.

"Feelings for, yes. Love, no," Eric went on. "It was infatuation that got way out of control."

"What are you talking about?"

"I'm talking about you and the walking, talking Ken doll."

"He's a doctor," I said, feeling compelled to defend my ex. "He's fucking brilliant."

Matt tried again. "Guys."

Eric made a jerking-off motion. "Yeah. A guy that fucks around on you is a goddamn genius."

"One has nothing to do with the other," I told Eric.

"And he's not," Matt chimed in gently, soothing me and then reaching out to put a hand gently on Eric's cheek. "A genius. Not by a long shot, which is the real point."

I was scowling; Eric had his arms crossed, glaring back.

"Let's just drop it. I see the girls."

I was going to argue with Eric some more—and he looked more than ready to keep going—but Matt told us both to shut up and plastered on a big smile as Courtney and her two best friends, April and Jennifer, crowded around us.

"Hey," I greeted Courtney as she leaned in to hug me.

"Oh, honey, are you sure you should be out? Aren't you hurt?"

I didn't know the other two girls well enough to make a judgment yet, having only met them once before, but Courtney I truly liked. She was so good for Ira—his champion, the whole wind beneath his wings and all that. "I'm fine," I promised her. "You remember Matt and Eric, don't you?"

"Of course," she cried happily, and I saw Matt thaw when she was so obviously delighted to see him again.

"So," Matt said conspiratorially, playing it up with an evil smile, "how big of a drink did you need after going to meet Mrs. Kohn?"

Courtney choked. "Ohmygod, no, she was lovely. Really."

Eric's smile turned even more sinister. "You can dish, g'head."

She was laughing and shaking her head. "No, you don't even know. She was so nice to me. Ira had me so nervous, and it was nothing like he said it would be."

"Ira can be a little… what," Matt said thoughtfully, searching for the right word. "Overzealous in his descriptions?"

"Oh yes," she assured us, giggling. "That's putting it mildly."

"Well, you'll help him with that."

Courtney threw her arm around Matt's neck, which, I could tell, both surprised and pleased him. It was always fun to watch his cheeks flush when he was happy and see the shy smile, the real one, come out.

"Oh my," Jennifer gasped.

"That was over a guy. I used to make that sound," Matt said seriously, leaning close to Jennifer. "Who are we looking at?"

"Right there," she answered, "in the red Henley. Jesus."

"Where are you looking?"

"With the shoulders and the muscles and—damn."

"Honey, what's red to you?"

"Right there," she squeaked out. "Okay, I'll be right—Oh, never mind, here he comes."

When we all finally saw who had captured her interest, Matt and I groaned loudly.

"No, no, no, that is not pretty," Eric said dryly. "That's related, as in brother."

"What?" Jennifer seemed confused.

"Really?" Ira groused at me, back from the bar long enough to hear what was going on. He passed out cosmos to all the girls and took a swig of the black and tan he'd gotten for himself. "Your brother the DEA agent had to come?"

"It's because of Wednesday," I told him. "He's still being overprotective."

He jolted suddenly. "Please tell me the partner isn't coming."

"They haven't been partners for a while," I informed Ira, "and to answer your question, no."

"Oh," Matt whispered, "is he? Is Cord coming?"

"I'm standing right here," Eric reminded him.

"Is he?" Matt pressed.

"That guy is your brother?" Jennifer asked me as her breath caught.

"Ira, how come I didn't know Tracy had a hot brother?" Courtney demanded to know.

"Ira, honey, you can date me," Eric told him. "Because apparently your woman wants the brother, and mine wants the brother's partner."

"As if I could ever get Cord Nolan's attention away from Tracy," Matt scoffed. "That'll be the day."

"What are you talking about?"

He gave me a patronizing look. "Gimme a break, Trace, even you are not that oblivious."

I squinted at him.

He stared at me for a minute, and then his eyes widened. "Oh shit, you really are."

"What are you—"

"Excuse me," Alex said as he reached the table, pushing around the women to step in front of me. "How're you? You feel all right?"

"I'm fine," I grumbled, glowering at him. "Now turn around and meet everyone."

He stared at me.

I widened my eyes, and he followed my directions.

"Ladies," he said, smiling.

All the men in my family but me were handsome. Somehow, as the middle child, I got my mother's birdlike bone structure and lean frame. Whereas my father and two brothers were tall, with swimmers' builds. I was shorter and skinnier, toned, with some definition, but no amount of cardio and weight training could make me into the perfect specimen of manhood that Alex Brandt was, or, even more so, Cord Nolan. Cord was hard all over, with cut, rippling muscles that—

"What about Cord?"

I snapped my head up and was faced with my brother's smirk.

"What?"

"You said something about Cord?"

"No," I said crossly, and then I took a breath. "I need you to be nice to Breckin when you see him, all right?"

He crossed his arms, which made his biceps bulge. "Why would Breckin be here?"

"Just don't be a dick," I warned him. "Go get a drink."

When he turned, Jennifer moved quickly into his personal space. "You're a DEA agent?" she asked him, clearly interested in his answer.

"Yeah."

"I'd love to have you come speak to my fifth graders if you could ever find the time."

I watched him get interested that fast. "Absolutely. Can I get you a drink?"

Shoving the barely sipped cosmo back at Ira, she smiled wide. "Oh yes, please."

Alex took her hand to lead her down to the opposite end of the bar, where the bartender seemed stuck.

"Oh, that was smooth," Eric agreed.

"Yeah, she picked him up like a pro," I told Courtney, impressed. "Damn."

"Fucking teachers," her friend April complained. "Would he have been as impressed if I said I was a lawyer on the partner track?"

"No," Eric assured her, putting an arm around her shoulders. "But you don't want him, anyway. Working class, blue collar... who needs the irritation."

She laughed with Eric, leaning into him.

"Besides," Matt said after clearing his throat, "Tracy has a better brother."

Courtney and April both turned to look at me.

"Evan's not better," I said, defending Alex; it was hardwired in me. "Just different."

"What does he do?" April wanted to know.

"He's an actor." Eric whetted their appetite.

"What kind of actor?" Courtney sounded just as interested.

"Why do you care about this?" Ira asked his fiancée.

"Go get some more drinks," Matt suggested.

"Somebody needs to drink Jen's cosmo," Eric reminded them.

"Pass it over," Courtney said with a cackle.

"Spill about the brother," April prodded me.

"He's on a show on HBO," I explained and watched them both perk up at the news. I smiled; I couldn't help it. "It's called *Cape Cod*."

It was about a political family, loosely based on the Kennedys, and their machinations to get their youngest son in the White House. My brother was not the golden boy. He was the other guy, the villain, who had more fun; the one all the women wanted.

Several minutes ticked by as I watched them absorb the information.

"Ohmygod!" April squealed. "I never miss that! I watch it every week!"

"Me too!" Courtney looked excited, a drink in both hands, as she rounded on Ira. "Why didn't you tell me?"

"It never came up."

"You liar!"

"Shit, Tracy!" he groused at me.

"Why is this my fault?"

"Who is he?" April was dying.

"Tracy, who does he play?" Courtney demanded, her focus back on me. "C'mon!"

I had to think. "Bradley Harrison?" Was that right? "Harrodsburg? No, Harrington?"

Shit.

"You're thinking of the wrong show," Matt apprised me.

"I am?"

He nodded.

"What one was that?"

"That was the one on CBS where he was an FBI agent."

"Oh that's right," I agreed, remembering. "Well, it's not like he's been on the new show that long."

"Three years isn't long?" Matt arched an eyebrow at me.

"Really? God, where have I been?"

"Tracy!" Courtney yelled at me.

"He plays Marco Dahlia," Matt told them, putting them out of their misery.

They both looked stunned, staring at him wide-eyed.

"Oh yes, that's the one." Matt snickered, grinning wickedly.

"Marco Dahlia?" April asked breathlessly.

"Yeah," I confirmed.

"Are you kidding me?"

I shrugged my shoulders and smiled at both of them. "No, I'm not kidding; he's my brother."

"Evan Brandt is your brother?"

"He is," I assured both women.

"So gorgeous," April said adamantly. "So beautiful. Ohmygod, when is he going to visit?"

"Where does he live?" Courtney asked me urgently.

"In New York," I informed them. "In Manhattan. He loves it there, and I love going to see him. I got to go last year with my dad and my boy—" No, I didn't have a boyfriend anymore. "But my brother the agent couldn't go."

"New York at Christmas," April sighed. "Was it awesome?"

"It was amazing."

"Does Evan ever come here?" Courtney pried. "Like, ever?"

I glanced over at Ira, and he threw up his hands in defeat.

"Oh, come on, Ira," Matt teased him. "The man's on TV. Let her be excited."

"Yeah, Ira, let me be excited." She laughed at him.

"I hate you all," he informed us.

I sat and drank while Matt hit the floor with April, and Courtney with Ira. Eric promised to go save Courtney if Ira's dancing started to look more like a seizure and less like he had any rhythm.

It was fun sitting there, watching the club fill up, finally not able to see the dance floor even from how close I was.

My brother came by to say good-bye; he was taking Jennifer and bailing. They needed to talk, and trying to communicate over the top of the charts and trance music was impossible. He said to call if I needed him, and then he was gone, Jennifer clinging happily to his hand.

"Well, that's just great." April groaned as she and Courtney joined me. "So who do I… oh."

From the way her eyes narrowed and her mouth went slack, I knew she'd seen something pretty behind me. When I turned, I saw the man who held her interest.

"Hey," Breckin hailed me as he made his way through the crowd and reached the table.

"Hi," April said, delighted.

He offered her his hand. "Breckin Alcott. And you are?"

Courtney moved close to me. "First your brother for Jen and now this guy for April—holy crap, Trace, my friends are going to jump at the chance to go anywhere with you all."

I watched April move in on Breckin, smile and laugh, and then ask him to buy her a drink.

"Sure," he agreed. "Any friend of Tracy's."

Her mouth opened as he turned to me, running his gaze over my face. "May I look at you?"

"Here?" I teased him.

"Out on the patio, please."

The man was really just stunning—the chiseled line of his jaw, the wide breadth of his shoulders, and his warm blue eyes. His T-shirt was too tight and clung to his sculpted chest and abdominal muscles

"You didn't do laundry," I commented, knowing he was out of clothes if he was wearing the tight T-shirts that normally were only worn under his scrubs.

He stepped close to me and put his hand on my face, stroking his thumb over my cheek. "I don't have anyone to remind me."

"Get a maid. I'm sure you can afford one now that you're working at an actual practice and not at County anymore."

"That's not what I need."

I nodded.

"Could you please come out to the patio so I can look at you?"

"I dunno know if I can afford you now that you've moved uptown."

He leaned close to my ear. "I'll take a kiss in payment."

"Only one? Deal." He opened his mouth to argue, but I patted his shoulder to stop him. "I'll meet you out there. I gotta pee first."

His smile made his eyes glow. "Hurry up."

I got up, told the girls to guard the table, and headed off to the bathroom. It was on the other side of the club, behind the dance floor. The door was heavy when I pushed on it, and the inside was smaller than I anticipated. There were no urinals, and most of the stalls were backed up. I found a working one near the back, and when I was done, I hunted for soap.

"It's official," I told my reflection, smiling at the brown eyes and hair I saw in the mirror. "My club days are over."

"Yes," a voice said behind me, and when I looked up to laugh with whomever it was, I only saw a mask.

I only had time to gasp before everything went black.

CHAPTER
Four

WHO THE hell was that?

Jolting awake, I would have sat up if there weren't hands there immediately to soothe and comfort me.

"Baby, you're okay."

But I wasn't, couldn't have been, because I was in the hospital. White walls, the cold, the smell of antiseptic, the bed I was in, everything let me know I was hurt. I had a tube in my arm as well, which was probably responsible for the lack of pain, which I knew, because I'd been hit, that I should have been in. The last time I'd been in the hospital, the feeling had been the same. Only really good drugs got administered through an IV.

Turning my head, I found Breckin, leaning down to wrap his arms around me. I grabbed hold of him hard, clinging, closing my eyes, and breathing him in.

"You're all right," he assured me, his voice a husky whisper against my ear. "I promise you're okay. Everything's fine."

I nodded but couldn't stop making a funny noise in the back of my throat. It was like when you're crying hard and winding down, the sniffling part that usually won't stop.

"I'm right here."

But that wasn't comforting, for some reason. I was still scared. I didn't feel safe.

"You're okay now, I'm here."

He took a seat beside me on the bed and leaned me against him, trying, I knew, to give me comfort. It was really very kind. But when Alex came striding into the room with a Styrofoam cup, I felt much better.

"Christ, Tracy, you scared the fuckin' shit outta me," my brother griped as he set the cups down, came around the bed, and leaned down to gather me in his arms.

I pulled away from Breckin quickly, needing family comfort, and was surprised when that too didn't take the hollow feeling in the pit of my stomach away.

I hugged him as hard as I could, and he held on to my hand when he straightened up. Courtney and April rushed the bed then, and each took a turn squeezing my other hand. Ira came last, and patted my shoulder. Matt had apparently gone for badly flavored beverages from a vending machine just like my brother, as he too had a Styrofoam cup. When he and Eric crossed the room to me, I knew from their faces that whatever I looked like was bad.

"What?" I asked Eric, knowing the sportscaster would give me the straight scoop.

"Were you beat up?" he asked bluntly.

"I dunno," I said, looking over at Breckin. "Was I beat up?"

"You were hit with something," he told me, shoving his hands in the pockets of his jeans, "something heavy, like a bat or a club of some kind."

I looked up at Alex. "You catch the guy?"

He shook his head. "I wasn't even fuckin' there." His tone gave him away.

"And you couldn't have prevented it if you were," I said frankly, wanting to assuage the guilt I heard in his voice. "So stop beating yourself up. Please."

"This isn't funny, you know."

I smiled suddenly. "Who said it was funny?"

Everyone gasped but Alex and Matt, the rest, even Breckin, not having been around long enough to know that when faced with a crisis, I laughed.

"Who would want to hit me with a bat?" I asked Alex, chuckling because I was imagining someone whacking me with a fruit bat. I was a little loopy.

"I dunno, maybe I'll go ask your scary-ass boss?" he yelled.

"I knew it," Breckin snarled at me. "You're quitting. Today. Now."

"Yes," Alex agreed. "That's what's gonna happen."

It wasn't. "Can you call my doctor in here?" I questioned the nurse who had appeared at the foot of my bed.

"Of course," she assured me, glancing over at Breckin. "It's nice to see you again, Dr. Alcott."

"And you, Angela," he replied. "And don't worry about paging Dr. Cutler; I just called him on his cell."

"Thank you. I'll be back to take patient history."

"I did that for you already."

"Oh, thank you." She beamed at him.

"Of course."

"Am I okay?" I asked Breckin the moment Angela left the room.

He nodded. "You're okay, you're just banged up. You have a concussion, so Tate's going to keep you overnight, but the brunt of the blow was to your upper back and shoulder blades, not your head. You were really lucky. If you had taken the full blow to the back of your head, things might have ended differently."

"Tate?" Matt asked him.

"Dr. Cutler," he informed my best friend since college.

"That's me," Tate Cutler, one of Breckin's old colleagues, said as he breezed into the room and up to my bed.

"So?" I asked him as he got out his penlight and checked my eyes. "Can I go home?"

"Tomorrow," he answered quickly. "I just want to keep you overnight."

"But he's going to be okay?" Alex pressed him, and I noticed how he purposely didn't direct his questions to Breckin or ask him his opinion. In the past two years, that would have been the case. And while Alex didn't know the specifics of why we were taking a break, it had relegated the man to a stranger in his mind.

"He is," Tate said resolutely, finishing up with me.

"He'll be fine?" Matt inquired of my doctor as well.

"Absolutely."

Matt turned to look back at me. "You feel okay?"

"I feel a little out of it," I confessed and was going to say more when I really looked at him. "Why? How bad do I look?"

"I just—" He trembled. "I was scared."

"Come here," I said, lifting my arms for him.

He moved fast, bumping Alex as he dove at me, breathing hard so he didn't cry, dragging air in and out of his nose "There's only Eric and you and… and… I have a lot of… but not you. Not Eric."

I nodded. "I know."

He had such a soft heart, which was why I was glad that Eric Harmon, the man who did the sports on Channel 5 at six and eleven weekdays, saw Matthew Sato's heart quite clearly and cherished it and kept it safe. After Matt came out in college, he'd had no family but mine. And yes, he adored my father and my brothers, but me—I was the one who really mattered.

After Matt pulled himself together, the nurse came in and announced that everyone needed to clear out of the room and let me get some rest. The only people she succeeded in herding to the door were Ira, Courtney, and April. I promised to call them as soon as I got home.

"Where did you leave Jennifer?"

"I dropped her at her place," Alex muttered as he got on his phone.

"Are you going to see—"

"Shut up," he barked.

I turned my attention to Breckin. "You okay?"

"Me?" He choked. "Who cares about me?"

"I do," I said, reaching for his hand. "And you look a little green."

He sucked in a breath, squeezing my hand. "I was scared."

"I'm sorry."

Leaning in, he kissed my forehead. "When I went to the bathroom to check on you and saw you lying there—I'm not ready to lose you."

"If you're gonna get hit," I teased him, tipping my head back to kiss his cheek, "doing it in front of a doctor is a good plan."

"Yeah, well, don't do it again," he insisted.

"I'll try not to."

He calmed, gave me another kiss, and then went to confer with Tate.

I asked Matt to entertain me, so he sat on the end of my bed and explained how the wedding he'd coordinated on Friday night had ended up not happening.

"Why? What?" I was dying to know. Matt's stories were legend. Most of his weddings came off without a hitch. They were either stunning, romantic, or kind of over the top, but every now and then there was trauma.

"The bride caught the groom with her sister."

"Oh shit," I groaned.

"Yeah. And then the sister—"

"Enough, you two," Eric said briskly, cutting us off by snapping his fingers. "Let's get the hell outta here, Matt. Tracy's got to rest. You heard the doctor." He indicated Tate with a toss of his perfectly coiffed head. "He's got a concussion and—"

"Okay, okay," Matt almost whimpered. "Please let's not go over and over it."

"Then come on," Eric pressed his mate before leaning over and kissing my cheek. "Forgive me."

"What?"

"About before," he reminded me. "At the club."

It took me a minute. "Oh, don't be an idiot," I soothed him, hugging him tight. "You just want what's best for me, I know that."

"Yes, but if that had been the last time we spoke…." He trailed off, obviously upset.

"Stop."

He nodded, kissed my cheek again, and then gave me an order. "Get better, baby."

"I will. Thanks for coming to check on me."

"Like we would have stayed away," he replied, walking around the bed to give Alex a hug. He forced a sort of smile, smirk, something in-between, for Breckin, but you could tell it was an afterthought, and for me. And, of course, my brother noticed. He narrowed his eyes, and I knew he was putting things together. There were only so many reasons people took breaks.

"Mattie, get up."

"I'll call you in the morning," Matt promised, rising from beside me, his eyes purposefully wide, like his boyfriend had flipped out. "And I'll keep trying until I get you."

"Good." I smiled at him as he kissed Alex on the cheek good-bye and ignored Breckin completely.

I made the mistake of looking at my brother, who tipped his head and met my gaze. He had it, then. Matt's icy demeanor was a dead giveaway. Once Breckin's biggest fan, the complete reversal could only mean one thing.

After they left, I was alone with Breckin and my brother. I hadn't noticed that Tate and the nurse had left.

"You two look decidedly grim," I said, as Breckin walked over to take hold of my hand.

"We're fine," he assured me. "We're both just tired."

"Speak for yourself," Alex said coolly.

Oh yes, he knew what Breckin had done.

"Then go home," I suggested. "I'll be fine."

"I'm going to stay a bit," Breckin informed me.

I scooted over in the bed to make room for him.

"Are you sure?"

"Yeah, go. I'll see you tomorrow."

He nodded, kissed me good-bye, and then left without a word to my ex-boyfriend.

"Well, that was fun," Breckin sighed.

"Sorry."

"Thank you for not telling him what happened."

"You're welcome, but I'm pretty sure he knows at this point."

He nodded.

I leaned back against the pillows, and Breckin did the same. He was warm there next to me, and he smelled like fresh laundry.

"Why don't you smell like cigarettes?" I asked absently. He should have smelled like smoke and beer, but instead he smelled like he always did, clean, like soap and a trace of vanilla.

"I wanted to stay with you, and I knew that if I smelled bad, you'd make me go home and take a shower. So I already went home and took one."

"Christ, how long was I out?"

"A while," he answered, shivering. "But I knew you were okay, so I went home so I could stay here with you once you woke up."

"You're a very considerate man," I assured him, patting his shoulder.

"No," he said, chuckling, "I just wanted to stay with you."

I sighed deeply, wondering about how well he knew me, and let him get comfortable beside me. I was suddenly so tired, the night catching up with me, and I didn't remember the last thing I said to him.

CHAPTER
Five

I WOKE up early in the morning, and one glance at the clock on the wall told me it was four thirty. The noise—dress shoes scraping over the floor—caught my attention. All the hair rose on the back of my neck. I hadn't realized how frightened I had been and still was.

"Who's there?" I asked the darkness, sitting up, careful not to jerk the IV needle in my left arm. My heart was pounding so hard I could barely hear anything. I started panicking as soon as I realized Breckin wasn't in bed with me. Where the hell had he gone?

"It's me," came the tired sigh from the shadows to the right of the bed.

When I turned, I found Cord walking toward my bed. It was a relief that it was him, and I let out a deep sigh as I sank back down on the pillows.

"You thought maybe I was your stalker?"

"I have a stalker now?" I asked him, annoyed. "Since when?"

He stepped out into the light from the hallway, and I saw him clearly. "Jesus," I groaned, "you look like shit."

He nodded. "Nice. Real nice. I'm going to forgive your rudeness since you're all hopped up on pharmaceutical-grade narcotics."

"Why are you here?" I asked pointedly, letting him hear clearly in my voice that I was only tolerating him, that I didn't like him.

"Because I have to talk to you," he said, his expression hardening.

I was about to ask the next logical question when his cell phone rang, and he shushed me to silence. I heard enough of the conversation to realize he was talking to some guy, and between his tone and his body language, I was certain he was blowing him off. I was not surprised in the least. Cord collected men and then discarded them; it had always been his way. And I understood how. The man exuded heat; everything about him was strong and hard. If I didn't know him, I would have wanted him too, but that was all surface appeal. Underneath, the guy was an asshat even if he looked like he'd been carved from stone. What I found more interesting, though, was that some men thought he was just okay. Unlike Breckin, who men—and women—found equally appealing, Cord Nolan worked only on the senses of those who liked that wild, rebellious kind of guy. He came off cold, dangerous, and untamable. He was not the kind of man you made a home with.

"Hello," he snapped at me, and I realized he had been done with his conversation for some time and my mind had been drifting.

"What?" I answered quietly, carefully crossing my arms over my chest.

"I have things to discuss with you," he said. Picking up the chair beside the table, he walked across the room and put it down beside my bed. Finally taking a seat, he got comfortable and looked up at me. "You look pretty good for a guy who almost got brained with a bat."

"Thanks," I said irritably. "Is that what you came by to tell me?"

He shook his head before taking a deep breath. "You're such a pain in the ass."

"Do you actually have something useful to say, or are we just going to have our usual—"

"Fine," he interrupted, exasperated. "Here it is. You got beat up in a club last night, and Celia Hughes got beat up at a football game the night before that."

I stared at him hard, waiting for him to go on. The silence stretched out longer and longer, and finally I had to cave. "Who is Celia Hughes, and what does she have to do with me?"

"I thought you'd never ask."

"Oh, for the love of God, just tell me what the hell you're talking about."

He looked past me then, to the doorway of my room.

I glanced over my shoulder and found nothing there. Returning my gaze to his, I waited only seconds. "What? What is it? You're making me nuts with this."

"I—"

"Speak!"

He cleared his throat. "Celia got beat up just like you did. The lights got turned off, and she got hit with something hard. We don't know what."

"She got hit at a football game?"

"Yeah."

"And?" It was like pulling teeth.

"It was a 49ers game."

Why was that important? "What's with you?"

"Nothing, I'm just telling you—you and Celia Hughes, same setup, dark bathroom, hit in the back, same outcome… except she's pregnant."

"Oh shit," I gasped, horrified, distracted from my annoyance by the possibility of someone hurting an unborn child. "Is she okay? Is the baby okay?"

"Yeah, the baby's fine. Celia had the presence of mind to roll into a ball and protect her kid."

"So it was a little different, because I got hit as the lights went out. I had no presence of mind to keep."

"You never have any presence of mind," he said matter-of-factly.

"Really?" I said flatly.

"Lest we forget how well I know you," he countered, grinning at me.

He knew events; he didn't know me.

Like there had been the time he and Alex had driven up to my apartment only to find me in a T-shirt and pajama bottoms on the front stoop, freezing, because I had locked myself out, and Matt wasn't home, and crazy Mrs. Fishman from next door wouldn't buzz me back in. Or the time I nearly fell off the pier at Fisherman's Wharf because I wouldn't let him help me carry the boxes of cracked crab I had been asked to pick up for my friend Denise's rehearsal dinner. Or the time Alex had sent me to pick Cord up from the airport, and I'd forgotten where my car was parked… for three hours. It always seemed like, sadly, he caught me at my worst.

"Moving on," I said, hoping my scowl showed clearly on my face and in my voice. "Are you allowed to tell me who Celia Hughes is? Or are you just trying to torture me."

He looked past me again to the door. "I was hoping I wouldn't have to tell you this stuff. I thought Alex would."

"It's almost five in the morning." I was incredulous. "I hope he's asleep. I don't even know why you're awake."

"Just am."

"Coming home from a booty call?"

"Shut up," he groused.

"Why Alex?" I said instead of escalating the discussion to a fight.

"Because I told him a little while ago, and he said he would be here."

"Okay, now I'm getting a little freaked out. Do you know where Breckin is? Was he here when you came in?"

He flicked his eyes to mine then, and I was swallowed up in his gaze. Caught off guard, I stared back and realized, as I always did, how beautiful his eyes were.

"Cord?" I asked as he moved closer to me, until our faces were inches apart.

"I called Alex last night to—" He checked his watch. "—yeah, last night, because I needed to talk to you, and I wanted to know if he wanted to be with you when I did."

"Last night when?"

"Like, just three hours ago."

"Jesus, Cord, are you sleeping at all?"

"Who cares, just…. I needed to talk to you, so that's why I'm here."

"So talk."

"We could wait a little," he stalled.

"You said you already told Alex, now tell me."

He inhaled sharply. "I was following up on a lead in the Stanson case that took me to Celia Hughes."

After a minute I realized that he wasn't going to clarify. "English, Nolan. Please."

"Well, you know I work Homicide now, right?"

"What do you mean now? You transferred to Homicide two and a half years ago, right before I met Breckin."

After a moment he nodded. "Yeah, that's right."

"I know it's right, so… what?"

"So I'm working a case right now involving a man who was burned to death in his home."

"Jesus," I gasped, horrified.

"Yeah, so I've been working it maybe three months, and I haven't been able to come up with anything concrete except for one thing."

"And what is that?"

"All I've got is the fact that Timothy Stanson had previously reported being attacked in a public bathroom and being beaten up."

I shivered and pulled the blankets up around me.

"As soon as I found out he'd been beaten, I checked to see if there were any matching reports filed within the last few months. One name came up a perfect match, and that was Celia Hughes. Are you following me so far?"

I nodded, unable to speak.

"As I was questioning Celia yesterday… wait," he said, stopping. "Is that right?"

"Technically it's Sunday now," I told him. "So you must've been talking to her on Friday."

He nodded. "Yeah, that's right. Okay, so when I asked her who might want to hurt her, or her baby, she gave me a name that surprised me."

"What name?" I choked out, shivering again and moving closer to the side of the bed, needing to be in his personal space for whatever reason.

"Yours."

"Mine?" I was stunned. My stomach twisted into a painful knot as my throat went dry.

"It seems your ex-boyfriend is the father of Celia Hughes's baby."

Time stopped. Terror gone, shivering gone, all pain forgotten.

"Tracy?"

Wait.

"Honey?"

Wait....

"Trace."

"What?" I choked out.

"Are you listening to me?"

I nodded slowly.

"Did you understand what I said?"

"No, I don't think so."

"Then I'm gonna say it again, okay?"

"Yeah." I felt like I was in a vacuum and all the air was being sucked out of the room.

He took a quick breath. "Your ex-boyfriend, Breckin Alcott, is the father of the child that Celia Hughes is carrying."

I stared at him.

"Did you hear me that time?"

"What?" I was confused.

"Did you hear what I said?"

I just knew I had misheard him. "One more time."

So he did.

"Tracy."

"Yeah?" I shook my head, trying to clear it.

"Baby." His voice was like crushed leaves, so hoarse.

"What, what are you... who?" I couldn't think. I could barely breathe. "What now? What?"

"Tracy," he began softly, his tone gentle, as I'd never heard it. "Listen to me. Breckin—"

"What?" I snapped at him, my voice high and unhinged. "What the hell are you saying?"

"She had pictures of the two of them together at some convention," he growled, suddenly aggravated. "She's a doctor too. A cardiovascular surgeon, and it's his baby."

"But I—he...," I started and then stopped, realizing I was beginning to hyperventilate. "We talked about having kids someday. I mean, I want kids. I think I would make a good dad."

"You would," he agreed. "I'm absolutely sure of that."

"We talked about—but that was down the road. He… and I, I wouldn't ever—he… he… oh no… oh no…."

I was surprised I didn't cry. It seemed like reason enough to. But I was gutted, hollow, and absolutely empty. The idea that Breckin, who I had trusted with my heart, could betray me not once, but twice, made me the biggest idiot on the planet.

Cord dropped the pad he was reading from on the rolling table beside the bed, stood up, and wrapped his arms around me. I couldn't get enough air, and I couldn't wrap myself close enough to him. He held me tight against him, and I started shaking. I felt like a cold wind was tearing through me, blowing me apart into a thousand of pieces.

"It's gonna be all right," he soothed me, and his breath in my ear, down the side of neck, was comforting, as were the slow circles he rubbed on my back. "I swear. You're gonna be okay."

At some point he released me. I watched him take off his gray wool overcoat, then bend and pull off his wingtips before walking around the bed and getting in beside me. We were face-to-face, and he yanked me up against him. He put one arm under my head so I was pillowed on his wide bicep and curled the other around my back. I wedged my knees between his thighs and pressed my nose into the warm hollow of his throat. Unlike Breckin, Cord smelled like stale air and coffee, but he was so warm, and I was freezing. I was shaking hard, trembling in his arms, snuggling tighter. I closed my eyes for a minute, realizing right before I did it that not once, the entire night, had I felt so safe.

I WOKE up slowly, the light in the room telling me it was still early, and when I looked around I noticed the pair of feet on the edge of the bed. When I lifted my head off Cord's broad chest, I saw the crossed ankles belonged to my brother, who was asleep in a chair.

I turned from my brother and looked down at Cord, who was yawning and stretching under me. He gave me a rare lopsided grin before finally speaking.

"You hurting?"

What did he mean? From what, my heart or my body? "A little."

"I'll go get the nurse and have her get you something," he said, and there was sand in his voice, all soft and husky.

"Just push the call button," I croaked out, my own voice gruff and nasally.

He did as I told him, getting off the bed at the same time.

The nurse's entrance woke Alex, and he was suddenly all over me. I put up my hand to hold him off, and the nurse made him wait while she unhooked my IV. That was the end of the good drugs. It would be all ibuprofen and Tylenol from there on out.

"Tell me the rest of it," I asked Cord after she left.

He was talking to Alex in the corner of the room and so didn't hear me.

"Nolan," I called over to him. "Please tell me the rest."

He crossed quickly over to me, and when he sat down I immediately noticed how different he appeared, how gentle. I had never seen him early in the morning. Maybe that was what he looked like first thing, before he hardened up in the course of a day. Amazing to see his eyes so warm and unguarded, and coupled with being rumpled and sleep tousled, you could almost mistake him for human.

"Where did I leave off last night?"

"About Breckin being the father of Celia Hughes's baby."

"You must have been really out of it for you to be able to fall asleep without hearing everything," Alex remarked, leaning across the bed to take hold of my shoulder. "And you must have been way doped up to let this asshole comfort you," he finished, tipping his head toward Cord.

I didn't have the strength to make Alex stop, so I let him hold on to me as my gaze stayed riveted on Cord's face.

"He was in shock," Cord explained to both of us. "But now you need to listen to me."

I nodded.

"Celia Hughes was Breckin's lover, but on closer investigation, so was Timothy Stanson. He knew Tim before you, Tracy," Cord told me, his voice hoarse. "All three—you, Tim, and Celia—have been attacked by obviously the same person. Tim is dead, so there's no reason to believe that the same is not planned for you and Celia."

"Did you tell Dr. Hughes your theory?" Alex asked.

"I did. She regretted having placed any blame on Tracy."

I took it all in even as I heard the rain start to pelt my window.

"I need you to not fall apart," Cord said gently, walking around the bed to face me as I had turned from both him and my brother. He raised my chin with his hand to look me in the eye. "Can you do that?"

"I don't fall apart," I promised, and then I massaged the bridge of my nose before nearly rubbing my eyes raw. "Al, would you do me a humongous favor?"

"Anything, anything, just ask me."

"Could you go home and get me some fresh clothes and clean underwear and my glasses. My contacts are killing me."

"Of course," he said gently, standing up. "I told Dad that you and I would be home tonight. I talked to your doctor, and he said he would release you later this afternoon."

"Where is Dad?" I asked him, surprised my father had not yet been to see me.

"He was fishing in Manhattan Beach with Uncle Rudy. He's on his way home now, though. I talked to him this morning."

"Okay."

"And Evan's coming in at six, so I gotta go pick him up at the airport."

I turned to look up at my brother. "What? Why?"

"Because somebody tried to kill his brother," Alex said flatly, shoving his hands into the pockets of his black leather biker jacket. "Dad called him. There was nothing I could do to keep him from flying out."

"Fine, whatever," I sighed. "I'll go with you. I'll call Tate—"

"Your doctor, Tate whatever?"

"Yeah, and I'll tell him I need to be gone by five."

Alex nodded and then promised he would be back soon.

"You have your key, right?" I asked him, stopping him at the door.

"I have your keys," he told me, jingling them for my benefit. "I'll be back."

"Hey."

Cord snapped his head up.

"We'll be in touch."

"Yep," he agreed, his gaze back on me seconds later. "You didn't ask me if it was true."

"What are you talking about?"

"You didn't ask me if I was telling you the truth about Breckin's affair with Celia Hughes," he said gruffly.

"Oh," I grunted. I threw the covers off my legs and swung them over the side so I was facing him. "Why would you lie? You don't lie. That's not one of your many faults. In fact, the opposite may be true—you're too damned honest."

He chuckled before giving me a devilish grin. "I guess with me you always know what you're gonna get."

"Yep," I agreed, raking my fingers through my hair. "Unless I was dating you, of course," I added. "People you date don't get to hear that one night is all you're after."

"That's what you think?"

"That's what I know."

He cleared his throat. "I'm just—Man, did I fuck this up."

I squinted at him. "What are you talking about?"

"Just—listen," he began, sitting down beside me so we were shoulder to shoulder. "I want you to call me if anything at all weird happens, okay?"

"Sure," I said stoically. "I'll call you."

He pulled his wallet from his back pocket and gave me a card with his name and number on it. "I wrote my cell on the back of that for you."

"Oh, okay." I was confused. "Why didn't you just leave it with Alex this morning? You didn't have to stick around and tell me all this stuff. He could've told me."

"It's okay, I wasn't busy."

"Liar," I grunted even though I was completely numb. "You're always busy. You're a homicide inspector, for crissakes, and this is the big city."

"It surely is," he agreed as he put an arm around my shoulders and squeezed me up tight against him. "But I will always make time for my friends."

"Are we friends, then?"

"We have more history than you obviously remember."

"Oh, I remember it all right," I said wryly, leaning my head against his collarbone. "I just usually see and speak to my friends more than once every couple of years."

"We don't run in the same crowd."

"The understatement of the year," I assured him.

"But you could invite me," he said softly, grazing my jaw, curling his fingers around my throat as he tilted my head up with his thumb. "It wouldn't kill you."

I scoffed at him. "And do what with my friends? They're all paired up. No one for you to fuck and forget."

"You're right: in the past I haven't done relationships," he acknowledged. "I haven't seen the merit."

"Right now I don't either," I said miserably, turning to look out the window at the rain. "I feel like I got the crap kicked outta me."

"You did get the crap kicked outta you," he said affectionately.

"Yeah," I muttered, crossing my arms over my chest, shivering suddenly.

He leaned close and pushed the hair back from my face. I closed my eyes, and he didn't move away. It was very comforting and almost undid me.

"Thank you for being here with me last night," I told him wearily. "I appreciate it more than you know."

"I know," he huffed, and I felt his warm breath on the side of my neck.

"Okay," I said quickly, squaring my shoulders and sitting up straight. "You go ahead an' go, and I'll call ya if anything weird happens."

He stood and put his coat on over his thick sweater. "Call me if nothing happens."

"That doesn't make any sense at all," I muttered, watching him grab his pad, his phone, and readjust his gun holster.

"Well, either your brother or myself or another officer is going to be guarding you from now on."

"How is that possible?" I asked him. "I mean, there's crime all over this city. How does one guy merit twenty-four-hour surveillance? All I got was beat up?"

"But you're obviously a target of someone with an agenda. You're in danger."

"I am?"

"Oh, for crissakes," he flared. "What the hell have I been saying for the past half hour?"

"So what you're saying is I do merit twenty-four-hour surveillance?"

"You merit watching, and because you're Alex Brandt's little brother and my friend, you merit more watching than would be regularly assigned." I could tell he was trying to inject an air of calmness into his tone. "Considering that one of the other people who was attacked in the same manner you were is dead now, I would think this news would give you comfort."

"I'm sorry," I apologized fast, motioning him over to me. "I didn't mean to sound ungrateful. I appreciate everything you've done so far." I clutched at his sweater.

He looked at me, and I saw his jaw tighten before he spoke again. "Okay, I'll see you."

"Am I okay to be here alone?" I asked, suddenly alarmed by his leaving. I looked up at him towering over me and felt safe. If he left, I wouldn't be scared, but I would be anxious.

He motioned behind me with his head. "You're not alone."

I turned to find my ex standing in the doorway of my room. He lifted his eyebrows in question, waiting for a sign from me that it was okay to come in. My hands fell away from Cord and I stared.

"Call me," Cord ordered, walking around the bed to the door. He shot me a look before he left, and I wasn't sure what I saw there.

Suddenly alone with Breckin, I felt my unease return.

"Can I come in?" he asked.

"Yeah."

He entered the room and closed the door behind him. It made me feel a little better that he looked terrible. As he crossed the room to my bed, I found myself shivering again. He stopped a few feet away and swallowed hard before carding his fingers nervously through his thick hair.

"You left."

"I had to check in at work and let them know I needed some time off."

"Time off for what?"

"For you, of course."

Of course. "You look ill," I croaked out.

"I feel ill," Breckin admitted, lacing his fingers behind his neck and then resting his arms against both sides of his face.

"How come?"

"You know how come," he answered woodenly.

"Tell me."

"It didn't mean anything," he began haltingly. "It was a mistake."

"That's what you said the first time," I reminded him.

"You forgave that; you can't bring that up now."

"I can, actually, but this one's different anyway: she's going to have your baby."

"It's her baby. You're the only one I'm having a family with."

For the first time I felt hot tears fill my eyes and then slowly slip down my cheeks. Not because we were really truly over—honestly, we had been since I'd walked through the door and caught him with his dick shoved up another guy's ass—but because all of it, even what had been hopes and dreams, had gone too.

"Tracy, don't—"

"It's not just her baby," I corrected him. "It's your baby too. Make no mistake about that. It's yours and hers."

"I don't love her," he said flatly.

"That makes it even worse."

"I told her I didn't want it."

"You need to do the right thing."

"Which is what?"

"You know."

We both went silent before I found my voice again. "When did you sleep with her?" I was interested. Was it before his indiscretion with Sean Granger, or after? Had we still been living together?

He took a deep breath before walking over to the chair on the other side of my bed. He picked it up by the back and then turned it around backward before he took a seat. I watched as he crossed his arms on the back before resting his chin on them. I saw all the pain in his eyes and that they were swollen from crying. "I slept with her in May when I was away at that conference in Florida."

It was mid-October, still a couple of weeks until Halloween. So five months ago. Before Sean. Celia first, Sean second. I had to wonder about that. So instead of me thinking that only for four months he had not been mine alone, it was actually a month longer. And I'd had no idea about either of them; my first instinct had been to trust.

"So you slept with her at the conference where you presented your case about how you saved that little girl in the ER with the holes in her heart."

He nodded.

"I wanted to go with you," I said, my voice sounding hollow.

"I was only there for two days," he returned quietly.

"So you didn't want me there because—"

"No," he interrupted, holding up his hand. "I had no idea when I left that something was going to happen. You have to believe me; I didn't plan any of it. I swear to God, Trace, I had no idea."

"So what did happen?"

"I cheated on you," he conceded, raking his hands through his hair again. It was an unconscious gesture I knew, one he did whenever he felt trapped.

"Which made it easier to do the second time," I said flatly.

"No."

"Then why did it happen?"

"I let myself be seduced."

"Isn't that what happened with Sean?"

He shook his head. "No. Sean… you know…. We'd been flirting for a year, just fun, didn't mean anything until that day. But we had a history."

Good to know.

"But with Celia—it just happened. Like I said, for once I let someone pick me up."

"Meaning that you're approached often and lots of people try to get you into bed," I concluded.

"You know it's true."

I did. He was eye candy. Both men and women always looked at him. "Go on."

"She was different and I was drunk."

"You've been drunk before."

"She was different, then."

"A surgeon, right?"

"Cord?" he asked, wanting to know how I knew.

"Of course Cord," I told him. "So she's a surgeon and really smart like you."

"Like me," he echoed, closing his eyes and resting his forehead against the palm of his hand. "Yeah, I'm fucking brilliant all right."

It was funny to think that I had been defending his brain to Eric the night before. "So she comes on to you, and you, what, ended up going with her to her room?"

"No," he sighed, letting out a deep breath. "We talked for hours. We closed the bar."

"Really," I murmured. "Those are the best kinds of talks."

"Tracy, it wasn't like—"

"What did you talk about?" I interrupted, ignoring him completely.

"I don't remember," he said, seeming to dismiss the idea that it was important enough to recall. "I just know that after that, she suggested we continue our conversation in her room."

"Oh," I breathed. "I see. What then?"

His gaze flicked to mine, and I saw the misery there and felt how acute it was. "Is this really necessary?"

"Oh yes," I replied, my voice sounding half-strangled. "It is."

His sigh was deep. He looked exhausted. "We were in the room, and we were sitting on her bed...." He trailed off, watching me, and I saw him deflate suddenly, the look in his eyes, the expression, pleading for me to stop. But I had to hear it all. "And then she said I was the most beautiful man she had ever seen," he finished solemnly.

"As I'm sure you were and still are." I swallowed hard, trying to dislodge the lump in my throat. Once I could breathe I prodded him to finish.

He squeezed the chair back, turning his knuckles white for a moment. "I remember laughing, and she leaned over and kissed me, and I didn't stop her."

I couldn't speak. I could barely continue to look at him.

"I didn't sleep with her," he told me, emphasizing the word "sleep." "I left as soon as it was finished."

Meaning he had not held her next to his heart as he did me. He had not snuggled her up tight against his chest; she had not slept in the crook of his neck. He had not woken with her tangled around him.

"And when did you know she was having your child."

"Well, the next morning, after we…." He trailed off again, shifting uncomfortably in the chair.

"Had sex," I offered, giving him the word he seemed incapable of saying.

"The day after, we had breakfast and she asked me what I wanted to do."

"Damn considerate of her," I snapped, finding my voice.

"She said she would be whatever I needed. I told her I didn't need her in my life. I told her it was a mistake. I told her how much I love you."

"Did she laugh?"

"No, she didn't laugh," he said crossly, defensive and annoyed. "She knows I love you."

"Oh, I'm sure she does."

"I can do without the sarcasm."

"And I could do without the cheating, but what are we gonna do?"

He scowled darkly. "She promised me I would never hear from her again."

"But? I hear a but coming."

"A month later she came to the hospital and told me she was pregnant."

"And you said?"

"I offered to give her money for the abortion."

"You don't believe in abortion."

"I did that day."

"And now?"

"And now even more," he confessed gloomily. "Because I know this is going to haunt my life forever."

"And you're sure it's your child?"

"I had a DNA test done."

"Wow," I remarked, my voice hollow. "You did want to be sure, didn't you?"

"I was hopeful."

"But?"

"But there is no doubt. He's mine."

"He?" I said shakily, my breath stuttering.

"She had an amnio done, and it's definitely a boy."

"Your son," I said breathlessly. I heard the chair scrape on the floor as he leaped to his feet and overturned the chair in the process. He wrapped around me, and I couldn't move. "Get off me."

He tightened his grip and buried his face in my hair. "Trace… Tracy," he chanted, on the verge of tears. "Please forgive me. Please, please forgive me. I'll do anything."

It was my fault. I had let him think we could be us again when it had never been a real possibility. "We're done, Breck," I said, pushing gently out of his embrace and slipping off the bed. "And honestly, I should be the least of your concerns right now."

On my feet with the bed between us, I felt better, like I could breathe.

"Trace—"

"You should probably go."

He looked cornered. There was a thread of panic in his voice, and the tears in his eyes spilled over. "Please, Tracy, please," he said over and over. "You must forgive me. You have to forgive me."

"It's not even about that," I insisted. "You and Celia have a lot of decisions to make, and what I do or don't should have no bearing on anything. I'm so insignificant in your life right now that it's laughable."

"No, you—"

"Go talk to her; don't waste your time here with me."

He came around the bed fast, and outside of flipping over it like a gymnast, I was stuck. So when he grabbed me and pulled me into his arms, I let him. "Trace," he said into my hair, his voice like a caress. "I need you. You need me. I belong to you. Don't throw me away. You love me. Don't stop, don't ever stop. I'd die—I would die."

But his words, which had once meant everything, now meant nothing. It was sad, the ending, and that's what I was feeling, nothing else. I had shed tears for him months ago. I was all out.

"Please. I need you to forgive me this one mistake. I need you to let me make this up to you."

But he'd made two mistakes, and the fact that I was more focused on his actual words than the feeling behind them spoke volumes. I was keeping score of his trespasses instead of forgiving him—it was ridiculous.

"I messed up, but it can be fixed if you just let me."

I looked up into the violet eyes I knew so well.

"Don't send me away, baby. Please don't."

But he was already gone—out of my house, out of my bed—done.

"Can I kiss you?" he asked me warmly, his gaze soft as he looked at me.

"No," I said softly, slowly, but firmly, extricating myself. I needed him off me, out of my space. He was too close.

"Tracy… baby…."

Again, I put the bed between us by walking around to the other side. "Listen, you need to do the right thing, the honorable thing."

"And what's that?" His voice, whisper soft, was imploring. "Please look at me."

"You should marry her," I directed him. "It's the right thing to do."

"I'm going to marry you."

"You should marry her," I repeated, sighing deeply, tired, ready to lie down.

"I can't ever marry anyone but you; that would make no sense. You're the only one I love."

"You should go now," I told him thickly, my voice so full of painful resignation that I hardly recognized it as mine.

"I want to take you home."

"I'm going home with Alex. He's coming back to get me."

"You're going to Alex's or your dad's?"

"My dad's, and, really, you don't want to be here when he gets back."

"I don't care. Let me come too."

"No. You should wait."

"I don't want to wait; I want to be with you."

"There's no more you and me, Breck," I said implacably, my gaze locked with his. "You know there isn't."

"Don't say that. Just give this some time. Don't make a decision today. It's too soon. Just wait. Wait a little while."

I shook my head.

"We're not over," he said, sounding scared even as he brushed away tears from under his eyes. "I won't accept that we're over. Just say you'll give it some time. Just say that, and even though it'll kill me, I'll go away."

"You should go see Celia."

He smiled at me then, and it was bittersweet. "Trace, I am not going to anybody else's place. I love you. You're my boyfriend. I'll come by your dad's tomorrow to see you."

"Is that wise?"

He shrugged his shoulders and gave me a rueful grin. "I have to face him eventually. And I want to see you in the morning."

"Okay," I heard myself saying because I thought it was the easiest way to get him out of the room. If I didn't argue, he would go.

"Okay." His smile brightened as he let out a deep breath. "I'll see you then."

I nodded.

He didn't leave, though, just stood there and looked at me.

"What?"

He stuffed his hands down hard into his pockets. "I can't help it. I want to bring you home with me. I want to take care of you."

It was a nice thing to say.

"You're hurt and I love you and so—I want to be with you."

I swallowed hard and looked at him. "I'll see you tomorrow morning."

"Can I hug you good-bye?"

The last thing I wanted to do was touch him. "Not today."

He took a step toward me, then hesitated a moment before continuing to the bed and leaning over and giving me a quick kiss on the cheek. I didn't recoil; I didn't have it in me to pull away and end things like that. No matter what it was now, once upon a time I had been in love with Breckin Alcott.

I watched him turn and leave the room without a backward glance, and then I lost it. It needed to come out, all of it—the sadness and the finality and the end. I grabbed the pillow and sobbed. And, really, they weren't tears for him, but for the whole shitty situation, for things that would never be. A minute later, arms wrapped tightly around me, and I was squeezed hard.

"Don't cry, Trace. It's okay. I promise, you'll be okay," Alex said gently, cajoling me.

He rubbed his chin across the top of my head and patted my back. I took a deep breath before moving the pillow away from my face, sniffling as the crying ceased.

"I saw him walking away, and you'll be happy to know that I didn't shoot him. I didn't even yell."

"No fun being a grown-up, is it?" I teased him, smiling through my tears, looking up into my brother's face.

"Nope. Not at all."

And minutes later, as I watched him unpack his army-green duffel bag, now full of all my stuff, something occurred to me.

"I'm having a bitch of a week."

His grin fired his eyes and made his dimples pop. "You really are."

"Maybe I need to be cleansed by a shaman or something."

"Maybe you need a new job and a faithful boyfriend."

"Or just a vacation," I threw out.

"Or that," he agreed, beaning me with a pair of my jeans and ordering me to go take a shower. Apparently he didn't want me stinking up his car on the way to the airport. I couldn't very well blame him.

CHAPTER
Six

MY FATHER, Raymond Brandt, did what he always did when conflict arose. He took no one's part and refused to pass judgment until he had heard both sides of the story. Alex related all this to me as we drove to the San Francisco International Airport to pick up my brother Evan. My father was going to wait and talk to Breckin before he said anything. That was his way. I had always looked to my father to be fair. He never let his emotions get the better of him. Alex and I, on the other hand, were much more like my mother, riding the emotional highs and lows at every turn.

"Can you believe it?" Alex asked me as we parked his Toyota Highlander and got out. "I mean, for crissakes, Tracy, it's about the hell time Dad got mad for once! This is a big fuckin' deal!"

"I know," I groaned, sagging back against the side of the SUV and leaning hard. "Hey, you got a cigarette on you?"

His eyes got big. "What?"

"A cigarette," I repeated. "Do you have one?"

"Not for you I don't."

"Oh, gimme the goddamn cigarette," I snapped at him, sounding more surly then I felt.

He pulled a pack from the inside pocket of his black leather biker jacket, pulled out two cigarettes, and lit them both. He nursed them for a second, making sure both were sufficiently burning, then passed me one. When I had been a smoker it had been merely recreational. In college there had been clove cigarettes and, of course, pot, and a few times things even stronger. I never got a taste for drugs, but I had really tried to be a smoker. It just never took. And I had been a lightweight anyway; it was all about the menthol. My brother did not know from menthol. He would have smoked them without filters if he could have found the time to roll them himself. As it was, I nearly coughed myself to death on the Camel he gave me. I didn't even know they made anything that full of toxins.

"Oh yeah, this is good for you," he snarked, rolling his eyes at me as we made our way across the parking garage to the elevators.

I put out the cigarette before we entered the building, then stood beside him as we waited with others to go down to the terminal and the gates. I noticed a woman and a man looking at me and wondered what they must be thinking.

Aviator sunglasses were hiding my puffy and bloodshot eyes. I had seen myself after I took a shower at the hospital. I was pale and hollow eyed. I looked like a refugee. I had on three layers—T-shirt, plaid shirt, and a slim brown leather jacket over that. Low-rise jeans and my ancient brown brogue boots completed my outfit. I was warm, and that was important. I couldn't seem to get my body temperature to regulate, so I needed to be piled with clothes.

The woman was still looking at me when it was time for us all to get on the elevator, and I noticed she and her husband had kind of drifted back away from us. Not huddled into a corner or anything, but damn close. Alex grabbed my arm as we got on, and when he held the door open so they could join us, the man politely informed him that they would take the next one. It was official: I was scaring people.

In the terminal I walked silently with Alex as we threaded through the crowd. He had his arm draped over my shoulder. I didn't even know where we were going until we reached the security check.

"Looks like we're a few minutes early," he sighed before turning to smile down at me. "You want me to get you a coffee or something?"

"Tea would be good."

"Yeah, okay, tell me what kind," he said, dropping his arm to pull his wallet from his back pocket.

"Get me an Earl Grey latte."

"Okay, I'll be right over here. Don't go anywhere."

He was worried, and it was nice. I turned back to the monitor as they announced the landing of my brother's flight. I knew he would be, like, the second one off, as he always flew first class. I couldn't remember a time that he hadn't.

Evan had graduated from Columbia with a degree in Art History but just barely—he had been so much more interested in his acting career. He'd done some theater work, but mostly he was not the kind of guy who did summer stock or Shakespeare in the Park or anything off Broadway. My brother was definitely the guy who did commercials, then walk-ons, then bit parts, then bigger ones. He was less about the theater or his craft and more about models and money. He was young, only twenty-seven, and maybe when he hit sixty he'd care about Broadway. But after a show on CBS playing a hot FBI agent, he'd moved on to HBO. He'd told Alex on the phone that he had news, so I was looking forward to hearing it. As passengers began streaming out from the opposite side of the security checkpoint, I looked for him. He wasn't hard to spot.

Alex and I looked alike; people always said so. We both resembled my mother—same brown hair and tanned complexion, the Portuguese and Spanish clearly evident in us, her brown-eyed children. Evan, being the youngest, somehow got mixed different. He pulled from my father's side of the family—Scottish, Irish, French, and German. He had gray eyes, dirty-blond hair, and a golden tan that he kept year-round. People always thought he was adopted until they met my father, who he looked just like.

"Tracy!"

I turned to the sound of the yell and found Evan striding toward me across the floor. I didn't know why, but seeing him made me feel worse. And maybe it was because the only reason he was home was because I was in trouble, or maybe it was the way he was looking at me, like he was sorry. Either way, I wanted to crawl under a rock.

"It's not your fault, idiot," he barked over at me.

I nodded as he reached me and let him wrap me in his arms and hold me tight against him.

"Hey, buddy, get your goddamn hands off my brother."

Evan pulled back, and his smile for Alex was radiant. They hugged hard, and Evan left his hand on the back of Alex's neck when they let go. Both pairs of eyes turned to me suddenly, and I waited.

"Here," Alex said, holding out the tea for me to take. I noticed he had even put the little protective piece of cardboard around the cup, so I wouldn't get burned. Damn nice of him.

I took a sip and sighed before returning my gaze to my brother. "Thank you."

After several minutes of staring, Evan finally spoke. "You feel okay?" he asked me, his voice soft, concern clear in his tone.

"As good as can be expected," I sighed. "C'mon, let's go, I'm beat." I watched Alex take Evan's carry-on and swing it over his shoulder before turning to go.

Evan walked between us, his arm around my shoulders and his left hand still on the back of Alex's neck. I watched people see us, trying to figure it out. Was he Alex's lover or mine? Alex and I sort of matched in our faded jeans and casual attire, but Mr. GQ didn't resemble either of us. He could have walked out of an ad for Calvin Klein. All he owned were labels: Donna Karan, Ralph Lauren, Armani, Cole Haan, Versace, Kenneth Cole. Not a pair of Levi's in there anywhere. And so we got the staring that usually went along with traveling with Evan.

I sat in the back once we got to the car, and I fell asleep on the ride to my dad's place in Sausalito. I woke up to Evan telling my dad that he was being ridiculous.

"What?" I yawned, stretching before I realized how sore I was. "Ow, ow, ow." I winced.

"You want a pill?" Alex asked from the driver's seat.

"Yes, please, kind sir," I said, catching his eye in the rearview mirror.

"In the small zipper pocket in my jacket I've got your eight-hundred-milligram ibuprofen, and there should be an Evian back there on the seat or on the floorboard next to my duffel."

"Thanks." I scrambled around and found the water and my pill and took it before leaning forward between their seats. "What's going on with Dad?"

"He's got that lady friend of his over at the house," Evan told me, "and he's trying to get rid of her before we get there."

"Why?"

"Because he wants to focus all his attention on you, and he doesn't think this is the best time for us all to meet her."

"I, for one, am dying to meet her," I told them both. "I have been trying to get him to invite me over when she's there for almost a month now."

"Yeah, but, Tracy, it's not the best fuckin' time," Alex reminded me. "We should maybe do it when you're feeling better."

"It will get my mind off other stuff."

"I'll talk to you, and you can watch TV. We don't need company," he groused.

I turned and looked at Evan and fixed him with a continuous stare. It took him a minute, but he suddenly got it, and I saw the recognition in his eyes. "Oh, you're kidding," he said warmly, curving his lips into a smile before he chuckled.

"What?" Alex asked, interested.

I turned back and looked at his profile. "You don't want to meet this woman because you don't want Dad to date."

"What?" he said defensively, his voice higher than I knew he wanted it to be.

"Alex," I began. "You—"

"Why don't you have your seat belt on? That's against the law."

"Really?" I asked, my voice steeped in sarcasm.

"Lean back and buckle up."

"I'm so not gonna do that just because you're using me to change the subject."

"Ohmygod," Evan croaked out, trying to stifle his laughter. "Jesus Christ, Alex, it's about goddamn time he started dating. Mom's been gone more than nineteen years now."

"I know how long she's been gone," he said solemnly, staring straight ahead, his knuckles turning white on the wheel as he drove.

I put my hand lightly on his right shoulder. "It's time, Al."

"I know it's time," he agreed indulgently, his tone condescending. "I just don't think that today of all days is the right one for us to be meeting her. We have important family matters to discuss."

Obviously, he was not ready for our father to move on. Alex, who had been with our mother the longest, being the oldest child, was not ready for our father to date.

"Dad deserves to have someone," Evan ventured, his tone gentle. "I mean, unless you're going to live the rest of your life with him and be his constant companion, he needs someone in his life to share it with. He's not a monk. He has needs too."

Alex turned from watching the road and looked sideways at me, completely ignoring Evan. "I just miss her."

"I know," I said simply, my eyes welling with tears. What I wouldn't give to have her back, to be going home to her right now. Not that my dad was lacking in any way. He was, in fact, much more nurturing than she had ever been. It was simply that you could sit with her and just be still and silent, and that was okay. She had been gifted with that quiet strength, and it had never left her, even when the pancreatic cancer had eaten her down to eighty pounds. Never had she complained, never had she blamed God or cursed her life. She had simply accepted the inevitable outcome, let my father nurse her in her final month, and told us all how proud she was of us and how much she loved us. She had made me promise to watch out for everyone, and at the time, I didn't understand why. Why me? How did that make sense? I wasn't the oldest. I wasn't the fixer, like Alex, or the showman, like Evan, who brought the whole family together to see him, to look at him. I was the middle child; all I knew how to do was negotiate and get along and....

Somewhere over the span of years I'd learned what she meant. I was the anchor, and both my brothers revolved around me. I was younger than Alex and so needed his protection. I was older than Evan, so he could reach out to me when he was in need. They all came running when I called. She had been counting on me to hold the family together. Normally I did a better job.

"So what?" I asked Evan. "Is the mystery woman staying or leaving?"

"I dunno. I told Dad to keep her there. Your guess is as good as mine, though. Maybe she'll be there, maybe she won't. It's a crapshoot."

Once we made it to the house my father had bought after he sold the big one we'd grown up in, we parked the SUV behind a silver Mercedes that was not my dad's. The woman had apparently stayed to meet the children of the man she had been dating for over three months. I was pleased; it would give me something to think about besides Breckin. I led the way, and before I got a chance to knock, my father opened the door.

"Dad." I smiled as I stepped into his arms. He hugged me gently, obviously not sure where I was damaged and not wanting to hurt me.

"Tracy," he said softly into my hair, rubbing my back.

I hugged him tight, remembering the last time I'd hung on for dear life. It was back in high school, when I had come out to him.

I had been so scared.

He had told me not to be, to just tell him.

When he'd heard I was gay he had stood up, thanked me for telling him, and then opened his arms wide.

He hadn't cared. It had changed nothing. Gay or straight, I was his son, and that was all there was to it. And I realized about the same time that I could call my dad at 3:00 a.m. if I was stuck somewhere. He would come and get me, and we would not talk about what had occurred to get me into that situation until the following morning. He never confronted me when I was drunk or embarrassed; he waited for a new day. And if I was hungover, then I had to endure breakfast. The same was true for Evan and Alex. The amount one had drunk was directly proportional to what he made you eat. Sausage, eggs, and biscuits and gravy were usually reserved for Alex. Evan and I mostly had chorizo omelets. The worst was menudo. You were in deep shit if he made you menudo after an all-night drinking binge. And he was always so damn cheerful when he served it, asking you all about your night, where you were, whom you were with, and what you had been doing in the wee hours. I absorbed all those life lessons.

He made us all self-sufficient and confident in our abilities. He was our touchstone if we strayed off the path. I loved his dear sweet face with the deep laugh lines in the corner of his light-blue eyes. Now, as I clung to him, I felt much better. Seeing him, I knew I was still me. I was still Tracy, and someday I would be okay. Just not anytime soon.

I pulled back gently, and he let me. Our gazes met before he turned to welcome Evan and Alex. I watched him cup Evan's face in his hands and really look at him, checking him over, making sure he was okay. He could tell if he wasn't. Nothing could be successfully hidden from my old man.

I became aware of someone looking at me, and I turned around slowly. Two women were standing beneath the arch that led from the foyer into the living room, one older, one younger.

"Hi," I said, sounding lame. "I'm Tracy."

The older woman came forward, holding her hand out for me to take. "Hello, Tracy, it's a pleasure to finally meet you. I'm Beth Segal."

"Beth." I smiled at her, taking the offered hand. "The pleasure's all mine."

"Here, here," my dad interrupted us as he walked around to stand beside her. He draped his arm around her shoulders. "Beth, I want you to meet my sons. This is my youngest, Evan, then Tracy, and Alex, my oldest."

My brothers both shook her hand, Evan cheerfully, Alex reluctantly.

"This is my daughter, Joanna," Beth said, indicating the woman who had come to stand beside her. She beamed at her daughter as Joanna shook hands with all of us.

"Come sit down," my dad said, herding us all into the living room.

My brothers took up bookend positions on the couch, and I flopped down between them. There was silence as Alex took off his leather jacket and Evan shed his suit jacket.

"I have to tell you," Joanna burst out suddenly, "I watch *Cape Cod* every single week. I have watched it ever since it started, and now I'm sitting here with you and it's totally amazing."

Evan smiled the one that did nothing for his eyes but looked mostly real. "Thank you," he said amiably, patting his leg at the same time, turning to look at me. "Why don't you rest your head, druggie?"

I would have told him where to go with the druggie reference, but I realized my head was getting fuzzier by the second. I still had the concussion thing happening. So I stretched out, legs on Alex, my head on the pillow on Evan's lap.

"Tracy, can I make up the bed in the spare room for you?" Beth asked me softly. I heard her, but I didn't see her, as my eyes had drooped closed, and I really didn't have the interest in opening them.

"No, no," my dad answered for me, "he's better here with us."

"He wouldn't be more comfortable—"

"No," my dad said, interrupting her. "He's plenty comfortable there and feeling pretty safe, as well. Safe is the important thing now."

"You don't know the half of it," Alex said petulantly, and I felt him taking off my boots.

"What does that mean?" my dad asked, his tone firm.

"I only told you he got attacked," Alex almost snapped at him. "I didn't tell you why."

"Then tell me why."

"Not right now." Alex sounded so peevish I wanted to kick him, but I didn't have the strength. He dropped his hand to rest heavy on the back of my right calf, and the warmth felt really good. I realized I was freezing again and mumbled something to Evan.

"What?" Joanna asked, trying to hear me, I guessed, but too far away.

"He's cold," Evan told her. "Could you grab Mom's afghan, Dad?" he asked, and I knew from the way he suddenly stopped speaking that he hadn't meant to phrase it the way he had. There was no agenda with him, no underlying hint of malice. I knew without seeing him that Alex was pleased with the wording.

The blanket was like heaven—so warm, so soft. I snuggled into it and shoved my cold feet under Alex's leg. I sighed my pleasure, and that apparently broke the tension. Everyone chuckled and relaxed. I tried to follow the conversation, but I nodded off, too content not to sleep.

CHAPTER
Seven

I STRETCHED and let out a yelp of pain. I had to stop doing that.

"Tracy, honey," my dad said gently. I looked up, and he was right there, looming overhead.

"Hey, Dad." I smiled up at him.

"What can I get you?"

"I'm hungry."

"Let's have some soup, okay?"

"Soup?"

"The instructions Alex has from the hospital say you should eat small meals because you have a concussion and you could throw up. I'm thinking soup is the safest thing."

"Okay," I told him, wanting to be agreeable. He left after smoothing my hair back from my forehead and bending over to give me a quick kiss. I leaned up on my right elbow, put on my heavy black-framed glasses that someone had been nice enough to take off me, and noticed Alex. He was sitting in the same place, at my feet, and he was snoring, with his head thrown back, his mouth open. I sat up and looked over the back of the couch and found Evan.

"And I was tired?"

He chuckled before throwing a card down on the table. I focused on the group then and saw that Beth and her daughter were still there. They were playing cards with Evan… and Cord.

"Hey," I greeted him, struggling to sit up. "What are you doing here?"

"Trace," Evan scolded me like I was being a brat. "Be nice."

"That was my plan," I snapped at him.

"I got off at six, so I came by to check on you," Cord answered.

"Yeah?"

"Yeah."

"Thanks," I said, lying back down. When I turned my head to the right, I realized football was on the TV, and I got confused. "Evan," I called over to him.

"What?"

"Is it Monday already?"

"No, it's still Sunday."

"And it's night, right?"

"It is," he confirmed, "why?"

"Why the hell am I looking at Green Bay and"—I squinted at the screen, still bleary with sleep—"Chicago, then?"

"It's called *Sunday Night Football*, dear; we do have something called night games in this country, ya know. Electricity for stadium lighting is an actual thing."

"Dad," I yelled.

"Yes, Tracy?" he called from the kitchen, which was just beyond the table where they were playing cards.

"I'm going to tell your son to go to hell now, okay?" I asked cheerfully.

"Okay," he said, and I could hear the smile in his voice.

"Go to hell, Evan." I told him, rolling over on my right side to watch the game. The screen was suddenly obstructed, though, as Cord came and took a seat on the coffee table, completely blocking my view of Aaron Rodgers.

"How ya feeling?"

"Like shit," I mumbled. "I'm sore all over. I'm such a damn pansy, and I always thought of myself as tough."

"When were you ever tough?"

I looked up at him to see if he was kidding. Hard to tell from his tone. But his smile was warm and his eyes glowed. Definitely giving me crap, and the normalcy of the interaction was good. "Hey, thanks again for being there last night. I know it couldn't have been any fun for you, but you stayed, and I appreciate it."

"Yeah, you sure got cozy fast," he said, reaching out to push my glasses up on my nose.

"What does that mean?" I asked defensively, annoyed. He always said something or did something that pissed me off, some stupid remark that got under my skin because of how he said it.

He shrugged his broad shoulders. "It doesn't mean anything."

I waited, because he wasn't done.

"But I guess you're all over Breckin Alcott, huh?"

"Come again?"

"I mean, the way you wrapped yourself around me, it was like we were sharing skin."

"You're complaining?" I said indignantly, propping myself up on my right elbow to look at him. "I can't believe you're complaining after I just thanked you. God, you're an ass."

His wicked grin made the laugh lines around his eyes crinkle. "No, I'm not complaining. I just think that if I were your man I would have a problem with how you were lying with me."

"Why?"

"It was too close."

"It was not. You're delirious."

He leaned close, so no one else could hear him. "At one point, Trace, I could feel how very happy you were to be near me."

"Oh, go to hell," I grumbled, rolling over so my face was against the back of the couch. "I'm tired."

"Okay," he agreed, his chuckle warm.

I heard the coffee table creak as his weight lifted up off it, and I wondered for the millionth time why he had to be such a dick all the time before I fell asleep again without my soup.

I HEARD clinking, and when I moved and stretched, my feet hit something solid. I lifted my head and found Cord staring at me from the other end of the couch.

"Still here?" I asked my voice gravelly and low as I reached out for my glasses.

"Yep," he answered, pulling my foot into his lap and squeezing it tight.

"Oh God," I groaned because the way he was rolling his knuckles under the arch of my foot was bliss.

"Your whole body is tense," he informed me.

"I'm aware," I grumbled. I pulled my foot out of his grip and sat up, putting both feet on the floor. "I'm sore, too."

"You hungry?"

I nodded as I put on my glasses.

"Tracy, honey," my dad called over from where he and my brothers and Beth were playing what looked like Texas Hold'em. "Do you want that soup now?"

"Chicken noodle will make me puke," I told him honestly.

"I made your mother's *sopón de pollo con arroz*," he said gently.

"You did?" I asked, standing up.

"Yes." He smiled at me. "Beth helped."

I turned my gaze to her. "Thank you."

She nodded quickly. "Oh, sweetheart, you're so welcome."

I felt like she was treating me like a child, but that was okay since I was hurt and everything.

"Just sit," my father ordered me. "I'll bring you some."

"Dad, I can—"

"Listen to your old man," Cord told me.

I was about to argue, ready to leave the living room, when he took hold of me, his grip like iron on my wrist. "What're you doing?"

His gaze met mine.

"Cord?"

"Siddown."

Instead, I stood there, staring at him.

"Please," he croaked out.

It was too much to look and not touch him. I gave up at the same time he gave me a gentle tug. I sank down onto the couch beside him. When he lifted his arm, I curled into his warmth and put my hand on his broad, muscular chest and my head on his shoulder. I craved his solid strength, and I closed my eyes when I felt him brush his lips across my forehead. The tenderness undid me, and I pressed in tightly against him. I was almost holding my breath, worried the moment would pass, but he seemed content to hold me, and I was content to let him.

"Thanks," he muttered, low and hoarse in my ear.

"What're you thanking me for?"

"The trust right here. I've been hoping for it."

"I don't think trust has ever been our issue."

"No?"

"Not in a physical way," I tried to explain. "I mean, I know you would never let anything happen to me—like you would never allow me to get hurt."

"No, I wouldn't."

"It's my heart that would have been in jeopardy," I said, hoping to sound playful.

"Not anymore."

I nodded.

"You don't believe me."

"Are you hungry?" I asked, changing the subject. He'd asked me, but I hadn't checked on him. "Do you want to eat with me?"

"I would love to," he said, nuzzling his nose against my temple. "But, really, Trace, I swear, your heart would never be in danger with me."

I stared at him, uncertain what I was supposed to say.

"You can count on me."

Could I? On Cord?

He smiled suddenly. "You think your dad will bring me some soup too?"

I turned and asked my father to bring a bowl for Cord as well, and he seemed pleased. "This is so weird."

"What?"

I brought my gaze back to his. "I'm in some alternate dimension where you, Cord Nolan, actually like me," I teased him.

"I like you just fine."

He was making my stomach flutter.

When my father brought over the chunky, spicy chicken soup, so much better than chicken noodle or something from a can, Cord inhaled the delicious aroma and smiled at me.

"You're gonna love it," I said, passing him his napkin.

"I'm already good," he said, his voice warm.

I nudged him with my elbow, and we ate together quietly while the others played. It was nice to just sit and talk with him and not feel like one or the other of us was going to run away, like we normally did.

"We should do this more often," I said after a few minutes.

"Yes. I would like that."

When I lay back down after dinner, Cord took the bowls to the sink. I wanted to talk to him some more when he came back and decided to just put my head down for a minute. I couldn't remember ever being so tired.

WHEN I woke up, it was dark. I rolled over and saw Alex asleep in the recliner in front of the fireplace. I thought for a minute about getting up and going over there and waking him—both of us needed to be in a bed—but I was too stiff and cold to bother. I lost my balance suddenly and put my hand down on the floor to steady myself, but instead of touching rug, I got dog.

My dad's mutt Bo turned his massive head and looked at me. The closest the vet could tell was that Bo was half Rhodesian ridgeback and half rottweiler. There might be some kind of mastiff in there, as well, but, really, just a damn big dog. He weighed a good hundred pounds and was all muscle. Every time my dad walked him he got offers to buy him. People just loved Bo. And as long as Bo saw my old man greet you, and smile at you, and better yet, hug you, he was fine. If, however, you startled my father, or if Bo thought you were trying to hurt him, you'd be in trouble. Not that there'd been more than some growling so far.

There were some guys in the park asking for money for drugs a while back, and my dad jogged by, and they reached out to get his attention. They didn't mean to trip him—even my dad said it was an accident—but he went down anyway, and at the moment one of the guys reached down to help him up, Bo came flying across the grass in a brindle blur. My dad had let him sit and play with some of the children while he did his laps around the jogging path, but apparently the dog was keeping an eye on my old man. He came with teeth bared, growling, snarling, and the guy forgot about my dad and ran. They both ran, and the women at the park with their children cheered. My dad called Bo back with a whistle and accepted some help from a few of the young mothers. They all knew my dad and Bo, and when the policemen came around and asked if Bo was a vicious dog, the chorus of outrage was almost deafening. How could a dog that patiently allowed himself to be buried in a sandpile by two three-year-olds be vicious? The two stoned college-aged guys had, in fact, frightened a few of the mothers with their belligerent requests for money. They all had their children with them, and it was creepy. If Bo had rousted them, well, good for Bo.

The loyalty Bo owed my father was well deserved. Returning home from his usual Wednesday-night bowling with friends, Ray Brandt had seen the dog lying in the gutter on the side of the road. Instead of racing by like everyone else, instead of driving on as the one who had hit Bo had done, he stopped. He carried the massive weight to the car and drove the dog directly to the emergency animal clinic twenty miles away. Amazingly, Bo's only injury was a broken back leg that the vet on duty said would mend cleanly. The water he had swallowed from what was rushing down the storm drain had been more life threatening, and he was in shock from hypothermia. He would need to be admitted to the hospital and monitored for perhaps as long as forty-eight hours. Two grand right there.

My dad paid the bill and two days later collected his dog. He put an ad in the paper, and when the owner called, my dad explained to him what had happened. The man was touched by what my dad had done and even offered to pay him the money for the vet bill, but then he pleaded with my dad to keep him. Sadly, the dog had been his daughter's pet, and she had been hit on her bicycle by a drunk driver and killed. She had named him Bo and had lavished much loving attention on him. It was painful for the man and his wife to see the dog every day, and, in fact, they had been on their way to the local shelter to drop him off when he had bolted en route to the car and leaped over their fence. The dog had been looking for the little girl for weeks, the man told my father, pacing the house anxiously. With a story like that, my dad was a goner.

My dad kept the dog's name and, of course, the dog. Bo was still a gem with children, but he was slavishly devoted to my father. In fact, the only time he left my father's side was when we all came to visit. Instead of sleeping on his favorite blanket next to my dad's bed, he was forced by either curiosity or a compulsion to protect, to go from room to room the entire night and make sure everyone was fine.

As I'd touched him he'd turned to check on me, and I anticipated him rising to his feet before he would thrust his muzzle into my face. I was surprised when he regarded me for only moments before turning his gaze elsewhere. It was strange, and so I traced where he was looking with my eyes.

I saw a black-gloved hand soundlessly try to remove the chain from the french door that led from the living room out into my father's large flower garden. The hand was attached to an arm clad in what looked like a black sweater, and more of it came into view as the chain was quietly rattled as whoever it was tried again and again. The dead bolt had been easily opened; the small chain lock was proving to be more of a setback.

I sat straight up but didn't make a sound. Bo came to his feet, and I was afraid if I yelled, the dog would go after the intruder, and I was afraid of what would happen then. I rolled off the couch, my gaze never leaving the door, and walked backward until I felt the recliner behind me. I sank soundlessly down onto the arm and put my hand over Alex's mouth.

Alex flicked his eyes open—he worked undercover, so maybe he was used to getting woken up like that—and looked up at me. He didn't do that surprised startle you always see in the movies, he just woke up.

I whispered for him to look, and as I said it, I rolled his head to the side so he could see the door. I felt him tense under my hand, and I moved away from him as he almost bounced up to his feet. He pulled his gun from the holster on his hip, and I had a moment to think that my brother was sleeping with his gun and that couldn't be good before he ran to the front door, threw it open, and charged out into the night.

It made no sense that he would leave me, but what was he supposed to do, let the guy in the house? That seemed like a worst-case scenario.

At the same moment the chain finally got worked loose, and I yelled as the door slowly swung open. I saw the outline of a large man framed in the doorway before I heard a command of freeze from outside.

He pivoted fast, and Bo began growling and snarling before launching himself toward the door. I lunged forward and caught Bo's collar so he couldn't go after the intruder. Having only about forty pounds on the dog, I wasn't certain I could hold him, but I managed to wrap my arms around him so he couldn't move.

"Tracy!"

The lights came on suddenly, and my dad was there, his hand on my back, and when I opened my eyes, and looked, there was nobody at the back door, neither the man nor my brother.

"Oh God, Alex," I gasped, and my heart stopped. I was certain the intruder had shot my brother.

Evan blew by us and flew out the door. Instantly I heard someone yell for him to freeze where he was.

I wanted to get up, to move, to go see, but I was frozen in place.

"Honey, let go of Bo," my father said gently.

I still had my hands clutched around Bo's collar, and I was shaking.

"Bo, sit."

The dog wanted to go see what was going on too, but one command from my father and he sat, waiting for what came next.

Slowly, gently, my dad untangled my fingers from Bo's collar and got me up off the floor and back down on the couch. Only then did he call Bo to him, and they both went out the back door.

Alone, I watched the floodlights go on around the property, saw a lot of shadows of people moving, and heard shouting as I sat and waited.

After several more minutes, Evan came back and took a seat beside me on the couch.

"Is Alex okay?" I asked him, holding my breath.

"He's fine," he said, passing me my glasses, which someone had taken off me and placed on the coffee table.

"You're sure?" I asked again as I put my glasses on, not turning my head to look at him, simply leaning against him heavily.

"Yeah, he's fine. Everyone's fine."

I nodded and then closed my eyes, trying to calm my racing heart, willing my stomach to unclench and my breathing to even out.

I heard a lot of sirens, and minutes later, when I opened my eyes, there was a new flood of noise from outside—voices, doors slamming, and just sound, too much for before dawn in my father's quiet neighborhood.

A policeman leaned in and closed the back door, so that drowned out the circus outside. I sat next to my brother and stared at the dying flames in the fireplace.

When Evan got up, I made sure I didn't fall over and watched silently as he threw one of those ready-to-burn logs into the fireplace with some regular wood and got the living room warm and cozy again.

We were sitting there quietly talking about Mom for some reason when the door swung open and Cord walked into the room. He looked strange: rumpled, eyes red-rimmed, and unshaven, which he never was. He crossed the floor to Evan and me and took a seat as he had earlier that night on the coffee table beside the couch, facing me.

"You look terrible." I said dryly.

"I've been with Celia Hughes."

"Why?" I asked him, concerned.

"Who's Celia Hughes?" Evan asked before I shushed him.

"The cops guarding her found a car bomb rigged to her Lexus tonight."

"Ohmygod," I breathed, leaning forward to put my hand on his knee. "Is she okay?"

He let out a deep sigh and covered my hand with his own. "She's no longer giving me shit about protective custody, I can tell you that."

"Cord," I pressed him, staring at him hard.

He nodded. "She's fine, just scared."

"Is the guy who just tried to break in—"

Cord cut me off. "No, he's not the car-bomb guy. I don't know who the hell this guy is outside, but he's definitely small-time. No professional hit man fucks around for ten or fifteen minutes with a goddamn Home Depot chain lock. He comes in, shoots the dog, kills you, and he's in and out without even waking up Alex. This was like having one of the Three Stooges come to kill you."

"I was still scared," I told him, my jaw clenching tight.

"I know you were scared, but between your dad's fuckin' monster dog and your trigger-happy brother, I don't really think you were in any danger even for a second."

"Is the guy dead?"

"No."

"What was he doing here?"

"Someone hired him to deliver a dead rabbit."

"I'm sorry, what?" Evan snapped at him.

Cord rubbed his eyes hard, scrubbing them with the heels of his palms before raking both hands hard through his short, thick dark-brown hair. "The guy outside was paid a grand to come over here, break in, and put a dead rabbit in a box on your living room table."

"Why?"

"How *Fatal Attraction* is that?" Evan pointed out.

I couldn't help smiling.

"It's not fuckin' funny!" Cord barked at me.

"No," I said, rubbing his knee, soothing him. "It's really not."

"But why a rabbit?" Evan pressed him.

"'Cause in the old days, a dead rabbit meant you were pregnant, right? That's how they checked; it was called the rabbit test," I explained to my brother.

"Wait, so that actually meant something in *Fatal Attraction*? I thought it was just about the kid's pet gettin' iced."

"Can you let this go?" I was trying really hard not to laugh for Cord's sake.

"Did the rabbits only die if a woman was pregnant?" Evan was like a dog with a bone; he had to know the why of things.

"No. All the rabbits died because to check to see if a woman was pregnant, the rabbit had to be opened up so the doctor could examine its ovaries after they injected it with a pregnant woman's urine."

"Gross that you know that," he said frankly, "and why couldn't they just put the bunny back together when they were done?"

"That's a lot of expense for a rabbit, right?"

"Are you kidding?" Evan was clearly revolted.

"I didn't say I thought it was," I said, defending myself, and then I coughed to cover the chuckling. "You know I would have saved every single one of them. I'm just telling you, that's what they did."

"That's horrible." He looked aghast.

"But a lot of advances in modern medicine happened that way."

"I don't like the sound of that."

"Ev—"

"Are you two done?" Cord snarled loudly at us, clearly annoyed that we'd been ignoring him. "Because a dead rabbit in a box just got collected as evidence, and neither one of you is concerned about the big picture!"

"So who sent the guy?" I asked, back on task.

"He doesn't know. He says he got a text on his phone, which led him to a locker in a bus station with the box and a thousand dollars in cash."

"And the phone the text came from?"

"No doubt a burner," Cord informed me.

"And are there maybe cameras in the bus station?"

"It depends on which bus station, but it's doubtful that even if they have some that they would be focused on the lockers."

"Okay." I took a breath. "So some psycho paid this guy to bring a dead rabbit over here, and since he doesn't even know who it was, it's a dead end."

"Yeah."

"So, really, he wasn't here to kill me or Alex."

"No. He's just a delivery boy."

His answer made me feel better even though the fear lingered. "You really do look like crap. You should go home and sleep," I told him seriously.

"No, I've got clothes in my truck, and your dad's gonna lemme crash here tonight so I don't have to make the drive back to the city."

I thought of something then. "Is it a bad sign that Alex sleeps with his gun?"

"I sleep with my gun."

"Oh, that's comforting," I said sarcastically with a strained smile.

He grinned widely and his eyes twinkled. "I'm kidding. I think Alex was strapped to protect you, that's all."

"Did he shoot the guy?"

"The guy wouldn't put down his gun; Alex had no choice but to put one in his leg."

"So he'll be all right?"

"Yeah, sure."

"Good."

"Why good?"

"'Cause I would've felt bad if Alex had to kill someone because of me," I confessed.

"He's had to shoot a few people, Trace, and they didn't all live, ya know? It's part of the job. It's not personal. If you do something bad, you run the risk of getting hurt. Alex is there to enforce the law. Sometimes the law must be carried out with deadly force."

"I hate guns," I said flatly. "If nobody had them, it would be better."

"That's ridiculous. Guns have nothing to do with anything. It's the person, not the gun."

"Who in the hell is Celia Hughes?" Evan asked suddenly, clearly annoyed.

I let myself fall back against the couch as Cord brought Evan up to speed on Breckin's latest affair.

I dozed off listening to Cord talk, and drifted in and out of sleep for a couple hours before all the policemen cleared out and my dad and Alex finally came back in the house. My dad made chamomile tea, and I got reheated soup and saltines. We all sat at the kitchen table and listened to Cord explain about Celia Hughes and the car bomb and how confusing it was to have amateur night being played out alongside the work of an obvious professional. The intruder was a nobody; the car bomb had been precisely planted. They only found it because Celia had first juggled and then dropped her keys on the way to the car, and because she was pregnant, one of the officers had volunteered to get down on his hands and knees and retrieve them from under her car. The keys had done the Murphy's Law slide and wound up way under the car, inaccessible from either side. As he crawled and reached, the officer had seen the bomb and alerted the others. Just plain dumb luck at work. So much C4 had been rigged to the ignition key, Cord said, there would have been nothing left of her to identify. I heard the room go silent and felt all eyes on me. I said nothing and didn't open my eyes to look at any of them.

"And you think Tracy is in the same danger?" I heard my dad ask suddenly, sounding frightened.

"I do," Cord replied solemnly. "I don't know what's going on yet, but I think it has something to do with Breckin and I'm not sure what else. Someone is killing the people he's been with, but what's really weird is that outside of us here and Celia and Breckin, I don't think anyone else knows he cheated."

"So the person who's trying to hurt Tracy must have been watching Breckin," Alex offered, his mind obviously clicking away in thought.

"Yeah, that's what I think," Cord agreed, yawning quietly, absently running his knuckles down the side of my neck. "I think one of two things is gonna happen: either the person who's doing this will eventually go after Breckin, or he or she will reveal himself or herself to him after everyone is dead."

"But Celia Hughes is still alive, and Tracy is certainly not going to die," Alex said adamantly, daring Cord to contradict him.

"Yeah, but Timothy Stanson is dead: he was killed in a house fire after he was beaten. Someone tried to blow up Celia today, and they were planning to up the ante with the delivery of the rabbit to Tracy."

"So did anyone deliver any dead animals to Celia?" Evan queried.

"No."

"Then why send the rabbit to Tracy?" Evan persisted.

Cord tipped his head back and forth. "I have a theory about that."

"Which is?" Alex prodded him.

"I think whoever this person is is mad at Breckin and wants Tracy to know that Breckin cheated on him. I think he's after Breckin. I think he's trying to punish him for some trespass that we don't know about yet, and he's upset on Tracy's behalf even though he, or she, plans to kill him."

"Jesus Christ," Alex whispered. "What the hell, Cord?"

"I know."

"I don't—" He took a breath. "You have to help me protect my brother."

I leaned across the kitchen table and put a hand on Alex's cheek. "I'm not gonna die."

"No, you're not," Cord said hoarsely, and when his gaze flicked to mine, I was surprised at the weight of his stare.

I reached for him, and he took my hand tightly, surprising me with his grip.

When he turned to Alex, he didn't let go of me. "There's a patrol car on the street night and day so everyone can get some sleep."

"Good," I said, yawning. "We all need it."

"Yes," Evan agreed, standing up. "Cord, the couch is yours, Tracy, you come with me."

Too tired to do anything but follow, I trailed after Evan up the stairs to the back bedroom, which had the other fireplace. I heard Alex mumbling something behind us as we all trudged along, but I couldn't make it out.

My last coherent thought of the night was that I had not slept in the same bed with both my brothers since I was, like, seven or eight. It was comforting to look from Alex, asleep on his stomach, over to Evan, who had his back to me, and see them both instantly sound asleep. I felt safe even as I looked over to the nightstand and noticed, in the flickering light of the fire, Alex's gun lying beside the lamp, on top of my mother's Bible.

CHAPTER
Eight

I DREAMED about Cord.

It was embarrassing and made no sense, but in my dream I was held down and woke up panting, which was not a usual occurrence. I had to get up, climb over Alex, wobble to the bathroom, and take care of myself before I could pee. I was thankful no one had been awake in the bed to notice my discomfort.

Back under the covers, I was lying there staring at the ceiling, trying to figure out why I was dreaming about Cord again after so many years. After we first met, I had gone through a stretch of time—six months, maybe a year, I wasn't sure—when he had been the focus of almost every nighttime fantasy. He had invaded daydreams as well, but it had been ages since Cord Nolan and his gorgeous green eyes had overrun my mind. When I finally got it figured out logically—he was there, in my space, so of course I would think about him—I was relieved. So when Alex rolled over and scowled at me, I was wide-awake, having been lying there for hours.

"Yes?"

"Do you not hear that?"

Evan was snoring and had been since I'd become conscious. "It's jet lag. He's tired."

"I don't give a fuck."

"Isn't snoring supposed to be bad or something?" I offered.

"It's goddamn annoying as shit," Alex said hoarsely, frowning at me.

"No, I mean it's supposed to mean something, like you've got a health problem."

"He's got a problem, all right," he said, sitting up in bed, "and I would not have stayed in here if you weren't because, Jesus, who can sleep with him doing that?"

"Me, I guess," I sighed, struggling to sit up beside him.

"You were all whacked out on drugs," he assured me, putting a hand under each of my armpits and hauling me up next to him. "Christ, no wonder he ain't got no woman. Who can take this every night?"

"There's no one woman," I told my brother, "but I'm sure there are many women in and out of his bed."

Much eye rolling accompanied my statement, but we both knew it was true.

Alex got up then and went downstairs to get me some coffee and my glasses. He came back a few minutes later with a stricken look on his face.

"What's the matter?" I asked as he passed me the two cups of coffee, one light as it had half-and-half in it, and the other black because Alex took nothing in his. He got back under the covers, careful not to spill either my cup or his, before turning slowly to look at me.

"I don't know what to say," he said, taking his cup from me before passing me my glasses from where he'd hooked them over the collar of his shirt.

"Just tell me. Something's obviously weird downstairs."

The bedroom door opened then, and Cord walked in. He closed the door gently behind him in deference to Evan, who was still dead to the world.

"Okay," I said, taking a sip of my coffee, looking up at him expectantly. "You tell me what's up."

He stood there obviously deciding what he wanted to say, looking uncomfortable.

"Cord?"

Still nothing.

"Maybe a skosh of a hint?"

He gave me the most pained expression I'd ever seen.

"Oh, for crissakes, what the hell is going on?" I snapped at him as Evan rolled over and nearly made me spill coffee all over him. "Jesus, be careful. I understand you actually need your face in your line of work."

"First thing in the morning?" he complained. "Sarcasm? Really?"

"Ev, I could've burned you."

"And whose fault is that?"

He had a point. I *was* the one drinking scalding liquid in bed.

"Where's my goddamn coffee," Evan grumbled irritably, which was obviously Cord's cue, because he told Evan he'd get it and left without another word.

I turned to Alex and gave him what I hoped was a searing look. "God help me, if you do not start talking in like one second—" My threat got interrupted by my dad, who walked into the bedroom with a cup of coffee—that I assumed would be for Evan since he was the only one without one—and a homemade scone probably meant for me. "Oh." I smiled at him, knowing that here finally was a man who would be blunt and to the point. "Dad, what's going on downstairs?"

"First," he said, smiling warmly at me, "try the scone."

"New recipe?" I asked, because I was always the guinea pig, which was how I knew the scone was mine. I'd never seen him make them before.

"Yes."

I tried it because it was my job and I knew I wouldn't get anything out of him until I did. "It's good, Dad."

He nodded.

"Downstairs?"

He cleared his throat. "Yes, well… were you aware that Joanna was getting married?"

"Who's Joanna?" Evan asked.

"Beth's daughter," I griped at him.

"Oh, yeah," he said with a yawn. "How come I didn't get a scone?"

"I can get you a scone," my father assured him.

"Or coffee?"

"Dad brought you coffee," I told him.

"No, I didn't," my father said, squinting at me. "This is mine; I just brought you the scone to try before I fed them to everybody else."

"Okay, so Cord's bringing you coffee, then," Alex chimed in. "Will you shut up?"

"Yeah, but—"

"Oh, for crissakes, here," I said, passing him my cup. "Will you shut up, please?"

"Is there sugar in here? I don't like sugar, only cream."

"There's only half and half in it," Alex explained. "Tracy doesn't like sugar either."

"Okay, good," he sighed.

"All set now, princess?" I asked sarcastically.

"Well, no, actually," he huffed out. "I thought Dad was getting me a scone."

At which point my father started chuckling and went for the door.

"Don't you dare leave," I threatened him.

The way he was smiling at all of us when he turned back, like we were all just the greatest thing, would have distracted me if I hadn't been having a nervous breakdown. "No, Dad," I said dramatically, "I wasn't aware that Joanna was getting married. Please tell me how that's relevant here."

"Well," he answered, "unbeknownst to her, Joanna's maid of honor, Celia, is the same Celia who has come between you and Breckin."

It took a minute. I wasn't really awake yet, and now I had no coffee. I squinted at him like maybe that would help with the clarity. "What?"

He cleared his throat. "Celia Hughes is downstairs in my kitchen."

"Celia Hughes is downstairs in your kitchen?"

He nodded. "Yes. She's there, and so are Breckin and Beth and a distraught Joanna. She's concerned that you might hate her, and while I've only just met the woman, I would say that Celia would rather chew off her own foot than stay here a second longer."

"So why is she staying?"

"Because presently she finds herself in the middle of a heated argument with your ex-boyfriend," he explained.

"Well," I sighed, "I guess I should go down and meet her."

"What?" Alex choked on his coffee. "No! What the fuck for?"

"Hold up," Evan grumbled from the other side of me. "Who's Celia whoever again?"

We all turned and looked at him.

"What? I wasn't listening. I can't even see until the caffeine hits my bloodstream."

"She's the woman Breckin cheated with, idiot," Alex barked at him, which was loud in the small bedroom and especially that close to my ear. "We talked about this all last night."

"Lower your voice," I ordered, crawling carefully over Alex since he was holding scalding liquid.

"You're actually going down there." Alex sounded incredulous.

"What am I supposed to do? Hide up here? Show everyone that I'm spineless and scared and weak? I haven't done anything wrong. I didn't cheat on anybody."

"But, Trace—"

"No," I interrupted, making a cutting motion across my throat. "Seriously, I'm going down there. I want to see her."

"Fine. I'll go with you," Alex said, throwing off the covers to get up.

"No, you stay here with Evan. Dad'll go with me."

He looked like he might protest, but Dad silenced him with a simple gesture to be still. I opened the bedroom door, and Cord was there, poised to come in.

"Hi," I greeted him, reaching for the cup. "That's mine now. Evan has his."

"I put half and half in it, and cinnamon, 'cause I know he likes it."

"Oh," Evan groaned behind me.

So we played musical cups once more, and Cord started chuckling along with my father.

"Did you bring a scone?"

"Eat the rest of mine," I growled but stopped when Cord pushed my glasses up a little higher on my nose. "What?"

"I like these on you."

I felt my face heat. "Thank you."

"Are you going down?"

"I am," I announced, passing by him and then descending to the first floor.

I realized as I walked into the kitchen what I was wearing. Sometime in the early morning I had woken up and changed into a white T-shirt and a pair of pajama bottoms. Everyone else looked great, as it was a little after eleven thirty, and I was a slob. Fantastic. Beth looked stunning, and Joanna would have looked good too if her eyes weren't swollen from crying.

"Good morning," I greeted her, walking over and staring down at her.

She looked up at me and sighed heavily.

I forced a smile before turning to my ex and his one-night stand turned baby mama.

Celia Hughes looked like she was maybe thirty, with a flawless golden complexion and straight blonde hair that had highlights of bronze and wheat threaded through it. It fell to her shoulders, and wisps of layers brushed her face. Her eyes were pale seafoam green with traces of laugh lines around them. She was a startlingly beautiful woman. Her face was simply luminous. I didn't know what to do. I had not brushed up on the etiquette for this situation. All I could think to do was to extend my hand to her.

"I'm Tracy Brandt."

She took my hand and squeezed it back. Not wimpy, not too strong, just enough to tell me she was there. "I'm Celia Hughes."

"Can we talk?"

"That would be great." She nodded, rising after I gestured for her to follow me into the living room.

Breckin started to say something, and I saw Celia wince. When I turned to him, I noticed how wrung out he looked. "It's fine. Everything's fine."

He furrowed his brows but nodded before I led Celia away.

In the living room, I took a seat in the overstuffed chair by the fireplace, and Celia sat on the couch where I had fallen asleep the night before. I told her to put her feet up on the coffee table, and she thanked me before stretching out her legs.

"How far along are you?"

She placed a maternal hand on her swollen abdomen. "Four and a half months, now."

I wasn't sure how that could be since she'd only slept with Breckin four months ago but I knew from other friends that there was a way to count back from when you missed your period, and it was math I didn't understand. When Ira and Courtney had kids, when my brothers got married, I would pay better attention to how that all worked. Right now, my interest in my ex's child, beyond hoping it was born healthy, was nil. "Can you feel the baby move yet?"

"Yes, I can."

I nodded, then took another sip of coffee.

She took a deep breath. "God, that smells so good."

"What? The coffee?"

She smiled and nodded.

"I thought caffeine was okay."

"Some say yes, some say no. I figure it's better to not tempt fate at thirty-six."

"You're thirty-six?" I asked, amazed.

She laughed. I could tell she didn't want to, but she couldn't help it. "Yeah. How old did you think I was? Forty?"

"No," I told her honestly, "I thought maybe twenty-eight, thirty."

"Oh, really?" I had caught her off guard. "Thank you."

There was silence then, and she finally fixed her gaze on me, not in a mean way, just straight in the eye, really looking at me. "I'm really sorry. It wasn't my intent to seduce your boyfriend."

"So why did you?"

"I have never met anyone like him."

"In what way?"

She thought a moment. "Gorgeous, smart, funny, dedicated, gentle…. I don't know what you want me to say. I went to the conference to recruit him for the Dedham Foundation, and I totally blew it."

"That's where he went into private practice."

"Yes."

The plot thickened. "So you both work at Dedham."

"I don't work there yet. I work as a cardiovascular surgeon now. I'm a resident, obviously, but I also do advisory work for the Dedham Foundation. After the baby's born, I plan to join the staff there full-time. They used to just be a pharmaceutical company, and then they expanded to development and research, and finally to what they are today, which is a privately funded facility for rare diseases. It's an incredibly prestigious company that subsists only on private donations from elite benefactors."

"But then why solicit Breckin? He was an ER doctor; he liked being in the trenches and helping out regular people," I explained flatly. "He doesn't do snooty fundraisers and fancy-shmancy hundred-dollar-plate dinners. He's a Democrat, for crissakes."

She smiled then and chuckled. It was a soothing sound. "Here's the thing," she began. "They need some 'in the trenches' people, as you call him. They need the perspective of the working doctor."

"I see. So how did his name come up?"

"By accident, actually," she said, and then she took a deep breath. "Fenton Deveraux, who sits on the board of directors at Dedham, had to take his daughter to County about a year ago. They were in an automobile accident close to Fisherman's Wharf, and due to the weather, they couldn't helicopter Marissa to Los Angeles to her regular doctor. Breckin was on duty, and he identified a pretty rare blood disease that she has right off the bat. Mr. Deveraux was all prepared to give Breckin her full medical history, and so when he didn't have to, he was simply stunned."

I nodded.

"Since then Mr. Deveraux has been really interested in the caliber of the hotshot young doctors we have in our public hospitals. He's impressed and has made a point of saying again and again how Dedham could benefit from an influx of new talent. He wants to specifically scout and hire the best, and for him that began with Breckin."

"Makes sense," I admitted. "So you went to the conference to plead Dedham's case."

"I did."

"But?"

She took a breath. "But... when we started talking, I was suddenly sixteen all over again. I'm not proud of what I did, but I couldn't stop myself. I didn't just see him there and decide to go over and seduce him. I went to him to talk about Dedham. I remember introducing myself, and I had all the literature with me and facts and figures for him."

"But?" I asked again.

"But then we started talking, and I started to notice things."

"What things?"

She scrutinized me. "You really want to hear all this?"

"I do," I said, and then I took another sip of my coffee.

"Well, like how warm his eyes were, and how funny he was, and how charming. How I could just sit there and talk to him and how easy and natural it was."

I nodded.

"I realize now that the ease and warmth he exudes is mostly due to you." I waited silently until she went on. "He's so very in love. He's not on the prowl at all, not looking to impress anyone, just content and himself with everyone all the time. He has no hidden agenda, and he isn't trying to get everyone he meets into bed, so he isn't careful, and he holds nothing back. He spreads this warmth and tenderness, and it's so…." She trailed off then, snapping her head up to look at me, afraid she'd said too much and offended me.

"It's so what?" I asked, staring at her hard over the rim of my coffee cup.

"It's so sexy," she said honestly. "He just exudes raw sex appeal. You must know."

Raw? No. Breckin was smooth and sensual. There was nothing dangerous or wild about the man. Not like Cord. "I do," I replied woodenly.

"You just look at him and your thoughts go carnal. His confidence is a magnet. I'm surprised you don't have to beat them off with a stick."

"I wouldn't know." I clipped my words. "Normally, if people persist in trying to get his attention, he gets a little hostile and cold."

"You don't have to tell me about hostile and cold. I am now clearly on the receiving end of hostile and cold," she told me, and she looked down suddenly. When she raised her head back up, tears had welled in her eyes. She looked as though she was ready to break down and sob. "I didn't mean to get pregnant. We used a condom; I can only hazard a guess that it broke at some point. It was a long night."

Really, I could have lived my whole life without hearing that comment, but she was being honest, and I had asked for the brutal truth. "Did he spend the night with you?"

"Yes."

"You two woke up in the morning together?"

"He was gone when I woke up, but when I fell asleep he was there with me."

There was a long silence before I asked her another question. "Why did you think I was the one trying to kill you?"

"For the obvious reason," she huffed out. "I'm sure that one case of infidelity you could forgive to keep a man like that, but the baby thing, that's a whole other ballgame, isn't it?"

"Actually, the infidelity in and of itself was enough. And not because of the act, or acts, themselves, but because of the loss of trust," I explained. "I mean, once the trust is gone, what do you have?"

She was silent.

"There has to be trust."

"If it means anything, he's always maintained his love for you."

"It doesn't mean anything at all," I told her.

She sucked in a breath.

"Listen, are you scared about all this with your car and everything? Are you okay?"

Clearly she was relieved we were changing the subject. "I'm terrified. But Inspector Nolan seems to have a good solution, don't you think?"

"I haven't heard the solution yet."

"Oh." She sounded surprised. "Well, he thinks that it's not safe for either of us to stay and be around our families because we might inadvertently put them in danger."

"That makes sense," I agreed.

"Yes," she said gently. "I mean, think about it. Some guy was here in your father's house last night. How many more of these would-be killers do you want to come here? That's really scary. I know I've been staying with my mother, and I don't want anyone to hurt her. So I'm going to do what the inspector suggests."

"Which is what?"

"He thinks that whoever is behind this wants to eventually confront Breckin, so where better to do that than at his parents' home in Fieldcrest."

"Which is where?"

"In Vermont."

"Funny. Breckin always told me that he was from Georgia."

"I guess that's where he was born, but they moved to Vermont before he started kindergarten."

"You know more about his family than I do."

"No, I simply spoke to Inspector Nolan before you this morning and heard the plan."

"Go on."

"Well, so he thinks that we should all go to Vermont to visit Breckin's parents and there, with us all together, he can protect us and draw out the killer."

"That's awful risky for Breckin's folks and his family."

"I guess the inspector has already spoken with them and they gave him the green light on it. I guess they're not too scared—pretty big in their community, apparently."

"Which does what for them? Is their house made of Kevlar?"

"I don't—" She looked flustered. "They're not worried, that's all I know."

"I wonder why."

"Like I said," she sighed, "I'm not sure. Inspector Nolan assured me that he will have a lot of local help. He seems okay with it, so I'm confident."

"Inspector Nolan makes you feel safe?"

"Ohmygod, yes. Doesn't he do the same for you?"

"Yeah," I answered thoughtfully, "he does." There was no denying that with Cord in the room, I felt protected. "So you're really okay with going?"

"I can't continue on like this," she told me seriously. "I'm having a baby. I will not have whoever is out there coming after my son. I need this to be over. I have a life to go on with. I have friends and family I want to spend time with, and I need to come to some sort of an agreement with your boyfriend about how he plans to help or not help with this child. If it's nothing, then it's nothing, but I need to know."

I nodded. "That's between you and him."

"No," she said, raising her voice for the first time. "It's between the three of us if you plan to stay with him. You have a say too."

"Dr.—"

She cut me off. "Celia. We should at least have that."

It was stupid not to. "Celia," I repeated, "I—"

"Listen," she began hesitantly, her voice trembling a bit. "I know it's hard, but I think if you told him to leave you that he would do the right thing and help me raise my son and be a husband and father."

"I already told him to do that," I informed her, rising from the chair.

"You did?" She was obviously shocked—the way the color drained from her face told me so.

"I did. You can ask him yourself if you don't believe me."

"Why would I not believe anything you say?" she asked sincerely. "You have been nothing but honest with me."

"Here's the thing: I know you want him. I'm telling you now that you should try hard to make it happen. Pull out all the stops; make him feel like he wants to be a daddy. You guys should be together. I firmly believe that."

"Tracy, I don't know what to—"

"Don't say anything. It's not necessary. Just know that your way is clear to him; I'm completely out of the picture."

She looked stunned. "You're amazing."

I was done was what I was.

Walking around the couch, I left the living room and went into the kitchen. Breckin was sitting at the kitchen table, head in hands, and didn't look up at me when I came in. If it had been my house, the cup I was holding would have been history—I would have smashed it into a thousand pieces. As it was, I used every drop of self-control I had to place it gently in the sink. I turned and looked from my father to Beth to Joanna and back to my ex again. They had all heard—maybe not every word, but enough.

I looked over at Joanna. "I'm not mad at you, okay?"

Her eyes were huge as she gazed at me. "You're not?"

"No, why would I be? You had no idea." I sighed deeply, suddenly exhausted as I turned and passed my dad to go to the stairs. My brothers were sitting on them, both with coffee, also having heard it all.

Alex looked up at me as I started up, and Evan squeezed my hand before I could get by. Cord was waiting for me at the top of the stairs.

"I am not going to fuckin' Vermont with my boyfriend and his pregnant lover. Is that clear?"

"We'll see," he said evenly, looking at me hard.

"No, we won't see," I assured him. "I am so done with this whole thing."

He nearly drilled his finger into my collarbone when he spoke. "You don't get to be done until your stalker says you are. Do you get it? You are not in control here. You might be in the driver's seat with this little domestic drama you've got going with your ex and his knocked-up dish on the side, but as far as the attempts on your life are concerned, you are not in control, and you are not the one calling the shots. Don't delude yourself; you will do what I say."

He poked me one last time for emphasis. I was sure I would have a bruise.

"Fuck you, Cord," I retorted. "I'd rather get shot than have to listen to you."

He was going to really launch into me, I could tell by the way he squared his shoulders and took a deep breath, but I walked around him, went back into the bedroom, and slammed the door behind me. I sank down onto the bed and then buried myself under the covers and closed my eyes. I was almost asleep when I heard someone come in and then felt them flop down beside me.

"You okay?"

Evan. "Yeah," I lied.

"You want the report?" he asked simply.

I threw off the covers and rolled over onto my back. "Okay."

"Well, Breckin plans to sit in the kitchen until hell freezes over or you come down or whatever. Basically, he's staying put. Cord needs to talk to you about Vermont, so he's staying. Celia, Joanna, and Beth left. Alex is having words with Breckin, or trying to over Dad making him be quiet. It's a lot of fun down there."

"She's pretty, huh?" I sighed heavily.

"Who?"

"Celia Hughes, of course. Who else?"

"I dunno. Joanna? Beth?"

"Oh," I said, looking up at him. He was right, of course. We hadn't actually discussed our father's lady friend. We had not given one another our opinions. I was more than eager to change the subject. "I guess. You think Beth is pretty?"

"Elegant and distinguished. Pretty doesn't really do it, does it?"

"No, no, you're right. And Joanna?"

He squished up his face like he'd eaten a lemon. "Mousy, I think. She must take after her dad because she sure as shit doesn't look a thing like her mom."

"You wouldn't date her?"

"She's getting married."

"No, I know, but you wouldn't have if you'd have met her before?"

"I don't date anybody. I just fuck," he made clear.

"Charming."

"You started it with the whole 'would you date her' bullshit."

"Yeah, I did," I assented, owning that.

"But to your original question, do I think Celia Hughes is pretty?"

"Yeah."

"She's a beautiful woman."

"Yeah, I thought so too." I sighed wearily.

"But a homewrecker nonetheless."

"Whatever. It takes two to wreck a home. She couldn't have done it by herself."

"Funny, though."

"What is?"

"You and Breckin."

"How so?"

"I never actually saw it. You and him, I mean."

"What are you talking about?" I asked, turning to look at him. "You loved Breckin."

"Past tense, yeah. Not anymore," he made clear. "He cheated twice."

"How did you know? Did Alex tell you?"

"Oh, come on, Trace, there's only one reason people take a break. Alex didn't have to tell me. I knew when Dad told me Breckin moved out that that's what happened."

"That's bullshit," I said, rubbing my eyes.

He scoffed. "Whatever you say."

"I knew Alex knew," I sighed, looking back at him.

"He's a cop, right? He's gonna notice shit like your friend treating Breckin like a leper."

"Yeah."

"And just so you know, even if you forgive him for all this bullshit—I won't. Not ever. Nobody treats you like this. He and I are done."

It was so sad to hear. One of my favorite things had been that both my brothers liked Breckin so much.

"But even before that, I never really got you guys."

"How do you mean?"

He shrugged. "He's a status guy, and you, you're happy with the working-class stiff. You're about the day-to-day and the work and the long run, and him, he's more about the fast rise and power and prestige."

"How can you say that? He was an ER doctor."

"*Was*," he emphasized. "Now he does research and decides who gets grants from the foundation he works for. He attends fundraisers and stuff like that. He's the face of Dedham; rolling in money now."

"I guess."

"But back in the day, when he was yours, did he really enjoy being an ER doc?"

"I thought so."

"But you're not sure."

"No."

He was quiet a moment. "So what does Breckin really want?"

I grunted. "Well, obviously I don't know anymore."

"But that's what I mean. I think Celia Hughes is more his kind of long-term commitment."

"Oh, this is helping," I groaned, rolling over away from him.

"I should shut up."

"Just… I wanna know what you think."

He sighed. "Well, to me, Celia looks like the kind of person I would imagine he would be with, if he were just a buddy of mine. She looks like she would look good next to him on a Christmas card. I wasn't surprised when Cord told us he came from a wealthy family; he's got that thing about him that tells you that's how he was raised."

"Like what?" I asked, my voice muffled in the pillow.

"Like I said before, you can tell he's about money and prestige. He wants more. He wants to be wherever he used to be. It chafes him that I make more money than he does."

"Oh, it does not; he could care less."

"You're deluded."

And maybe I was and had been so the whole time.

"I always thought you'd end up with a guy like Cord."

"Cord," I scoffed, rolling back over so I could see my brother. "Oh, for fuck's sake. Why?"

"Because you're exactly alike."

"Yeah, no," I grumbled. "We're nothing alike."

"You're wrong. Everything he wants, you want."

I shook my head.

"Yes."

"How do you even—"

"What?"

"You don't know Cord."

He scoffed. "I've known him just as long as you have, but unlike you, I've been out drinking with the man. I've sat and listened to him and Alex talk about what they want their futures to be and about their dreams and everything."

"You have?"

"Of course I have."

"Huh."

"He wants a home, he wants kids, he wants to coach soccer, vacation at Disneyland, and have someone to come home to who wants to take care of him. Period. End of story."

"You—"

"And you want all that same stuff."

"So does Breckin."

"Breckin wants a yacht and to belong to a country club."

"Where are you getting this from?"

Evan smiled down at me warmly. "Most of all, Cord wants you, Trace."

I rolled my eyes. "Man, whatever you're taking you need to fuckin' share, 'cause all they gave me was giant Motrin."

He laughed softly. "I always thought you'd make a really good husband for a policeman."

"Why?"

"Because you know it's dangerous, but you wouldn't let that run your life. I think that's how a policeman's mate has gotta be."

"Cord, right," I placated him. "You and Cordell Nolan could have a contest for dog of the year. See which of you could break more hearts and fuck more people."

"There's no contest there." He grinned wickedly, moving close and then lying down on the bed right next to me so we were touching down the lengths of our sides.

We were silent for several minutes before I turned and looked at him. "So... what? We're just going to stay up here and wait out the storm?"

"Why not?" He yawned. "What the hell else you got planned for today?"

"Matt's supposed to call me and maybe come by."

"Who's Matt again?"

"My best friend since college."

"Oh yeah."

"You know you really do have the attention span of a two-year-old."

"If that," he scoffed, grinning crazily. "But I do know what's truly important."

"Like what?" I teased him because I was getting tired.

He thought a moment before he answered. "Like that your favorite ice cream is chocolate chip and that Mom's was coffee, and that Dad is afraid of loving Beth, and that Alex almost got strung out on heroin the last time he was undercover."

"Holy shit," I gasped, rolling my head to stare at him. "I should know that. How come I don't know that?"

He shrugged.

"I didn't think he talked to you more than me about stuff that went on at work."

"You thought wrong," he said gently but firmly.

"How come?"

"It's because he wants you to think of him one way—he needs it to be that way, counts on it. It makes him feel safe. He can share the garbage with me and know that nothing will change."

"He has more faith in you than he does in me," I said sadly.

"No. He counts on you for his emotional support and me as a sounding board."

"I worry about him."

"Hell, so do I. I'd really like him to quit."

"He's like Cord, though—fat chance of either of them ever quitting."

We were quiet then, and I realized how sick I felt thinking of all the things I couldn't fix or change.

"Say something else."

He lifted his left wrist. "You want this?"

Alex and I had banned Evan from buying us things, gifts, because he didn't have to, we loved him no matter what. What he wanted was to pay off my mortgage, Alex's, and to send my father around the world. None of us allowed that, not wanting to take advantage. So lately, he had started to leave things when he visited or swap Alex a Ralph Lauren leather jacket for whatever he had in his closet, and steal my bracelets and watches and apologize by sending ridiculously expensive replacements. At the moment he was tempting me with the black-faced, distressed-brown-leather strapped Luminor Panerai he had on his wrist.

"No," I lied.

He took off the watch, which cost more than I made in a month, and passed it to me. "You could just borrow it."

"Evan, you don't—"

"I'll get it at Thanksgiving."

Arguing was futile. He knew me, had seen my eyes light up, and I recognized in him a desire to make me even a little happy. When I put the watch on, his smile made his eyes glow.

"It looks good on you."

He was so transparent.

"So now you wanna hear about this movie part I read for?"

"Oh fuck yes."

And so I listened for hours about the war movie he was excited about that sounded horrific to me. There would be sacrifice and unrequited love and death, lots of that, all in the future where World War III was a done deal. The longer he talked, the worse it sounded. I liked the other one he had already signed up for—a big sprawling urban-fantasy epic, steampunk vampires, lots of layers, some of them good, and some bad. He made it sound like a cross between *Underworld* and *The Matrix* with *Hellboy* and *Firefly* thrown in for good measure.

"So do you get to wear leather?"

"Lots."

"Awesome."

"I'm leaving *Cape Cod* too."

"No shit."

"Yep. I'm moving back to regular TV."

His new show sounded a little spooky and a lot graphic. In fact, it was going to have to have one of those cool disclaimers at the beginning of each episode that warned you to get your kids the hell out of the room so they didn't get the crap scared out of them. I was pleased with him and his choice. I'd been worried that he would forever be cast as the pretty boy, and his latest choices were not that.

"You're gonna do more than show off your abs."

"Oh, I suspect the abs are still damn important."

"You know what I mean."

His smile told me he did.

I TOOK a shower around five, and right after that Matt called to check in on me. He had called before I woke up and I had missed it. I stayed on the phone for an hour and was surprised how much easier it was to tell when I wasn't living through it at the same time. Even a little bit of distance helped.

My explanation came out in staccato bursts—"And I said and he said, and I said and he said"—until the whole thing was out. The baby part was too much for him, and I found myself relating that piece to Eric instead. I had no idea Matt's beloved could swear like a sailor.

When Matt got back on the phone, after he breathed into a paper bag for several minutes, I got to the part about the psycho trying to kill me. Since it became an episode of *Criminal Minds* at that point, he calmed down. Police drama, he understood.

After I got off the phone with Matt, I went downstairs and found my dad and Alex having a couple of Coronas in the kitchen while they fixed dinner together. Breckin was asleep on the couch, with Bo lying down beside it, as if guarding him, and Evan was watching *Monday Night Football*. It seemed so normal that I almost lost it. I went directly to the back door and walked outside to my father's flower garden. It was nice outside, and I was warm enough in a long-sleeved T-shirt, jeans, and socks. I took a seat on a chaise and stretched out my legs.

"Can I come out here and sit with you?"

When I turned, I found Cord staring at me with a beer in his hand.

"Sure."

He sat down in front of me so I had to sit up, cross-legged, as he faced me, his own long, muscular legs draped over the sides.

"You all right?"

I shrugged.

He reached over and brushed my hair out of my face. "I like seeing your eyes, and this got a little long, huh?"

"It's gotta be cut. It's on my list."

"Or you could leave it," he rumbled, sliding his fingers down my cheek.

I grunted.

"So, listen, I wanna talk to you about Vermont."

I exhaled a deep breath. "I'll go."

He scowled as he studied me.

"What? That's what you want, right?"

"I do, yeah, but why the sudden change?"

"Like you said, I don't want anyone near my dad or Alex or Evan. I can't have that."

He nodded.

"And you."

"Me?" He was surprised—it was clear in his voice.

"Yeah. You're protecting me, I don't want to just stay here and have you with a giant bull's-eye on your chest. I need to do something."

"I should be the least of your worries."

"Yeah, well, you're not," I said softly. "I need to do whatever I can to get this over with. I mean, I know you're coming with me and you'll be in danger too, but there's no changing that. To fight with you and not go, that draws everything out much longer and increases the chances of you getting hurt."

"Jesus, Tracy."

I unfolded my legs, turned, and got up. I put a hand on his shoulder to brace myself as I stood. "Can we talk about all of this later?"

"Whatever you want."

"When do you want to go?"

"The sooner the better."

"Tomorrow?"

"That's what I was hoping."

"Can you get tickets by then?"

"Of course."

I nodded. "Okay. I'll call Dimah and tell him. You let everyone else know."

"Good."

"Man, I'm beat."

"Emotional stuff can really take it out of you."

I shot him a look.

"I wasn't trying to be a dick that time," he snapped defensively. "I swear."

Studying his face, I realized he really wasn't. "I'm gonna go in and talk to Breckin and tell him to go home."

He didn't say anything, and I would have stepped away, but he caught and held my hand as it slipped from his shoulder.

"What?"

"I can make him leave."

"In cuffs and transported in a police car?" I chuckled, turning my hand in his grip, sliding my palm over his callused one.

"Why not?" he teased, drawing me closer.

"I'll make him go. I need to talk to him anyway."

"Okay."

"So you'll call me later and tell me what time to be at the airport and what airline, all right?"

"Yep."

I meant to walk away from him, but I really liked the feel of his rough, callused palm skimming over mine.

"So, you and Breckin," he said, his eyelids fluttering as I lifted my hand away from his and put in on his stubble-covered cheek.

"What about it?" I asked, tracing my thumb over his left eyebrow.

"What?"

I stroked over his cheekbone and watched his eyes narrow like he was drugged. "You have a question about Breckin and me."

"Is it over?"

I could get far too addicted to touching the man if I wasn't careful. The way he responded, the feel of him… it was dangerous. "It is."

"That fast, huh?"

"Not really, not if you think about it," I said, the sudden urge to touch his short sideburns nearly overwhelming me. "We've been apart for four months already, so—"

"What?" he said quickly, his gaze clearing as he stared at me.

"What did I say?" I asked, taking a step away from him.

"How long have you guys been taking a break?"

I scoffed. "Let's call it what it is, Cord. We've been done for—"

"Done?"

"Well, yeah. It's been four months. Almost five."

"Are you kidding?"

"Why would I kid about that?" He was so strange sometimes. I gave him a faint smile before I walked away. I turned at the door. "Don't let Alex hit Breckin, will ya?"

"I promise," he said, seeming distracted. He probably had a lot on his mind.

Walking back into the house, I didn't say anything until I reached Breckin at the kitchen table. He was sitting with my dad having tea, and he looked up at me.

"You need to go home and pack; we're getting on a plane tomorrow."

He stood up and faced me. "I just want a chance to talk to you. How come Cord gets time and I don't?"

The answer seemed obvious to me. Cord had never made promises and broken them. Cord had never made me wonder what was wrong with me or why I wasn't enough to satisfy him. Cord had never cheated on me.

"There's nothing for us to talk about. Just go home; I'll see you tomorrow at the airport."

"Tracy—"

"Make sure you get the flight information and stuff from Cord. You should actually go out and talk to him now."

"I don't want to talk to Cord; I want to talk to you!"

"Tomorrow," I insisted, squeezing my dad's shoulder when I turned away.

I was upstairs and safely ensconced in the bedroom minutes later. Sleep came fast after that. When I woke up a couple hours later, a little after seven, Matt and Eric were downstairs, and they had brought us all dinner from Molinari Deli. When I asked Alex if Cord was coming back, he said no.

"Why?" my brother asked. "Are you disappointed?"

"No, I was just wondering."

But from the look in his face I guessed I hadn't fooled him at all.

CHAPTER
Nine

AT THE airport on Tuesday morning I was thankful Evan was flying out too, so he could stay with me a little longer. It was also a nice distraction to watch people see him, do a double take, and then approach slowly. I enjoyed having my mind occupied.

"What's it like, Evan?" I asked him when he took a seat beside me.

"What?"

"To look like you?"

"I dunno." He shrugged, pushing his sunglasses down to the end of his nose to look at me. "Never known anything else."

I smiled at him; I couldn't help myself. My mother always used to stare at him in wonder and tell him how beautiful he was. She did that with all of us; mothers were like that.

"Better'n being ugly, huh?" He grinned wickedly.

"It is," I agreed as Celia joined us in the boarding area and took a seat across from me.

"Not that you would know."

"What?" My attention returned to him.

"Please." He made a face. "You know what you look like."

"Yeah. Not you."

He gestured at me. "Oh, come on. You got Mom's dark coloring, her big brown eyes, and her thick eyebrows and long lashes. You came out prettiest of all."

I groaned. "Yeah, 'pretty' is what every man strives for."

He snorted. "Don't knock it."

Smiling at him, I watched his face grow serious.

"I will come at a moment's notice if you need me."

"I know," I soothed him.

When Evan had to go catch his plane, I held on to him tight. I had left my dad and Alex at the house, not able to do the whole "waving through the security checkpoint" thing that day.

"This will all pass and just be an interesting sound bite in your life," he promised me before kissing the top of my head and giving me a tight squeeze.

"So, I've got my phone and I'll call you."

"You'll call me every day," he made me promise, holding me out at arm's length. "Every goddamn day, so I don't worry and make myself mental."

"I know, I know: you, Dad, Alex, and Matt. I promise."

"And if you wanna get out of there, just call and I'll get you on a plane."

I nodded with tears stinging behind my eyes, my throat dry, and my stomach in knots.

"Don't cry or you'll dry out your contacts and have to take 'em back out."

My father had made me pack my glasses just in case, but I had eye drops, so in theory I was back to round-the-clock living in my contacts.

"It'll be okay," he told me again, grabbing me hard and then hugging me against him. "I love you more."

I nodded. I couldn't speak, just put my wire-rimmed aviators on as soon as he turned and walked away. He knew better than to look back; he just smiled his dazzler at me before he left.

"I love you more?" Celia asked gently as I sank back down into the chair across from her.

I looked up at her but said nothing.

"It's nice," she said, smiling ruefully.

"It's something my mom always said," I explained. "She would look at us and say, 'I love you more than my eyes.' After she died, I finally understood what it meant. Evan knows too, and so he tells me."

"You guys are all really close."

"We are."

"You're very lucky."

"Yes, I am," I said softly, glad I had my sunglasses on so she couldn't see what a mess I was. I needed to get it together, and soon.

Cord and Breckin were still not there by the time we boarded, and my seat number put me in business class behind Celia, two and two, both of us with a window. Finally, Breckin appeared and moved quickly to put his duffel in the overhead bin above me, but before he could climb in, Cord was there, directing him into the seat beside Celia.

"You guys need to talk and get your stories straight before we land," he advised Breckin. "Tracy's out of this."

Breckin looked annoyed but gave me an affectionate smile before dropping down beside Celia.

Cord shoved his much bigger duffel into the overhead bin, along with his overcoat, and then took his seat next to me.

"You all right?" he asked, checking on me.

"Yeah, fine."

"You look like shit."

Charming. "So what do Breckin and Celia need to coordinate?"

"I had Breckin tell his folks they were married, so I need them to be able to tell his folks when they met and all that."

"Why?"

"Why do they need to know about you? Why do they need to know he's bi? How is any of that important? In this case, the simplest explanation is the best."

"No, I don't mean why that. That makes perfect sense."

"Does it?"

"Like you said, why do his folks need to know anything about me at all? What's the point?"

"Then what's your question?"

"What's my cover? What am I doing here? Who am I to Breckin and Celia?"

His smile was wide and made his eyes glint. "What's your motivation, you mean?"

"Yes." I chuckled, then added dramatically, "Line, please."

He looked good grinning at me, enjoying the playfulness, sliding closer and lifting the armrest between us. "You're Breckin's best friend, who's also been threatened."

"Okay, that's good. I like it. And you?"

"Baby, why would I need a cover?" he said, like I was stupid.

Spell broken, I groaned and turned away from him.

"What are you doing?"

I ignored him.

"Turn around and look at me."

Rolling my head back, I noticed how clear his eyes were.

"What happened?"

"Do you even realize what you did?"

"Obviously not," he said, opening his legs wider so his knee and thigh wedged up against mine. "Tell me."

"Why do you always treat me like an idiot?"

"I don't."

"Yeah, you do, all the time. You always answer me like I'm so fuckin' annoying."

He was scowling.

"Why can't you just speak to me nicely?"

"You could do the same."

I turned in my seat to face him. "See? That's what I mean. You always justify how you treat me. How come you being nice to me is dependent on me being nice to you?"

"That question makes no sense."

"Sure it does," I pressed. "You should just be nice to me because it's what you should do and not for any other reason."

He thought about it a moment. "Be nice to you on general principle, you mean."

"Yes."

He shrugged. "Okay, I guess."

"You guess?"

"Fine, I'll be fuckin' nicer to ya."

"Don't strain yourself."

He pointed at me. "Now, was that necessary?"

I studied his face.

"Well?"

"No."

"Okay," he sighed, crowding me a bit more even as he noticed my regard. "What?"

"It would be nice if you pretended to like me just a little."

"I like you more than you know."

The man made no sense.

I stared out the window as we took off, and after that I was quiet, watching the flight attendants bustle around the cabin. Trying to figure out Cord Nolan was futile, so I pulled out my laptop and prepared to work once we were given permission.

Cord interrupted me getting started. "I wanna talk about Dimah."

"What?"

"You said he's such a great partner, but he doesn't seem worried about you."

"No, he's plenty worried."

"How so?"

Dimah didn't at all like the idea of me traveling to Vermont alone. He wanted to send someone with me, but when I explained about being, technically, in protective custody, he stopped worrying.

"So what was Dimah gonna do, send some goons with you?"

"I can assure you we have no goons on our payroll."

"You're such a wiseass."

"One does what one can, Inspector," I said dismissively and thought that would be it, but he jabbed me gently with his elbow. "What are you—Cord?"

The smirk I was getting made my breath catch. So much arrogance but sexiness at the same time, and the way he was looking at me was really hot.

"Just unclench already. I'm sorry I opened my mouth about Dimah. You're fiercely loyal, and I forget that sometimes."

"I—thank you."

"Don't sound so surprised, I can be nice to you."

I nodded, almost dazed with the change in the man, his willingness to call a ceasefire.

He bumped me with his knee and then didn't move it away after.

"Maybe we can both try harder," I offered.

"I would love that," he husked, his smile kind and unguarded.

Cord got on his laptop then, and after a moment I was able to tear my attention away from him so that we could both do some work. Breckin turned around in his seat and asked if he could switch places with Cord so he could talk to me, but I told him we both had too much to do.

"Tracy, I—"

"Talk to Celia," I instructed him. "You guys don't want to mess up."

"I—"

"And what are you going to do about a ring?" I questioned him. "The devil's in the details."

He cleared his throat as he looked over the top of the seat at me. "My mother told me I could have my grandmother's ring when I got married. I just have to ask her to get it from the safe-deposit box for me."

And it was a girl ring already, so win-win. "Oh, that's perfect."

"It's supposed to be yours."

I shook my head. "This way it can just slide right on Celia's finger."

He glared at me. "We're going to talk at my folks' house, Trace."

"Sure," I agreed.

Cord said nothing about the exchange, but he gently gripped my upper thigh. His touch was comforting, and I appreciated the gesture.

Drinks came, and then the meal was served. It didn't look appealing, but I watched Cord wolf down what appeared to be lasagna.

"I promise to feed you when we get there," I said playfully, "because that is so not going to hold you."

"Oh yeah? You're gonna take me out to dinner?"

"I will," I sighed, bumping him with my shoulder.

"It's a date."

I smiled at him as I went back to my Excel spreadsheet.

When the lights went out for the movie, I saw Celia and Breckin lean their heads together. It was good they were talking; they had a lot to figure out.

"I'm sorry."

"What?" I mumbled, not turning to look at Cord, still busy with work.

"I know this is hard on you. You probably thought you'd be meeting his folks someday, but not like this."

"It doesn't matter," I said softly, opening QuickBooks, ready to start paying people.

He leaned close enough to breathe down the side of my neck. "How come?"

"We're done."

"Yeah, you said that yesterday."

"Then why the question?" I asked, turning my head to squint at him.

"I just wanna be clear."

I tipped my head at Breckin's chair. "It's just stupid at this point. We're not even married, we don't live together—it's time for this to be over," I said solemnly. "Like I told you, it's already been close to five months."

"Why?"

"Why what?"

"Why be done?"

"How come we're going over this again?"

"Humor me."

I huffed out a breath. "Trust," I replied flatly. "It's all gone."

"Yeah, but you can rebuild that."

I tried to imagine being back in my cozy little A-frame with Breckin or moving to Pacific Heights with him, but the images just wouldn't come. I couldn't picture us together anymore. Somewhere during those four months, everything had changed.

"I think," I began, turning to him, "that truly a one-off of infidelity can be forgiven. Like, you messed up, and you're really sorry. And you promised you'd be faithful, but there was a moment of weakness. I get that."

He was silent, but he put his big, heavy hand back on my thigh.

"But, see, I caught him, right?" My voice dropped low, and I leaned close to Cord's ear to whisper, "He didn't tell me. And now… Celia. She was actually the first. Sean Granger was the second."

"What the hell are you talking about?" He clipped the words as he leaned back.

And it hit me that he didn't know. Neither of my brothers had told him, which was kind of nice. "Breckin slept with a friend of his four months ago; it's why we were taking a break in the first place."

He stared at me a second, taking that in. "So you're telling me there were two women?"

"No. Sean's a guy."

"So one guy, one girl?"

It sounded even worse that way.

"Trace?"

I nodded, rubbing the bridge of my nose. I started chuckling because it was so ridiculous.

"Lemme get this straight," he began. "After Breckin slept with Celia but before he knew he knocked her up, he fucked a buddy of his?"

"Yes," I said flatly.

"Are you kidding?"

I was suddenly giddy. Between being scared and getting beaten up and having to fly out of the state to try and trap a killer—the ridiculousness of my situation had finally caught up to me. I began giggling.

"He fucked around on you twice?"

Yes. God. I was that guy, the one who got cheated on. "I'm pathetic."

"Jesus, Trace."

I rubbed the bridge of my nose and then closed my eyes and breathed. The laughter subsided, and after a moment, I felt a hand on my cheek. "I'm an idiot."

"Yep," he agreed, tracing his thumb over my eyebrow.

I breathed in and out, concentrating, his gentle touch helping me focus, his thumb smoothing over my lashes.

"These look fake."

"I'm sorry?"

"Your eyelashes," he growled softly. "They're so long and really beautiful resting on your cheek."

I swallowed down the lump in my throat.

"They look like glossy black feathers."

It was helping, how he was talking to me. I could feel myself calm. "Should you be worried about Sean Granger?" I asked, opening my eyes.

"The person responsible for the death of Tim Stanson and the attacks on you and Celia doesn't give a shit about some guy Breckin fucked."

"But didn't Breckin just fuck Stanson?"

"No; they were in a relationship, which is why he's dead."

"Okay. So you're sure Sean Granger is safe?"

"Considering I had no idea there even was a Sean Granger before you just told me, yeah, I am," he assured me. "You're on the list because whoever this is knows that Breckin wants you, and Celia's on the list 'cause she's knocked up. Only you two matter."

"That makes sense." I took a shaky breath.

"But for the record," he whispered, "I'm only worried about you."

"What?"

"Don't get me wrong, I will protect Celia," he explained softly. "But you're the only one I'd take a bullet for."

"That's a terrible thing to say."

"Why?"

"Because I'd prefer no bullets were near you at all."

"Well, hopefully they won't be, but that's the point, right?"

"What is?" I pried.

"I'm here for you."

"So if I wasn't in danger, you would have let someone else come with Celia?"

"Yes."

I tested the water. "You're such a good friend to do this for Alex."

"It has nothing to do with him."

"Oh? What does it have to do with?" I had to ask. I had to know. And with my innocuous question I was out in the deep end, swimming into the wild, wild sea.

"It has to do with there being no one for four months."

"Why are you so stuck on that?"

"Why didn't you tell me?"

"What would have prompted me to do that? We're not close, yeah?"

"Four months?" he repeated, sounding almost annoyed. "Fuck."

I lifted my hand to his cheek, meaning to pat it, to say it was okay, and thank him for worrying, but he covered it with his, turned his head, and kissed my palm.

Everything stilled.

He licked his lips and swallowed like he was nervous. I took in his hooded eyes and heard his breath catch, both reactions causing a quiver of excitement to run through me.

"Cord," I whispered, sliding my hand from under his, around the back of his head, tangling my fingers in the thick hair, taking hold. "You want me."

He closed his eyes, exhaling, and I felt the shudder go through him.

"You want me bad."

"I just need a second to—"

Easing him forward, I sealed my lips over his. I wasn't sure what he would have done; he always got close to me and then something or someone would pull him away. We had been interrupted more times than I could count. Just once, I wanted to taste him.

It was simple: there was a mere breath separating us. I lifted and captured his mouth, taking what I wanted, kissing him hard, slipping my tongue between his parted lips, rubbing it seductively over his. The low moan from the man suffused me with heat as I registered that he was kissing me back roughly, mauling me, hands on my face, holding tight.

The soft whimper from the back of my throat sounded greedy, full of want, and I scared myself with my own hunger. Some of it was the sex drought, I could own that, but mostly it was Cord. I didn't have the same kind of history with any other man, no lurking unfulfilled passion, no sexual tension that you could cut with a knife. Five years of desire had flooded me, and because I was surprised, I tore free, panting softly, afraid of what I would do if I kept kissing him, so close to throwing my arms around his neck and climbing into his lap.

He was staring at me, and even in the low light I clearly saw his blown pupils and swollen lips.

I had to swallow before I could speak. "I'm sorry. You were being nice and I took advantage."

He got up abruptly, and I felt like such an ass. Groaning, I turned to the window even though the shade was down because the movie was on.

Normally I would have run. Faced with an embarrassing situation, distance and time would have fixed it. But I was stuck, and even as I ran through scenarios, my mind kept tripping back to kissing Cord.

Dear God.

I always assumed the man knew what he was doing in bed. Everyone wanted him; he was quarry everywhere he went. I'd been witness to that more than once. Men who had been in bed with him once always wanted a repeat performance. But I also knew the man never stuck around. He was the king of the one-night stand. None of that mattered, though, as I relived the kiss. The searing heat, his teeth on my bottom lip, how hard he sucked my tongue… I had gone boneless and needy in his arms. There was no question: whatever he wanted, I would give. I could only imagine what he must have thought. There I was telling him that Breckin and I were done only to basically assault him.

I was horrified by my behavior. Now was the time to trade seats, before I died of embarrassment.

Leaning forward, I was going to peer through the seats, but the armrest was raised between Breckin and Celia. And while I was surprised, it didn't bother me.

"What are you doing?"

My head snapped up, and I found Cord looming over me.

"Nothing," I assured him. I turned in my seat, grabbed the flight pillow, leaned sideways and closed my eyes. Not that I could sleep, but it was the only escape I could see.

I felt him take his seat, heard the seat belt buckle, and then gasped when he reached across my chest, grabbed my right arm, and wrenched me around to face him.

"Cord," I huffed out.

He took hold of my chin. "I was gonna come right there with you all over me, so that's why I left. I had to take a quick walk and calm down so I could talk to you."

I had gotten him worked up. Me. His confession was dazzling. I'd been so humiliated when I had walked in on Breckin and Sean because my boyfriend had chosen someone else over me. I was obviously not as sexy as Sean Granger, not as hot or funny or smart. Those were the reasons Breckin had wanted him instead of me. I must have been lacking.

But Cord…. Him, I mesmerized, and he wanted me. A surge of heat burned right through me as I stared at the man studying my face.

"I fuck everybody because I don't fuck you."

I wasn't following.

"Things change, things we want, and five years ago I was different than I am now."

Easing closer, I heard how rough his breathing was, felt the slight tremble in his touch, and saw his gaze move to my mouth.

"I think about you all the time," he said on an exhale, cupping my cheek. "But you don't see me now; you only see how I was."

"You're telling me you don't sleep around anymore?"

He shook his head. "Not for a long time."

I studied his face and saw a yearning there that I had not before. "I'm a mess right now."

"No. You just think you are."

"What are you talking about?"

He lowered his voice, crowding me so we were cheek to cheek, his lips next to my ear. "The second you found out Breckin cheated, you threw him out and reclaimed your space."

His breath in my ear broke me out in goose bumps, and coupled with his lips pressed to the skin behind it and his hand sliding up under my shirt, my cock was thickening fast.

"You've been figuring out what to do—cut him loose or work it out—for several months, but in that time, he hasn't been back in your bed."

He was rolling my left nipple and it hardened under his touch. He pressed his forehead to mine and dropped his other hand to my upper thigh.

I wasn't a horny teenager anymore; I could control my own body.

"I know you love hard, so I get that it'll take time for you to be over Breckin and have your head and your heart clear."

He cupped me through my chinos, squeezing my cock, and I writhed in his grip, wanting more—more friction, more pressure, more everything.

"So for now, I'm gonna claim the only thing I can," he growled, opening his hot mouth on the side of my neck.

I jolted under his hands, loving the kiss that quickly became suckling before he added his teeth.

"Pull the blanket over your lap."

It was bunched beside me under the window, so I moved it quickly as he yanked on my belt buckle with his left hand.

"Tracy."

I leaned my head back so he could suck and nibble whatever skin on my neck and throat he wanted. At the sound of my name, followed by the man's seductive chuckle, I bent forward. He was right there, staring at me, and I closed my eyes and kissed him.

"You keep," he rasped as I tugged on his bottom lip, "kissing me."

"You're finally letting me," I ground out, putting my hands on his collarbone, inside his shirt, and tracing over warm sleek skin. The need to wrap both arms around his neck and lock him tight against me was nearly overwhelming.

My belt buckle loosened, the button and zipper fly gave way, and he slid his hand under the waistband of my briefs to my rigid, leaking dick.

"Oh fuck," I whined softly, bucking up into his fist, shivering with the desire to come and see it on him. The idea must have shown on my face, because he narrowed his eyes in a look that was all predator.

"Tell me," he demanded, and the darkness in his voice made my breathing falter. "And don't fuckin' lie."

As if I could.

"Now," he rasped.

"I want to come on your skin… on your gorgeous abs and your beautiful chest."

"Because?"

My voice was ragged and choppy. "I've always wanted to, to see… to watch."

"While you're riding my cock," he growled low in his chest. It was a statement, not a question, because he knew the answer already, probably always had.

"Cord," I whined softly.

But he had me, literally, and I saw his hooded eyes before he began to slowly nibble along my jaw. "I've been waiting for this—for you."

He wanted me too, and suddenly I was dizzy with the implication.

"All the time," he said, his voice going out on him. "At night, in bed... it's you."

It was too much. I couldn't go from nothing to having the deepest wish in my secret heart granted.

Yes, I had loved Breckin Alcott, and if he hadn't cheated the second time, I might even have forgiven him. The man had been a gift, someone I thought I'd never have being simply me, plain, ordinary Tracy Brandt. But the tucked-away dream, the one covered under layers of denial and banter and indifference was this, was him: Cord Nolan.

Even if nothing worked, even if we crashed and that killed all semblance of civility so we wouldn't even be able to stand to be in the same room together ever again... even then, it was worth it to try. I would gamble my heart because it was time to leap and not look.

"I will beat you if you ever go near Breckin Alcott again."

I nodded and suddenly realized that he had to get his hand off me; I was susceptible to him, to our history and his strength, to my endless hunger for him. "Let go."

"No."

"Please," I begged, trying to stop my body from surging toward climax even as I writhed in his grip.

"No," he repeated gruffly, milking my length, stroking fast, expertly, the vise of his hand and the drooling precum making the motion fluid and perfect.

I tried to stifle the sound of his name as I wiggled and shifted in my seat, going suddenly rigid as I came, spurting thick ribbons of cum over his clenched fist, wrist, and heavily veined forearm.

"When we're alone, I expect you to scream if you need to."

He was trying to kill me, saying things like that.

As I stared at him, trying to keep from panting, from making any noise at all, he ground his mouth down over mine; taking in my soft, decadent moans as he kissed me and smiled at the same time. Shoving away from him, I met his heated stare. "I'm funny?"

"No," he assured me with a low chuckle. "I am."

"Why?"

"Because I should have done this a long fuckin' time ago," he said crossly, recapturing my mouth and devouring me. I had never, ever, kissed anyone like Cord. His kisses were seductive and rough and ravishing, and I wanted more.

He let me go, my flagging cock slipping from his cum-covered fingers, and I adjusted myself fast, tucked in, zipped up, and buckled as he wiped himself off with the napkins from dinner he'd stuffed in the pocket of his seat.

I couldn't look at him—the only image in my head was me under him in bed.

"Talk to me."

Turning, my head, my gaze met his. "I'm at a loss, Cord."

"Lucky I'm not," he said, taking my hand and lacing his fingers with mine. "Wherever we end up tonight, you're sleeping with me."

My heart fluttered. "You're sure?"

"Never been more."

I nodded.

"How's your head?"

I could feel my face heat, and I was sure I was blushing.

"Not your little head, idiot," he said through quiet laughter. "You have a concussion—what I did wasn't that smart. I hope I didn't hurt you."

"Even if you had," I informed him, "who cares?"

He lifted my hand to his mouth and kissed my knuckles. "I wasn't thinking."

"Good."

We sat there in silence, and after a while I got sleepy. He lifted his arm, and I snuggled close like I'd been doing it forever. He anchored me there, holding me tight, and leaned his cheek against my forehead. Why that felt so normal after only a half-a-day flight I didn't know, but after years of lead up, I was finally going to start something with Cord Nolan. I was excited and terrified at the same time.

CHAPTER
Ten

THE INTERNATIONAL airport in Burlington, Vermont, looked like many other airports I'd traveled through in my life. What changed was what was sold. In San Francisco it was sourdough bread and Alcatraz key chains or trolley-car magnets. In Vermont, there was maple syrup for you to grab, and Green Mountain Coffee, and, of course, Ben & Jerry's merchandise. The shops went by in a blur as I followed everyone else.

"You look nice, by the way."

Glancing over at Cord as we walked, I wondered if this was how it was going to be from now on. Would he simply blindside me with compliments? I knew I looked ordinary in slim-fitting chinos, a sweater vest, a long-sleeved button-down, and a brown leather jacket topping it off.

"I like all the stuff too."

My new watch compliments of Evan, the brown leather cuff bracelet on the opposite wrist.... He was noticing it all, and I stumbled for a second because I didn't even know the stranger walking beside me.

"You all right?" He checked with a hand on my shoulder, the concerned look in his eyes not completely foreign. Now that I was clear of my detritus where Cord was concerned, I was noticing things as well. The affection on his face had always been there, I had just seen something else. I had always thought the worst of him. Now that I wasn't, he had dropped his guard. It was brand new.

"I'm fine," I told him, catching his hand before he withdrew it, squeezing tight a moment.

"Stay close to me," he ordered, and clear as day I heard the possessiveness in the tone. How had I missed that?

"I will."

My simple words drew a smile I had never seen before from the man, and I was reminded again that yes, Cord Nolan was into me. I needed a little time alone to process it, but I wasn't going to get any.

When we walked out through security into the main terminal, I heard several people call Breckin's name. The crowd there was a surprise, as was seeing his parents. His mother was a stunning blonde, and his father just as gorgeous with his gray hair and piercing blue eyes. They were straining to see their son. Once he was close enough, Michelle Alcott threw herself into her son's arms and covered him in kisses. His father watched them, waiting his turn. I saw his tense posture, his anxious anticipation. Breckin emerged from his mother's embrace and went quickly into his father's waiting arms. Everyone standing there clapped—Breckin was at the center of his family. I saw his sister, his brother. It was amazing how similar they all looked; easy to spot any of them anywhere.

When he was released from the cocoon of homecoming, he turned, and for the first time, everyone saw us: Cord. Celia. Me. He introduced us without a moment's hesitation.

"This is my wife Celia," he said, looking right at me as he spoke.

A month ago, a week ago, even a couple of days ago, that would have hurt. But it was strange how clarity came at odd times. Ever since I found out five months ago that he'd cheated on me, I had been moving toward the end… and suddenly I was there.

His family surged around Celia, putting hands on her stomach, on her back and shoulders, Michelle crying now, smiling through her tears and hugging Celia tight. They loved her. Loved her! You could have put it up in neon lights. She was, after all, the ideal of feminine beauty, and she had come bearing the greatest gift: his child.

They remarked on the fact that she didn't have a ring, and Breckin said her hands were swollen with the pregnancy, but that what they had at home was a small and inconsequential diamond. His mother promised him the ring she had at home, retrieved from a vault in hopes that he would want to give it to Celia.

"Wow," I said, impressed.

"What?" Cord asked, looking down at me.

I gazed up into his face, as always leaning my head back to see him. "They certainly got their stories straight on the plane. That's some slick lying he did there."

He squinted at me.

"What?"

He scoffed. "Breckin's always been a world-class liar."

"I didn't know that."

"No?" He grinned and put a hand on the back of my head, tangling his fingers in my hair. "That's so cute and clueless of you."

Normally I would have defended myself, thinking he was taking a dig at me, but I didn't feel the need to anymore. I leaned, instead, into his space, wanting to be closer. As focused on Cord as I was, I missed the others around me until I became peripherally aware that everyone was staring at the two of us. Breckin had a strange look on his face that I couldn't place, and Celia looked stunned. Cord extended a hand to Mr. Alcott.

"Cord Nolan," he said huskily, taking a deep breath. "San Francisco Homicide."

Mr. Alcott took the offered hand and shook it, furrowing his eyebrows across the bridge of his nose. "Good to meet you, Inspector, though I do wish the circumstances were different."

"As do I, sir," he agreed before turning to indicate me. "May I introduce Tracy Brandt."

Mr. Alcott turned and smiled at me before offering me his hand. "Mr. Brandt, a pleasure."

"And you as well, sir."

"Tracy, is it?" Mrs. Alcott asked me, coming forward to shake my hand.

"Yes, ma'am."

"I'm so glad that in the absence of his family Breckin has such a good friend in you."

I smiled back at her as she introduced me to Breckin's sister Bethany and his brother Brian. They made a beautiful family. I was glad Cord had given me the rundown on everyone while we were on the plane so I knew who I was looking at.

Minutes later I watched Breckin put his arm around Celia and follow his parents out of the terminal. I didn't move until Cord picked up his duffel and turned to me.

"You okay?"

I nodded.

"You look sad."

"No," I assured him, moving forward to put my hand on his cheek. "I'm not sad one bit, Inspector."

"Not for long," he said gravely, "at least not the kind I am now."

"Please tell me what you're talking about, 'cause you lost me there." I teased him.

He draped his arm across my shoulders as we walked. "I mean, I won't be an inspector anymore, so you gotta stop calling me that. I'm leaving the force to take a job as an in-house investigator at a law firm."

I was stunned. "You are not."

His low seductive chuckle made my cock twitch. "I am. I'm out at the end of next month."

"Why didn't you tell me?"

"Well, until these past few days, we haven't exactly been close, have we?"

No, we had not. "Okay," I said, leaning into him.

He tightened his arm, putting his hand in my hair. "I can't seem to stop touching you."

"I'm not complaining," I sighed, savoring how demonstrative he was. "Why leave the force?"

"I'm not happy."

"How so?"

"I have no balance in my life. I do the same thing day in and day out, and I don't want to transfer to the DEA like Alex did, and—I'm just over the whole thing."

"Why?" I asked, tipping my head back and giving him a quick kiss under his jaw.

His step faltered, and if I didn't already know that he liked me, I would have from the sudden staggered step. That fast, I had him flustered.

"I want more," he choked, clutching at my hair.

"Like what?"

"Like, since I'll be an investigator and not a cop, I would be home at a decent hour."

"And?"

"And so I could take you to dinner and stuff."

"Oh."

He coughed softly. "So, you think you'd wanna do that with me? Eat dinner?"

"I would."

"We could even take a weekend trip somewhere, since I wouldn't work those."

"That sounds great."

"The money's way better, double my salary, and I have room to move up, and there's incentives and amazing insurance."

"It seems to me you have everything worked out," I said, leading him around the back of one of the agent counters at an empty gate.

"What are you—"

"Will you miss being an inspector?" I asked, taking hold of the scarf he was wearing around his neck and easing him down to me.

"I—no," he admitted. "I want to do a job but not have it be my whole life like Alex's is. I want more."

"What do you want?" I asked, my lips a hairsbreadth from his.

"I wanna see you," he rasped.

"Who was it gonna be since you didn't know I was even available."

"I was getting things lined up so I could make my play."

"For me?"

"Yes, idiot. It was always gonna be you."

The deluge of honesty was staggering.

"Tell me I can see you."

"Yes," I murmured, "you can see me."

He bent, and I lifted up and sealed my lips over his, kissing him hard, taking what I needed because the man was making my heart hurt. I'd had no idea he could be so romantic, so serious, and the idea that I had brought it out in him was overwhelming. I couldn't seem to kiss, touch, or breathe him in enough. I needed more.

One kiss became another and another, and as I whimpered and whined against him, grinding my hard groin into his thigh, he put his hands on my ass.

"Bathroom?" I whispered hotly against his lips.

He shoved me off him, both of us panting, his dilated pupils a treat to see. "I am not fucking you in a bathroom stall at the airport." He looked indignant.

"Why not?" I complained.

He grabbed my wrist and yanked me after him back across the carpet to the concrete. "Because I don't do that anymore."

I scoffed.

"I don't! I'm a grown-up now."

"I see," I pacified him.

He growled. "You're special. I won't fuck you in someplace that's not."

The man was a grouchy mess, and I loved it. "That's not what you said the first day I met you," I taunted. "You were gonna do me in your car."

"Five years ago!" he reminded me loudly.

"Oh, okay." I chuckled.

"I know your family, for fuck's sake."

"Which has what to do with anything?"

He rounded on me. "Your father, both your brothers—they like me. Do you know when I've had that before?"

"No."

"Never," he announced. "I've never had that. So I have a chance here to have everything I've ever wanted: a man I love and a family that wants me. Why would I do anything to fuck that up?"

He had no idea what he was really saying to me, but that was okay. I knew. "Okay," I soothed him, leaning in and wrapping my arm around his waist. "Let's catch up with the others."

"Okay," he agreed, exhaling a sharp breath, wrapping his arm back around my shoulders.

"But, um," I pried playfully. "I can get laid in bed tonight, right?"

He untangled himself from me, scowled, and walked quickly away.

I cackled as I followed after him. "Please, baby."

"I will end you!" he shouted as he strode quickly through the terminal.

"No, you won't," I said playfully.

His growling was actually really hot.

Everyone was still waiting for luggage, and when we got there and Breckin saw us, I smiled automatically. I saw no reason to be combative with him, so I promised myself that I would concentrate on getting along.

When Cord bent to ask me what my luggage looked like, I put my hand on the side of his face when I answered. Now that I could touch him, I didn't plan to miss out on any opportunity to do so.

Outside the baggage claim, two cars were waiting for us. Cord and I went with Breckin's sister Bethany and his brother Brian in a Lexus SUV, and Breckin and Celia went with his parents in a limousine. Cord chatted with Breckin's siblings about pretty straightforward stuff. They hadn't seen Breckin in more than eighteen years, and the fact that he was suddenly home was a little overwhelming for them. Though they had heard from him through sporadic phone calls and the occasional e-mail, he had not returned home. He had left for college, and it was as though he'd left the family. Neither Bethany nor Brian knew why.

It was a beautiful drive to their home from the airport. The countryside was breathtaking, awash in fall colors.

"Vermont is gorgeous," I said in awe.

"It is," Brian agreed, smiling into the rearview mirror.

"Wait until we go through the covered bridges," Bethany announced, turning around in her seat. "You're going to love it."

We took 89 from the Burlington Airport past Colchester and kept going north.

"What are we close to?" I asked.

"We're passing Malletts Bay," Brian informed me. "You can't see it from here, but that's where we are. I'll turn off soon, and we'll head west toward Lake Champlain."

"So your house is on the lake?"

"No, we're further inland, but it's only, like, a half hour or so to the water if you want to go," Brian explained. "We're going to pass over three or four covered bridges on the way."

"Oh, I can't wait. I just love it here," I told him, reaching over to take hold of Cord's hand. I felt him squeeze back gently, but I didn't turn to look at him.

When we finally turned off the highway, we drove down country roads, and all I saw were the colors of fall—auburn, gold, red, mahogany, and brown. The birch trees, aspen, and dogwood were like something out of a magazine.

"Here we go, Tracy." Bethany pointed, and I saw the beautiful bridge.

"It's not a big deal," Cord said, nuzzling my ear, covering me in goose bumps.

"It's a huge deal," I assured him, marveling at the backdrop of autumn. "This is amazing."

"No," Cord whispered, gently nibbling the side of my neck. "It's you."

I suddenly felt overwhelmed. Between the man at my side and the splendor outside, a bad day had turned into a wonderful one.

We passed the sign welcoming us to Fieldcrest, Vermont, population just below five thousand. The Alcott home was a Vermont log house with a saltbox roof that sat on ninety acres of rolling hills in lush green and orange. Once we got out of the car, I could see down toward town from the hill the house sat on.

The streets were lined in sugar maples, there was a church with a high steeple, and I could see from one end of town to the other. In the Alcotts' yard, I saw a gazebo out back, as well as a shack that I was informed was for storing the maple syrup extracted from the trees around the grounds. I had never seen a more beautiful home, and I wondered how, as Breckin had obviously come from something so grand, he could have ever enjoyed life in my tiny little fifteen-hundred-square-foot A-frame.

Cord bumped me, and when I looked up into his eyes, I saw a glow in them as he smiled down at me.

"What?"

"When we get back," he said hoarsely, "will you let me sit on your couch in your sweet little house?"

How did he know?

There was no way Cord Nolan was perceptive enough to know what I was thinking. But somehow he did, and I couldn't have stopped my lunge if my life had depended on it. I threw myself at him and wrapped my arms tight around his neck as I eased him down for a kiss.

It was fast—I didn't ravish him, but I bit down gently, and tugged on his bottom lip before I let him go. No one was paying any attention to us, too wrapped up in Breckin and Celia. It was nice; I liked that it felt like Cord and I were all alone.

"Is that a yes?" he prodded.

"That's a yes."

"Inspector."

Mr. Alcott—"call me John"—offered me and Cord rooms at the house, but Cord explained that we had reservations at the bed-and-breakfast in town.

"We're not all staying together?" Celia asked Cord.

"No," he told her. "Chief Ripley is sending an officer here to stay at the house with you and Breckin. Tracy and I will be at the Den of Antiquity off Main Street, which is apparently an excellent B&B as well as a top-notch antique shop for the serious aficionado of all things dated."

I turned and looked at him and could not hold back the laughter. "The Den of Antiquity?"

He was trying not to smile. "Yep."

"You made that up."

He was smiling at me as he shook his head, stepped into my personal space, and took hold of my chin.

"Can we get a room together?" I asked breathlessly.

"Oh yes," he promised, his voice silky and low.

I stifled the whimper as Michelle invited us all inside.

There was a maid there, Rita, and she welcomed Breckin home before walking over with a tray of spiced cider and hot chocolate. I wanted neither, but I thanked her for the offer.

"Oh," I said, amazed when I stepped into the stunning house.

John walked up beside me. "You like my home, Tracy?"

"I do, sir, very much."

"Would you like the tour?"

"If you don't mind," I said, taking off my sunglasses and putting them in the pocket of my jacket, leaving on the chunky scarf and my wool beanie.

John was pleased to play tour guide; it was written all over his face.

I was the only one who went with him. We started one floor down, in the basement, which was finished, decked out with a library, offices for him and Michelle, a game room and a media room.

"Your basement is bigger than my whole house." I grinned at him.

He walked me out to the garage and pointed out the door to his wine cellar and his workshop, where he tinkered with brass and silver. He made wind chimes, which he sold on eBay.

"Huh," I grunted.

"I'm crafty," he teased me.

Up the stairs we went back in the kitchen and then moved into the great room, where everyone was now sitting.

"Tracy, I hope he's not boring you to death," Michelle called over to me.

"Oh no, ma'am," I assured her, smiling at Cord.

He tipped his head at me before I followed after Mr. Alcott, and he showed me the wood-burning stove and the antique Revolutionary War musket that hung over the fireplace.

We went up a flight of stairs to the floor with all the bedrooms, six in all, plus a sitting room and a two-person sauna.

"These windows are beautiful," I remarked.

"Thank you, Tracy. It's wonderfully satisfying to show you around my home."

He led me up last set of stairs into a loft that was basically an open floor that looked like it had once been a play area and was now cozy with pillows and a privacy screen and small windows that opened at the bottom and pushed out.

"It's very 'oasis in the desert' up here," I said, pointing to the hammock, the throw pillows, and the low table.

"It is, you're right, except for that side."

He pointed, and I saw a reading nook, a window seat, a rocking chair, and a love seat stacked high with plaid blankets in fall colors.

"I love it," I sighed, and he clapped me on the shoulder.

Back downstairs, I followed Mr. Alcott into the great room, unwinding my scarf while I took off my hat.

"Oh," Michelle Alcott gasped, looking at me. "Why, Tracy, you're just gorgeous."

"Thank you," I said, thinking that if she thought I was pretty, Evan would give her a heart attack.

"Tracy," Breckin said as he got up and crossed the floor to me.

"Yeah?"

"I'd like to speak to you in here, please," he said tightly, grabbing my arm and pulling me out into the foyer. The floor was black marble, just beautiful. He turned me around to face him. "What the hell are you doing?"

"When? I—"

"With Cord." He cut me off fast, furious. I realized I just hadn't noticed he was seething. "With goddamn fuckin' Cord!"

He didn't yell, but it felt like it. "What are you talking about?"

"Staying at a hotel with Cord? What kind of game are you playing?"

"What?" I was confused.

"Is this what you want? Are you giving me a taste of it?"

I sighed deeply. "Oh, for crissakes, Breckin, I'm not gonna stay here. Get serious."

"I am serious."

I launched into him. "I'm not trying to give you a taste of anything. I'm not like that," I finished quietly. "You should know better."

"I guess I forget when my ex flirts right in front of me," he said tightly.

"You shouldn't care," I reminded him.

"So you are flirting with him."

"Why does it matter?"

"Since when, Tracy?" he asked, his jaw clenched so tight he could barely speak.

"Since when what?"

"How long have you been fucking Cord?"

I was incredulous. "Are you serious?"

"Answer the—"

"Never," I said, glaring at him. "The answer is that I have never fucked Cord Nolan."

"But you've always wanted to."

"Yes," I answered honestly. "I've always wanted to."

He drew his arm up to backhand me, but I caught it and held tight. I was so stunned, I just stood there and let my eyes fill with the realization. I was still hurt from my attack, and he'd tried to hit me. I had no idea who he even was.

"You're so pathetic," he snapped at me scornfully, yanking his wrist free. "You think Cord Nolan wants you for anything more than a quick fuck? You know better, but because you can't stand to be alone, even for a short time, you'd let him do whatever he wants to you."

I couldn't speak. I could only stare at him.

"What? Are you going to fall apart now? Cause a scene?"

"No," was all I could find the voice to say.

He shook his head disgustedly. "Whatever, Tracy, do what you want. I'm through groveling. You don't want me, fine. It's your choice."

He turned and stalked away, and I was left standing alone in the hall, staring at the empty space where he had been. It was all so confusing. First he loved me and wanted me to take him back, and now it was fine that I wouldn't. Most of all, I wished that I'd thrown out some zingers too.

If I'd still needed any sign to know I was altogether over Breckin Alcott, God, that would have been it. In the face of losing the supposed love of my life, I wanted to make sure I returned fire. If you wished for a scriptwriter when you were fighting, maybe you shouldn't be fighting. Maybe it wasn't worth it.

"Hey."

I turned to find Cord leaning in the doorway.

"You want me to shoot him? I can make it look like an accident."

I smiled at him as he closed in on me, finally taking my face gently in his hands.

"I don't want you for a quick fuck."

"You heard," I mumbled, ashamed.

"I did," he whispered, tilting my head back so he could bend and kiss me. It was soft, tender, and when I opened for him, he slipped his tongue inside to mate with mine.

He walked me backward, behind the stairs, and once there, he made the kiss long, slow, and deep, licking and sucking, nibbling on my lips until I was whimpering under the tender assault.

When he tore free, I was left shivering and panting, wanting the man almost painfully.

"Stay."

I nodded and leaned back into the alcove, into the darkness, concentrating on calming my racing heart.

Minutes later, Cord came back. "So apparently there's some sort of cheese festival here this weekend."

I chuckled, and his smile was instant.

"As God is my witness, there's a whole thing, so the bed-and-breakfast is all full."

"I thought we had a reservation."

"Apparently they could cancel at their discretion."

"Or," I said, surmising what had happened, "if the folks at the B&B had someone standing right in front of them willing to pay them, say, double or even triple?"

"Right."

"Small towns," I teased him.

"Yep."

"So we gotta stay here."

"Yes, we do."

"In the same room?" I asked hopefully.

"In rooms that share a bathroom," he told me. "So I can attack you in the middle of the night."

"Is it an attack if I'm begging?"

He pounced on me, putting his arms around my waist as he lifted me off my feet and kissed me almost savagely. "No—" He explored my tonsils. "—begging necessary."

I went boneless in his arms and wrapped my legs around his hips as I told him to take me upstairs to the bathroom.

He shoved me up against the wall, telling me in broken whispers and sharp inhales of breath that bathrooms were for kids; beds were for grown-ups with serious agendas.

"Oh yeah," I teased him, sucking his bottom lip into my mouth, feeling a shudder tear through him. "You're serious?"

"Don't talk to Breckin anymore. You don't belong to him."

"No?"

"No, Tracy. He was never gonna keep you."

And he was so very right.

CHAPTER
Eleven

THE ALCOTTS had insisted on feeding us. They had a whole spread of turkey with all the fixings, as if Thanksgiving had come a month early. It was all beautifully presented, all the flourishes just gorgeous, no detail missed. I had never seen a more lavishly catered meal. Cord and I sat together at the kitchen table while everyone else was in the great room, spread out over couches and love seats. When we were done, I offered to help clean up, but Michelle dismissed me and said that the service was paid to leave her kitchen immaculate as well.

I went upstairs with Cord, who yanked me inside his room and shoved me up against the door as he locked it. He kissed me before I could get a word out.

There were things I wanted to say, but as much as I knew we needed to talk, I couldn't stop kissing him long enough to form words. When he finally pulled away from me, I was absolutely aching.

"Come back," I uttered hoarsely, my voice crackly with need.

"I gotta go," he said, clearing his throat, not sounding happy about it.

I crossed quickly to his bed and sat down, patting the space beside me. "C'mere and talk to me."

"I can't," he insisted, pulling his brown corduroy blazer over his gray cable-knit sweater with the button neck. "I have to go check in with the chief of police here in Fieldcrest."

"Who's gonna watch over me?"

"Officer Dennis Cumberland," he explained, "who I think is downstairs already. I'll make sure before I go. You know I wouldn't leave you alone."

"Yes, I know," I whispered, gesturing for him. "Come here."

"No." He chuckled, his smile decadent.

"Cord, I—"

"Now listen, do not leave this house for any reason," he ordered. He walked to the door and stood there, poised to leave the room.

"You're really going?" I said irritably, getting up, ready to intercept him

"Yes," he answered, opening the door before I made it halfway to him.

"Cord!"

"Take a nap," he ordered gruffly, walking out.

"Come back here and blow me," I demanded in a sharp whisper.

"Later," he called back.

I ran to catch up and caught him at the top of the stairs, taking hold of him. "Seriously, why the hell are you leaving? You can't touch base over the phone?"

"No."

"Why not?" I asked, my hands on his sides, feeling the steel strength in the man beneath my palms.

"Because that's not how things are done," he said, slipping his hand around the back of my neck and easing me forward.

"Cord," I whined without meaning to, lifting as he bent to kiss me.

He was not a gentle kisser, not yet. Everything between us was brand new, so when we connected it was explosively, not gently. He drove his tongue deep, dragging it over mine, and I opened, loving the feel of him, his taste, wanting to get closer, my body pressed tight to his.

I wanted to go to bed with him, feel his weight on me, holding me down, and have him buried inside my body as hard and deep as he could.

When I whimpered in the back of my throat, he tore free, pressing his lips on the side of my neck before he shoved me back out of his reach.

"What?" I rasped.

"God, you're cute," he said, smiling quickly before he leaned in and kissed my forehead.

I was what? "I'm sorry?"

"When I get back, you better be ready for me," he said, taking the first step down.

"Maybe I'll be asleep already."

His laugh was lusty and rich. "You'll be pacing the floor."

"You're so sure?" I grumbled to his back, watching him descend to the first landing.

"I'm sure."

My jaw muscles tensed. "Fine."

"Yeah, that's what I thought." He snickered, turning to look up at me.

"You're so smug," I said flippantly.

"Only 'cause you're lookin' at me like you'll die if I don't do you."

"You're such an ass."

"Don't forget it," he said, and I could hear him chuckling as he went down the second flight of stairs before he called out to me, "Hey!"

I moved quickly down the first three steps so I could lean over the railing and look down into the great room at him. Everyone else was outside around the in-ground fire pit, roasting marshmallows and making s'mores.

"I'll be back as soon as I can. Do what I said and stay here."

"If you're so worried, maybe I should come with you."

The man's eyes, the way he was staring at me… I really had no idea anyone would ever gaze at me like I was simply too dear for words. The urge to keep him, put a ring on his finger, took a deep bite out of me.

"I'll be back soon."

I nodded.

"I'm taking your scarf 'cause I like it better'n mine."

"Yes, please."

He gave me a grin that made his dimples pop, and then he was gone. It was probably good he was leaving me for a little while; I had lots of calls to make.

It took the better part of two hours to talk to my dad, Alex, Evan, and Matt. I talked to Dimah, as well.

"You are fine?"

"Yeah, I'm good."

"Thank you for e-mailing payroll to me."

"Of course."

"When will you be home?"

"Hopefully someone will try and kill me quick."

"This is not funny."

"Sorry. Bad joke."

He was quiet for a few moments. "You like that police officer very much, yes?"

"What?"

He chuckled. "You are a bad actor."

I grunted. "I am going to see if I can invite him to my house when I get home."

"That sounds promising."

"Thanks."

After I hung up, I decided to read for a bit, since I had no intention of going downstairs and seeing or talking to Breckin. I tried really hard not to fall asleep.

I WOKE up starving because the time was off by three hours. So eight in Vermont was only five at home. Cord still wasn't back, and when I tried his cell it went straight to voice mail. After changing into a pair of jeans and a T-shirt, I went to find something to eat. Downstairs in the kitchen, I rummaged around in the refrigerator until I came up with jelly and milk. I checked the pantry and found peanut butter and honey-wheat bread. I was standing beside the counter having my little feast when Breckin came into the room. He didn't stop when he saw me, but walked straight up to me and would have wrapped his arms around me if I hadn't moved quickly around the island with copper pots hanging over it, putting that between us.

"I'm so sorry."

Was he kidding?

"Baby," he said softly, taking a step toward me. "I'm so sorry. I really am."

I moved quickly, keeping distance between us. "Jesus, Breckin, you treat me like shit, you change your mind about stuff every two seconds, and you spend the day acting all lovey-dovey with Celia. Are you fucking kidding me?"

He looked at me hard. "I already told you why."

"No, no, I think I would have remembered that. I think your reasoning for being a total prick would stick in my brain."

He shook his head. "Cord."

"Cord?"

"Yeah, Cord. He's all over you, and I can't stand it."

"Cord is being a gentleman. I'm the one all over him."

"Because he's letting you, and the only reason you're giving him the time of day is that I have just trashed your life."

"You didn't trash anything," I assured him. "Everything's fine."

"If it's so fine, why won't you let me touch you?"

"For what reason?"

"For Christ's sake, Tracy, I love you."

But he didn't. "Just let it go."

"Let it go?"

I nodded.

He was quiet a second and then a look crossed his face, like he'd had an epiphany. "You want Cord."

"Yeah," I admitted. "I do."

"Since when?"

"Since forever, like I told you earlier, it's just—"

"You would have let it go and never acted on it if I had stayed loyal."

"Which," I said, "if you think about it, is kind of shitty."

"How so?"

"I would have always wondered what could have been if I'd just had the balls to start something with him. But he was never ready, and then there was you."

"So now he's finally a grown-up, and you're free because of my infidelity."

"Yes," I said flatly.

"Tracy, I—"

"And anyway, I'd forgotten things about Cord."

"Like what?"

"I'm sorry?"

"Like, what did you forget?" He sounded exasperated.

I sighed deeply. "I forgot that he makes me feel safe."

"And I don't?"

Once upon a time he had. "You used to, but Cord never stopped."

He inhaled sharply. "I don't want this to be our end. Do you understand?"

"I do. Of course I do," I replied gently. "But it already is. Was."

His eyes darkened as he looked at me. "I think we can fix this if you'll just allow us to take the first steps."

"You said earlier you were done talking. I think that's for the best."

"Tracy," he began.

"I'm so sick of all of this, of you and me," I confessed tiredly. "You have to be too."

He stepped in close and cupped my face in his hands. "No. I was mad, and I'm so sorry I tried to—I wasn't thinking. I should have been charming instead of letting my frustration boil over, but I just couldn't manage it. I was too pissed."

I changed the subject, easing free of his hold. "You really fit with them, Breckin," I said, walking around the kitchen island to the other side, putting the barrier between us again.

"What does that mean?"

"You're very comfortable being rich."

"You make it sound like a bad thing."

"It's not, just different."

"Well, different is good, and you could be comfortable too."

"I don't think so," I assured him, my voice low. "My dreams are small. Celia's are more like yours."

"You have no idea what you're talking about. You don't know shit about Celia's dreams."

"But you do, right?"

"Yes, I do," he snarled, annoyed all over again. "Celia's dreams are all riding on me, that's it, the beginning and the end. All she wants for her life is me."

"Then that's perfect for you."

"No, it's not perfect for me. *You* are perfect for me!"

His words sounded so automatic, and empty. It was like he knew what he was supposed to say, and so that was what he did. Why he was trying so hard, I had no idea. Maybe I was the first person who'd ever walked away from him, and his pride was ruffled. But whatever it was, it had nothing to do with me.

As I studied his face, I tried to see the old Breckin in the man now dressed for bed in monogrammed pajamas. With me he'd worn only the bottoms, and they were cotton, not silk. And the slippers he was wearing; I'd never seen him in a pair before. Normally, he wore crew socks, like me, if his feet were cold. Dumb things I noticed, things no one else would care about. But I cared; I saw it for what it was.

"You belong with me."

"What about your family? Everyone loves Celia so much."

"I don't care."

"That's bullshit. Of course you do."

"What are you talking about?"

"I see you, Breckin," I said, and I could hear the chill in my voice. My disbelief was showing, and my anger. I was trying to be cool, but it was not working at all. "I see how you're acting."

"Oh? How am I acting? I would love to know."

I waved a dismissive hand at him. "Whatever, fine. You wanna be a jerk, be a jerk. I'm going to bed."

He came fast around the island and grabbed me. He dug his fingers into my upper arms and pulled me in close. "This is our whole life we're talking about here, Tracy. You ready to just throw that all away?"

"You threw it away!" I yelled at him. "You, not me. You. I did not fuck someone else. I did not go looking for someone else. I—"

"I didn't go looking for her! It was an accident, it just happened. There was no plan, there was no scheme, and I didn't do it on purpose! You have to get over this, you—"

"I don't have to," I began, and then I saw a face at the window. "Oh shit!"

"What?" Breckin yelled, spinning around, frantic because I startled him with my yell.

Just for a second I had seen a white mask in the darkness. "Someone was there."

"Outside on the deck?"

"Yeah."

We froze, both of us glancing from window to window until the floodlights suddenly went on because some motion outside had triggered them. That was the scariest part of the whole thing—knowing for certain that I had not imagined it, that there had, in fact, been someone looking in at us.

By the time Officer Cumberland came rushing in from the living room, gun drawn, I had already calmed, and moved across the room so I could see outside to the now-empty deck. There were two police cars outside in the grass, both with their red and blue lights cycling.

"Are you two all right?" Officer Cumberland asked, checking on Breckin and me.

"We're good," I answered quickly before he opened the door and went outside.

"Tracy," Breckin said as his family started coming down the stairs. "Maybe you should stay away from the glass door, huh?"

If the intruder had wanted me dead, I would already be dead. I dismissed his concern. "I'm fine."

I got a pained look from him as I stood there, off to the side, as his parents and siblings and Celia clustered around him. The mother of his child walked up to him, and he took her in, hugging her close. His parents rubbed his back, offered to get him something, anything. He stroked Celia's hair, shushed her gently, and told her he was okay. The way his mother looked at the two of them together was really sweet.

"Trace!"

Everybody started, Michelle even gasped, and I smiled without meaning to, because, really, who came into a house and bellowed like that?

Cord charged into the room, his Glock drawn, scanning the room before his gaze met mine. He was holstering the gun as he reached me.

"You all right?" he barked, sounding scared. I opened my arms for him, and all pretense was gone when he grabbed and crushed me against him. And I wasn't so much smaller than him—he had only six inches on me—but still, when he hugged me, I felt the strength and power in his hard, muscular frame and loved how I was being held. "Trace?" he whispered hoarsely close to my ear.

"I'm fine," I assured him, clutching at his jacket.

"What were you doing down here?" he asked, leaning back far enough to see my face without letting me go.

"I was hungry."

"But you ate dinner didn't you?" he asked as though that were logical, leading me from where I was by the door near the others toward a quieter spot.

"I was peckish," I teased him.

"What?"

"It's only, like, five our time now. I normally eat dinner around nine."

"You're not supposed to eat after seven."

"In what world?"

He laughed.

"I eat late," I said.

"You do?"

I nodded.

"You usually eat out? Or grab something and go home."

"Either. It depends."

"Where do you go?"

And that fast we were having a conversation.

"Sometimes Rosamunde," I explained, only peripherally aware that people and cops were moving around us. "I like the andouille or the chicken habanero sausage."

"Oh yeah?"

The smile he gave me was gorgeous and made his eyes glitter as he gently slid a hand around the side of my neck. "I like Kvetch in Crocker-Amazon too. I always get the lobster mac 'n' cheese or shrimp and grits."

"I'll take you over to the Swan Oyster Depot when we get home."

"It's a date," I said, grinning, hands on his hips.

"So you were hungry is what you're telling me."

"Yeah."

He sighed suddenly, both hands on my face. "There are footprints out there in the mud."

"Oh yeah? Big ones, little ones, what?"

"Big."

"Okay, so, a man."

"Yeah," he said, and I heard him purposely trying to infuse his tone with normalcy.

"I saw someone at the window—freaked me out."

"I bet. I'm sorry I wasn't here with you. It won't happen again."

"You were doing your job."

"My job is you," he said, drawing me back close. I curled my arms up under his and put my hands on his shoulders as I rested my head on his collarbone. "I've been waiting so long to get you; I don't wanna lose you now."

I put my nose up to his throat and inhaled his warm male scent, and he chuckled, which I felt more than heard. I almost purred.

People got closer, Breckin and his family crowding toward us, probably wanting to talk. Cord didn't want that, as evidenced by him pulling away from me only to tug me after him.

"Come over here and siddown," he grumbled, but I heard the smile in his voice as he led me to the great room and took a seat beside me on the couch. "So what was Breckin doing down here with you?" he asked casually.

"Convincing me to take him back," I said as seriously as possible.

As he furrowed his brows, I snorted out a laugh.

"These are questions important to the investigation; I would appreciate your cooperation and truthfulness."

"Yes, soon-to-be ex-inspector."

He growled at me.

I cleared my throat. "He wanted to yell at me about you."

"I'm sorry?"

"He doesn't like me all over you."

"Well, he better fuckin' get used to it."

"Like it matters," I soothed him, reaching up to trace my fingers over the stubble-covered jaw. "As if you care."

"I don't," he admitted, smiling shyly, seemingly pleased with me.

"Something else."

"What's that?"

"The sensors for the floodlights didn't work the same as they do at my Dad's house."

"How do you mean?" he asked pointedly.

"Like, the lights didn't come on until the guy was leaving. He was all the way up here on the deck, and they didn't come on. That's weird, right?"

Cord nodded. "That means whoever the guy was, he knew where to walk so he wouldn't trigger the lights, or the lights were on a timer or—I should check. I'll be right back."

I greedily accepted the kiss he leaned close and gave me before he rose and strode from the room. It was strange, but as surreal as the situation was, being with Cord was the opposite. In the middle of the craziness, I was grounded because he was there. I could look at him and be reminded of who I was, of my life and my family and my friends. Never had I thought he would provide stability.

"You're deep in thought."

I was surprised he was back already. "I thought you were checking on something?"

"I did." He chuckled, sitting back down beside me, too close for us to be anything else but lovers. He took my hand in both of his and stared at me.

"Cord?"

"Sorry," he said quickly, clearing his throat. "I just can't get over it."

"What's that?"

"That you see me, that I have your attention."

"I'm sorry."

"No. No reason to be sorry," he told me, lifting my hand to his face. "So the lights aren't set to go off with movement, they're on a timer."

"So it was just time for them to go off when they did."

"Yes."

"That's stupid."

"I agree, which is why now they're set on the motion sensors."

"So the security company does their part—"

"But Mr. Alcott got tired of them going off for foxes or stray dogs, cats, whatever, and so he changed it to specific intervals."

"That's great," I said sarcastically.

"Yeah, it is," he rumbled softly, pressing his face down into the crook of my neck and opening his mouth on my skin.

I made a noise I didn't intend, a groan, moan, whimper all rolled together as he kissed up behind my ear.

"It was good that you noticed that—that it struck you as odd."

"Was it?" I asked, fishing for the compliment.

"Yep, I would have never known otherwise."

"I should be rewarded, then."

"Uh-huh," he said, pulling me into his arms for a hug.

So fast.

I could get used to being crushed against him very, very fast.

He let me go after a moment, but not without a kiss on the forehead. Everyone else slowly trickled in, until they were all there.

"You should probably bring us up to speed, Inspector," John Alcott suggested.

"There's nothing new to tell," Cord informed him, taking my hand in his.

A knock on the door sent Officer Cumberland out to the foyer, and a moment later we were looking at the chief of police of Fieldcrest, Martin Riley. Cord got up to go speak to him, and then, when Chief Riley came to talk to Mr. Alcott, Cord gestured for me to come over.

I crossed the room to Cord, and when I was close enough, he grabbed my hand and yanked me forward into the foyer and into his arms.

"What are you doing?"

"The chief's gonna talk to the Alcotts, but there's no news."

"Okay," I said, waiting for more.

"So this is your point of no return."

I smiled at him.

"No, don't just jump in," he cautioned me. "You need to really think about this. We're moving really fast, and if it's too—"

His protest was cut off when I leaped at him, wrapping my arms and legs around him tight.

"Tracy…." He was scolding me and smiling at the same time.

"You have a really odd idea about fast," I said hoarsely, tightening my legs, wriggling against him. "And all I want to do is go upstairs and put you on your back."

"Yeah?"

"Yes," I said, uncoiling, regaining my feet before I took his hand in mine. When I turned to tug him after me, he didn't move. "What's the holdup?"

He cleared his throat. "We don't—we could take—"

"Stop," I whispered, lifting his hand to my lips and then kissing his knuckles. "You're scared. I promise not to hurt you."

"Don't you think that should be my line?"

I studied his face. "I think you're the one who's worried."

"How can you not be worried?" he groused.

"Because I'm not," I said simply, drawing him after me to the stairs and up. At the door to my room, I told him to go to his, lock it, and then come through the adjoining bathroom and meet me in bed.

"Just like that."

"Yeah," I said as I slid a hand around the back of his neck and pulled him down to me. "Just like that."

He kissed me, and I sucked his tongue into my mouth, stroking slowly, seductively, running my hands all over him, then tugging his shirt up and exposing all that warm, sleek skin. I mapped the rippling muscles in his chest and abdomen with my palms, missing nothing as I broke the kiss and pressed my open mouth to the base of his throat.

"Tracy," he rasped, shoving his hand down the back of my jeans and then sliding his index finger over my crease.

"Go do what I said," I croaked out as I pushed back and saw how ravished he looked with his lush swollen mouth, blown pupils, and bated breath. "Hurry up."

I didn't give him time to answer, instead leaving him alone in the hall as I went into my room and locked the door behind me.

In minutes he was there. He opened my bathroom door, then quietly shut it behind him and turned to face me.

I smiled. "Come here—I won't bite."

"You can bite," he rumbled as he crossed the floor to me.

As soon as I could touch him, I pulled his sweater up over his head and off, followed by the strangely sexy white T-shirt he wore underneath.

"God, look at you. You're so beautiful," I groaned, putting my hands on his massive chest and sliding them over the hard pecs and pebbled nipples.

"Take everything off," he ordered, going to work on his belt as he toed off his biker boots.

I watched him, mesmerized by how quickly his jeans were being shoved down his long, muscular, fuzzy legs.

"What are you doing?" he snapped, looking up at me from where he stood bent over, taking off his socks.

"I've never seen you naked before. I wanna look at you."

Straightening to his full towering height, he spread his arms wide so I could look at all of him. The man was a gorgeous, carved specimen of heavy, cut muscle, roping veins, and dark golden skin. Even his feet were stunning.

"You about done stalling?"

"I am *so* not stalling," I said as I stepped forward, took hold of his long, thick cock, and squeezed gently.

"Oh fuck," he growled, instinctively shoving into my fist.

I went to my knees.

"No, I want you in bed, I don't—Tracy!"

He knew me, but he had no idea what I was like behind closed doors, and licking over the flared head of his rigid shaft had been enough to tear a deep, guttural moan up from his chest.

"You can't just... oh God," he moaned, low and deep, tangling his fingers in my hair as he stared down at me.

I swallowed his crown, and he tightened his hold on me.

"I'm not—selfish," he rasped. "I can take care of you too."

He smelled good, like musk and faintly of soap, and he felt good on my tongue, his silky flesh and the thick vein that ran the length of his rigid shaft, so swallowing him down the back of my throat took no effort at all.

"Tracy!"

Pulling back, making the suction strong, I wrapped my hand around his base and licked and laved, swirled my tongue over his length, and showed him how desperate I was to taste every last inch of him.

"No," he growled suddenly, shoving me off the end of his dick, panting as he stood there.

"No?" I teased him.

Grabbing me under the armpits, he yanked me to my feet before giving me a hard shove down onto the bed. He opened his mouth to say something, but I lifted my arms to receive him, and I watched, amazed, as the man's eyes bled to black, his pupils dilating instantly.

"You like to be wanted," I whispered hoarsely, "so come here."

He dove onto the bed, scrambled over me, crossed my wrists over my head, and held them pinned to the mattress with one hand. He used the other to tug and rip at me—my belt, trouser stays, and zipper surrendering fast. When he smoothed a hand up my abdomen, I arched up under his touch.

"I wanted—" He gasped. "—but you fight me all the time."

I did. "Not anymore," I promised, starting to shake, my body heating. "Get the lube from my bag."

"Yes," he agreed, but instead of moving, he bent and slanted his mouth down over mine in a long, hard kiss.

I fought because I wanted to touch him, and he released my wrists so he could take my dick in his hand and stroke and squeeze me from balls to head.

"Cord!" I pleaded, breaking the drowning, devouring kiss for seconds, needing to speak to him, but wanting him all over me at the same time.

He wrenched away from my clawing hands, rose off the bed, strode over to my duffel, and dug around until he came up with my lube. I enjoyed watching him move, the fluid roll of his hips, the muscles rippling under his sleek gold skin, and the wicked grin when he noticed my gaze on him.

"You love looking at me."

"Yes," I agreed.

"This is it for you," he promised gruffly. He fell back into bed, then rose over me, put his hands on my thighs and parted them. Then he snapped open the cap of the tube and pressed slick fingers inside of me.

I had always imagined that being in bed with Cord would be rough and bruising, with power I had guessed at but never seen. But the deliberate movement paired with his words told another story altogether. I would be taken, yes, but not with any kind of force.

"Please," I whined as he rolled me to my hands and knees and pressed against my entrance.

"I won't move," he promised, curling over me, plastering his chest to my back, coiling his right bicep around my neck, and closing his other, lube-slicked hand around my cock. "You take me inside when you're ready."

It was up to me to lean back and impale myself on his thick, leaking dick. The control he was giving up to me, the caring, and the tenderness—all of it was a wonder to me. And as I sank slowly over him, feeling the burn and stretch, how full I was, I couldn't keep from trembling in his embrace.

When I had swallowed him to the hilt, I leaned forward and then pushed back, rising and falling, realizing instantly that I needed much more.

"Cord," I husked, turning my head, twisting as far as I could to offer my mouth.

"If you give me permission, you can't ever take it back. You're done and I'm moving in and you're getting a ring. You're stuck with me 'til you're dead, so you better think."

"How come I can't just get laid?"

"Because that was never you, and now it's not me. So let me love you or I'll go."

"You don't play fair," I gasped, trembling, my body having broken out in a cold sweat as he began a slow, deep, thrusting that I never wanted to stop.

He was nailing my prostate each time he shoved inside, and the burn was gone; only the sensation of his long, thick cock pushing in and pulling out remained.

"I wanna hear your answer," he said, increasing his speed, thickening inside of me, my muscles clenching around him.

"Cord," I choked out, barely able to hold myself up as he took my mouth.

"Tell me now," he demanded, breaking the wet, hungry kiss just long enough to speak before sealing his lips back to mine.

It was all too much: he rubbed his tongue seductively over mine, shoved my cock in and out of his hot, slippery fist, anchoring me to him with his arm, pressed himself along the length of my back, and drove his enormous dick up into me again and again. I had never been used so hard in my life, and I could feel my balls tightening, the familiar buzzing, and the tingling roll begin shooting down my spine. My orgasm was building, and I had only seconds of lucidity left.

"Oh fuck," I cried out as he fisted his fingers in my hair, releasing my dripping cock, and shoved me facedown into the bed.

"Now," he yelled, hammering into me, gripping my hips tight, allowing for no wiggle or squirm, no movement of any kind. "Do you want me to love you? Yes or no."

"Sex talk means nothing," I reminded him even as my voice cracked.

"It means everything," he roared back. "Now, Tracy!"

"Yes," I whispered brokenly, tears there before I even realized. "Yes, Cord, just don't break my heart."

"Never," he promised, and then he reached under me and tugged on my dick, his grip almost painfully tight, and just that much stimulus sent me right over the edge into a splintering orgasm that flushed my whole body hot and cold in a matter of seconds.

It was ridiculous that at thirty-three I had just discovered what sex could truly be. Every muscle in my body clenched, and the ones in my ass clamped down hard on his cock.

"You're so tight and hot, and I am going to fill up your sweet little ass."

I spurted hard under me on the bedspread as I felt warm liquid fill my channel. I had never thought to ask for a condom, my brain short-circuited with heat.

We froze together, a study in sated lust, until he grabbed me and we rolled sideways, the man still buried to the hilt in my ass.

He wrapped his left arm around my stomach and slid his right hand under my arm, and across my chest, then closed it around my throat, tipping my head back. "You swore, Trace, and in bed is where promises are made."

I was trying to start breathing regularly again. "Actually, lying is what usually happens in bed."

"No. Not with us. Never with us."

And he was right. My soul had been on display moments before, more naked than I had ever been in my life.

"Say it," he prodded me, nuzzling his face into the side of my neck. "Tell me you're gonna keep me."

I chuckled softly and felt him tense behind me.

"Trace." He growled.

"Of course I'm keeping you," I soothed him, clutching his forearm, turning my head so his lips touched my cheek. "I want you in my bed and in my house as soon as we get home."

He hugged all the remaining air from my body, but that was okay; I didn't need to breathe. I had just claimed the man I'd always wanted: body, soul, heart, head. All of him belonged to me. Oxygen was a secondary consideration.

MY PHONE softly buzzing woke me up, and I realized my cheek was plastered over Cord's heart. Somehow I had wound up draped on top of him with his arms wrapped around me. And while it could not have been comfortable for him, I had slept like a rock, which was probably what I felt like on his chest.

Gently, slowly, I extricated myself from his arms, rolled free, and reached for my phone on the nightstand. It was late, four in the morning, and I had a text from Ira telling me I needed to call him the following day and give him an update too. Apparently secondhand information from Matt was not making him happy. I noticed I had a new e-mail as well, something that had come in hours before. When I checked, it was from Cord, and I had test results in my inbox from a month earlier. It was sweet of him to have sent it even though I had missed it entirely. I too had a document at home that proclaimed me disease free, mine from five months ago, when I got myself tested after Breckin cheated on me. And as there had been no one since him, I knew I too was in the clear.

"What are you doing?" Cord rumbled sleepily.

I turned to look at him and smiled before leaning close and tracing a finger down the long, straight line of his nose.

"Don't worship me now. Close your eyes."

I snorted out a laugh. "Worship you?"

"Yeah, well, you think I'm gorgeous, so it's gonna happen."

Grunting, I bent and kissed him. He opened for me, sliding one hand in my hair and using the other to untangle the blankets and sheets between us until we were once again skin to skin.

"I have a piece of paper at home too," I said between kisses, "so you know what we did wasn't dangerous."

"It never crossed my mind to worry about you. You're too much of a Goody Two-shoes."

"I beg your pardon?"

His husky chuckle was very sexy, and when he rolled me to my back under him, I parted my legs so he could slip easily between my thighs.

"You're not the fuck-around kind of guy, Trace, it's never been you."

I would have argued, tried to make myself sound more adventurous, but I had a sneaking suspicion my need to have more than five minutes of connection before fucking in a bathroom stall was something he liked about me.

"So that's how I know taking you to bed without protection was no big deal," he husked.

"It's a big deal to me."

"You know what I meant. Don't bait me."

"Okay," I relented.

He cleared his throat. "Are you sore?"

"No," I answered, wiggling under him, edging up enough so that the head of his cock bumped against my hole. "Why?"

"Don't tease," he groaned softly.

"Who's teasing?"

Even in the darkness, he easily found the lube, and I heard the cap open with a loud snap in the quiet room.

"I'll be gentle this time."

"I don't remember complaining."

"I just—the first time had a five-year buildup. Now I know you're not going anywhere."

"No," I said softly. "I'm not."

My body didn't tense with the breach, just took him in as he pressed forward slowly, steadily.

"Trace," he breathed out before he opened his mouth on the side of my neck, then sucked hard as he slid out of my clasping channel only to slide back in, the motion smooth and languid. "I have wanted to sink inside of you and just be for so long. I feel like I'm finally home."

Never would I have guessed I could be Cord Nolan's whole life or, even more, that I would have ever wanted to be.

CHAPTER
Twelve

CORD HAD to leave me first thing the following morning, but he checked my tonsils before he left, and having him all dressed and me naked under him, rubbing his thighs with my hands as he straddled my hardening groin, was absolute agony.

"Stay here."

"I gotta go," he grumbled, mauling my mouth. "But I don't want to."

"That's a nice thing to say," I said, fisting the lapel of his suit jacket with one hand while I slid the other up into his hair.

"There's extra security around the house," he said softly, kissing along my jawline. "Do not leave. Stay here until I get back."

"Isn't the point supposed to be to lure this psycho out?"

"The point is to make him so nuts over not being able to get to you or Celia that he messes up. I need you to wait here and not leave."

"All right," I agreed. I took his hand and slid it down my abdomen to my dick. "But before you leave…."

The deep, filthy groan from the man as he squeezed my cock made me buck up off the bed.

"Nobody's ever wanted me like this."

"I don't get that at all," I replied truthfully because, really, given his moss-green eyes, chiseled jaw, and big, hard body, how was that even possible?

"Don't—" He gasped. "—change."

"I promise," I said before I went to work on the buttons of his dress shirt.

I WOKE up from my postcoital nap, showered, and then went downstairs. When I arrived, I realized there were a lot of visitors in the house.

"Good morning, Tracy," Brian Alcott greeted me. "I'm sorry you didn't sleep well."

"What makes you say that?"

He pointed at my eyes. "You have some serious baggage there."

I had, truthfully, not gotten much sleep, but the reason was not to be shared. "So what's going on down here?"

"My folks are hosting a brunch for some of Breckin's old friends."

"Got it."

"Feel free to mingle, and there's food and drinks out on the deck."

There was, in fact, a huge spread out there, monitored by a whole host of catering personnel. It was a security nightmare, and I wondered vaguely if Cord knew.

Breckin stood with Celia, his parents, and friends in a small huddle. When I drifted by I heard him sharing stories. Celia was holding his hand and shot me a look as I walked by. It wasn't necessary—I had no claim on the man anymore, and I wanted to tell her that. But from the way she visibly bristled, I decided the best thing was to just stay away. The next circle was discussing country clubs, trust funds, and European vacations. It was all over my head, so I walked on.

Out on the deck, I filled a plate and took a seat at a small table by myself. A member of the staff came by, dropped off a goblet of water, and asked me if I wanted something else as well.

"Ice tea?"

"Flavored, sweetened, or non?"

Dear Lord. "Just regular unsweetened black, if you have it."

"Of course."

It was impressive, really.

"Hello."

My head snapped up because I had been eating—voracious sex created quite an appetite—and met a pair of soft blue eyes.

A man held out his hand to me. "I'm Lucien Ritter, an old friend of Breckin's, and I understand you're a new one."

"I am," I said, smiling up at the handsome man as I shook his hand. "I'm Tracy Brandt."

"It's a pleasure."

I invited him to sit with me since he was holding a plate in his other hand. Once he was seated, the waiter delivered my ice tea and asked Lucien what he wanted. After he'd ordered and we were alone, I asked him how far he and Breckin went back.

"To high school, actually," he said, smiling at me. "It was me, Breckin, and Turi."

"Who?"

"Turi Carrera. The three of us all swam together, played soccer, and ran track."

"Oh. Like the three musketeers."

"Yeah."

"And where is Turi now?"

He cleared his throat. "He died—" He made a quick noise. "—is easiest to say."

"What's harder?"

His gaze met mine. "He committed suicide."

"Oh, I'm so sorry."

He nodded. "Yeah. Right after that, Breckin left for college without a word. This is the first time I've seen or talked to him in eighteen years."

"I'm so sorry," I said sincerely, reaching across the table to squeeze his shoulder briefly. "Not only did you lose Turi, but Breckin too. That had to have been so hard."

His gaze locked on mine. "You're very kind; no one ever said that to me before."

I was surprised, and my look must have conveyed as much.

"I think it's because we're guys, right? I mean, how connected could we have been?"

"That's nuts."

"It was, but no one knew until Turi's funeral that he and Breckin were in love."

I leaned forward, grabbed his hand, and held it tight. He rolled his hand in my grip so he was holding mine back. "Is that when you found out too?"

He shook his head. "No. When his mother sent me to his room before the funeral to get what clothes I thought he should be buried in—"

"What *you* thought?"

"Yeah," he replied softly, squeezing my hand tighter. "She was… she was upset because in his note…. She had no idea he was gay."

"Oh. What did she do?"

"Almost all of his stuff went to Goodwill the following day. I took his journals, his letters, his drawings, some of his clothes—everything I could grab when I left."

"And whatever he was buried in."

"Yeah."

"And then what?"

"I took the clothes to the funeral home."

"Fuck, I'm sorry."

His eyes had filled and were sparkling with tears as he stared at me. "I saw the rest of his things getting picked up the next day."

I sat quietly, listening.

"She saw me out there, in my car, watching, and when she came to the window, she gave me his gold St. Christopher medal."

"That was nice."

"Yeah, I'd wondered where it was, but I guess he had taken it off before he hung himself in his closet, so she had it. She told me she was glad that he died because his choice to love men went against God's law, but that she knew I wasn't filthy like Breckin, so she wanted me to have it."

"Oh. She didn't know about him and Breckin before she read the note?"

"No. Nobody did except Breckin's folks. He told me he came out to them, like, a week before, and then at the reception after the funeral at the country club, he came out to everyone."

I could only imagine how hard that had been for Breckin.

"You know, Mr. and Mrs. Carrera would have disowned Turi if he'd lived, so it was just so hypocritical to see them at the reception talking to me and all his friends, other parents, acting like they gave a damn. I hated every minute of it."

I cleared my throat. "So he left a note, and in it he said he and Breckin were in love."

"Yes."

"Then I don't get why he would kill himself since Breckin loved him back, right?"

Releasing my hand, Lucien leaned back from the table. "Like I said, Breckin had told his folks about Turi a week before, and I guess they dropped a bomb on him."

"Which was what?"

"They told him if being gay was his choice, he could pay for college on his own because they certainly wouldn't. They didn't approve of what they felt was his lifestyle choice, so they were cutting him off."

"But Breckin paid for college himself. I know he did. He never had any contact with his parents, so what the hell? I'm so confused."

"Well, I guess he and Turi had this big coming-out planned at Breckin's graduation party, but Breckin broke up with him instead."

"Why?"

"If Breckin wanted to go to school, he needed his parents' money."

"But wait." I had to get it straight in my head. "Breckin broke up with Turi, Turi committed suicide because of that, and then Breckin left, cutting ties with his folks anyway?"

"Yes. After Turi died, he couldn't take their money."

"Holy shit."

"Yeah. I remember he called me, told me that he was sorry he and Turi had kept their relationship a secret from me, but now that Turi was gone, he couldn't live a lie. He owed it to Turi not to do that."

"Not to be trite," I snapped, "but it's too bad he didn't have that revelation when his boyfriend was still alive."

"Yes," Lucien agreed, nodding. "I've always thought the same thing."

"Man, that is a fucked-up story."

"I'm sorry to have—"

I stopped him. "No. Are you kidding? Thank you for sharing it with me. I just… I feel so bad for you and for Turi."

"Not Breckin?"

"Yeah, Breckin too," I said thoughtfully. "I mean, the guilt had to have been just staggering."

"I think it was for a while, but I think now, with friends like you and his relationship with Celia... maybe he doesn't think about Turi much anymore."

I was about to argue when he said, "Has he ever mentioned Turi to you?"

"No. This is the first I'm hearing of this."

He nodded. "You see?"

"I do," I assured him. "May I ask you a question?"

"Of course."

"Were you in love with Turi?"

His smile was huge as he wiped at his eyes. "How did you know?"

I shrugged. "It just seemed like it."

"I was, very much."

"Did Breckin know?"

"Yeah, he did, because I told him."

"It must have been hard to find out they were in love."

"It was."

"I mean, Turi killed himself over Breckin. Did you ever tell him you loved him?"

"No. I was waiting until after graduation. I wanted him to come with me when I left for Cornell. He was accepted to the University of Vermont, but he told me he had other plans. I had no idea he meant leaving with Breckin. I thought I could get him to go with me."

"Sure."

"He was so smart; he could have gone with me, done the community college thing for a year, and then got into Cornell, or done something else. I just wanted us to be together."

"Of course you did," I groaned, and I got up, walked around the table, bent, and hugged him. He looked startled, but after a minute he hugged me back.

"Tracy, you have a really soft heart."

Pulling back, I stared down at him. "It's a tragedy, and I hate those."

He patted my shoulder before I retreated back to my seat.

"You must have been furious with Breckin," I said.

"I was too devastated over losing Turi; Breckin was the last thing on my mind for so long," he explained sadly. "I thought, if only I had been brave enough to tell Turi, maybe he would have fallen in love with me instead and still be alive today."

"It's not your fault. It's nobody's fault. It was Turi's choice to take his own life. I wish he had talked to you. Even if he was done with Breckin, he still had you to turn to. I so wish he had."

"Yes. If only."

"So, was it hard for you in high school? Being gay in this small community?"

"No one knew," he told me. "So, no, it wasn't. I was a big jock, right? So were Breckin and Turi. And like I said, we were always together, and there were always cheerleaders."

"Was Breckin bi then too?"

"Yeah, he was."

"You and Turi too?"

"No, just Breckin," he confirmed. "But Turi and I dated a lot of girls. Both of us just made sure we picked the ones we knew were saving it for their husbands or at least college."

I smiled at him. "So, not only did Breckin have Turi, but cheerleaders as well."

"Yep. You know him—he likes to have his cake and eat it too."

"I wouldn't know," I lied.

He lifted his eyebrows. "No? You're gay, Breckin's bi…. Not once?"

"How did you know I was gay?"

His smile was sheepish. "I saw you kiss the inspector in the foyer last night."

"You were here last night?"

"I was."

"I don't remember seeing anyone but Breckin's family."

"I'm a little invisible," he teased me. "But I'm also in private security here in Fieldcrest and work closely with the police."

"Oh." I chuckled. "Well, that explains it."

He reached out and patted my shoulder. "Yes. I'm under contract with the police department as we speak. The chief hired my company to do backup surveillance for them since he has a total of himself and four officers."

"That makes sense."

"Yes. We're supposed to be walking around checking out all the guests, but since there are so many of us here, I thought, I'll go sit with Mr. Brandt. I apologize for the subterfuge—I already knew who you were when I walked over here."

"That's okay."

"And I didn't mean to burden you with my ancient history."

"No, thank you for telling me."

"You're welcome."

I coughed. "So you went from Cornell and came back here to work in law enforcement?"

"No. I went and got a degree in chemistry, then a master's, as well, at Cornell, and finally a PhD in chemistry from Dartmouth."

"And came back here to do what?"

"I tried teaching in Burlington at the University of Vermont, but it just didn't agree with me. Then I tried high school, and that was worse."

"You didn't want to get a job at a lab somewhere?"

"No."

"So you came back to Fieldcrest."

"I did, and after taking a look around, I decided private security was what was needed in this town. I mean, it's a small community, but we get a lot of tourists, a lot of people coming through all the time, and people need to have their homes protected."

"Sure."

"I've been back about seven years."

"And is there anyone in your life?"

"Not yet."

"Because of Turi?"

He looked pained. "There have been a few people but... no one important."

"I'm really so sorry."

"My whole life just stopped that summer. I've done things, gotten my degrees, traveled, but as far as…." He trailed off, his gaze flicking to me and then away.

"What?"

"I'm rambling, and you're a complete stranger. I'm surprised you haven't gotten up and run away yet."

"No," I said, reassuring him. "I feel very privileged that you've trusted me with this."

He was silent for a minute or so, and I stayed quiet, giving him time. "You know, his parents never once went to his grave."

"I'm so sorry," I said sincerely.

"It was their choice."

And then it hit me that there was something odd about his sentence. "Went? Did they move away?"

"No, they died."

"Oh, that's terrible."

"Yeah. Seven years after Turi died, I guess they hit a patch of black ice and went right off the road. I heard they both died instantly, so that was some comfort at least."

"Was that before you moved back or right about the same time?"

"Right around the same time," he answered. "I didn't go to their funeral."

"I think it would have been hypocritical if you had."

"Thank you. Some people thought it was odd of me."

"I don't."

His gaze locked on mine. "You're a very understanding man, Tracy Brandt. If you weren't already involved with the policeman, I would ask to take you to dinner."

"And I would have accepted." I smiled at him.

He was a handsome man with his short blond hair and dark-blue eyes, but there was a sadness that clung to him. His regrets would never go away.

Changing the subject then, he asked me what I'd seen, and I gestured around me.

"You haven't been off the property?"

"No."

"There are some lovely covered bridges to see, and just walking down Main Street is a treat. You should let me take you and the inspector out."

"I'll ask him."

"Excellent. Let me give you my number."

He excused himself a few minutes later, and I wandered the grounds, sat in the gazebo, and eventually drifted back into the house and through the crowds. I finally walked into the great room and took a seat on the couch. I was just about to get my phone out when Bethany took a seat beside me.

"Oh, hey," I greeted her.

She was studying me.

"What?"

"You know, I was really surprised by you."

"Sorry?"

"I just—and I don't mean you to take this the wrong way, but... when I first saw you," she said thoughtfully, "I was certain my mom got it wrong."

"Got what wrong?"

"She told me what the inspector said on the phone the day he called, but when I saw you and Celia, I thought maybe Mom misheard and that you were Breckin's husband and Celia was *your* friend who was also your surrogate or something like that."

"What?"

She cleared her throat, leaning forward, closer to me. "He told me he was bi in high school. I've known forever."

"Oh."

"And you're totally his type."

"His type?"

"Well, yeah. You look just like him; you must know that."

"Like who?" I asked, even though, after talking to Lucien, I could hazard a guess.

"Turi Carrera. He was this guy Breckin fooled around with in high school."

"And what happened to him?"

"He killed himself because Breckin wouldn't come out to, like, the whole town."

"Oh yeah?"

She nodded. "Yeah. It was really sad. I guess he thought Breckin was going to take him to college with him, but that wasn't going to happen if Breckin wanted my folks to pay for it."

"Go on."

"But my folks didn't know that Breckin borrowed money from my grandparents against his trust fund. Plus he had a couple of scholarships for track."

"So he had the means to go to school when he disappeared."

"Yes."

"Do you think he had the means when he told Turi he wasn't going to take him with him?"

"No. I think he was still working it out when he told Turi he couldn't go. That was before the graduation ceremony. At that point, I think he was still thinking all he had was our parents, so what they said went."

"It's too bad he didn't wait to talk to Turi until he actually knew something."

"Yeah. I think so too. But I also think, maybe either way, Turi wasn't going to get taken along with him, you know?"

"What makes you think that?"

"Because when Breckin used to talk about college with me, he never talked about taking Turi along, and I used to ask him, 'What about Turi?'"

"Why?"

"I caught them a million times, kissing, all hot and heavy, and it looked like love to me, so when Breckin started talking about California, I was like, what about Turi?"

"And what did he say?"

"He said Turi would be okay with him or without him," she explained. "He told me they weren't serious, so I never figured they were."

"Turi must have thought so."

"Yeah, he did, poor guy. The note he left was just heartbreaking. Lucien—he was another friend of Breckin's that used to hang out with him and Turi—he was given the note by Turi's folks, and then he gave it to Breckin."

"What did Breckin do?"

"He left the next day. No word, no nothing."

"So it's been eighteen years since you guys have seen him?"

"Yeah. He didn't want to see any of us. But, I mean, he called, told us he was okay. He e-mailed my parents, and then a couple years ago, he and I started corresponding, and then he and Brian. So we've been in touch."

It had been an interesting bit of news when she and Brian had shared it with me in the car the day before. What struck me as odd was that Breckin had never said a word to me about any member of his family beyond telling me that they were not close.

"So you and Breckin have been in touch for a while now, as you said."

"Yes, but he never mentioned either Celia or you, so this all just came as a bit of a shock."

"I bet."

"And like I said, I was so surprised when I saw you," she said, smiling at me. "Yesterday when you came downstairs and took off your scarf and hat and your sunglasses, I said to my mom after, 'Doesn't he look a lot like Turi Carrera?' My mom was amazed at the resemblance too. I bet if Lucien saw you, he'd be blown away."

Funny that Lucien had not mentioned it. I was betting that maybe the similarities were superficial—maybe the same brown eyes, brown hair, tanned skin.

"Turi was really stunning, and so are you, Tracy."

"That's nice of you to say."

"I'm not trying to flatter you. It's true. I wish my nose was that perfect and my eyelashes were that long, and I would need implants to have cheekbones as high as yours."

"I actually met Lucien," I said, ignoring her comments.

"And did he say you reminded him of Turi?"

"No."

"That's so weird, because like I said, the first thing I thought when I saw you was how funny that Breckin found a new guy who was the spitting image of Turi."

"Do you have an old yearbook? I'd love to have a look."

"We do," she said slowly, and I could tell she was thinking at the same time. "I just have to figure out where they are."

"Well, if you can."

I hoped she could, because my mind was reeling, wondering if that was what it was, the reason that Breckin had been attracted to me in the first place—my resemblance to Turi Carrera.

"I'll look tonight after everyone leaves."

"Great."

"So tell me, Tracy, what do you do?"

We had a nice talk. I told her all about bookkeeping, and she told me all about her party-planning business. Event coordinators worked for her, and she put on big extravagant parties for a thousand people down to lavish, intimate gatherings for ten. Her brother Brian had gone into the family business with his father, which was maple syrup.

"Really?"

She smiled and nodded. She walked me to the kitchen pantry and pulled a bottle of Alcott Farms maple syrup from a shelf and gave it to me. The glass bottle was heavy.

"It feels expensive."

"Six bucks a pop," she said, waggling her eyebrows at me.

"No shit."

"We ship it all over the world."

"Nice."

"I'll ship a case home for you," she said cheerfully. "They make good gifts for people you gotta buy for but don't really want to. Tie green and red ribbons on the top and stick them on people's desks. They work great."

"Thank you."

"No problem. Text me your address."

"I will."

"Do it now."

"Oh, okay."

We were standing there, Bethany giving me her number, me texting, when Breckin reached us.

"We're all going to an art exhibit in town," he explained, putting his hand on the small of my back. "You guys come with us."

"Cord told us to stay here," I reminded him.

"He said for us to all stay together and listen to the police," he argued. "And since they're coming with us, we'll be fine."

"Where are you going?" Lucien asked as he walked up beside me.

"To the old dairy they converted into an art gallery," Breckin informed me, turning to look at Lucien. "Please come."

Lucien smiled at Breckin, who suddenly grabbed him and hugged him tight. "I missed you too, buddy."

It was nice to see them hugging, and when Breckin turned and saw the look on my face, he smiled the smile I had fallen in love with, the one that made his eyes glow.

"You come too," he said gravely, and when he touched my face and I let him, he got bolder and slid his hand around to the back of my neck and dragged me close. "Say yes."

And I did.

Once we were all piled into the car, I called Cord.

"What?"

Really, the man's social skills were for crap. "Meet me at the old dairy that was converted into an art gallery. Everyone is going there now."

"What did I tell you to do?"

"Yeah, but, I mean, the whole place is emptying out. There would be no one home to guard me against crazed psychopaths."

"Are you kidding?"

"Nope."

He growled on the other end.

"Meet me."

"Fine."

"And don't be mad."

He grunted. "No promises."

THE GALLERY had a rustic feel to it, and it was really big. As soon as we got there, Breckin and Celia were swarmed by people. I noticed two policemen hovering close around them as well, which reminded me that I wasn't at home meeting Cord out on a date. Someone was actually trying to kill me.

But no matter how I tried to stay on guard, I wasn't scared. It seemed like ages since the bathroom incident and the intruder trying to leave me a dead rabbit. Seeing someone outside the window had been alarming at the time, but not really that scary in the bigger picture. Logically I knew that whoever had killed Tim Stanson was dangerous, but if whoever it was had really wanted to hurt me, he could have shot me right there through the glass. Everything I knew about the case was running through my head, and so I decided to remain vigilant, thus turning down the champagne-filled flutes the waiters floated by with.

"So? What do you think of the gallery?" Lucien asked as he reached me.

"It's nice," I said, looking for Cord, hovering close to the front door so I wouldn't miss him.

"I wish I could ask you to dance," he said, smiling at me.

"Well, that would be odd in the middle of an art gallery," I reminded him.

He was staring at me.

"Lucien?"

"I'm sorry; you just look so much like Turi."

"You didn't tell me that at first."

He nodded. "And I should have."

It hit me then that waiting for Breckin's little sister to find an old yearbook was a waste of time. Surely Lucien was a quicker source. "Lucien."

"Yes?"

"Would you happen to have a picture of Turi in your wallet?"

"I do."

Of course he did. "May I see it, please?"

Immediately he pulled his wallet from the breast pocket of his suit jacket. Inside, tucked in the compartment right behind his driver's license, was what must have been a senior-class picture of Turi Carrera.

The tuxedo jacket Turi was wearing was terrible: dark royal blue with a black collar. Underneath, the pale-blue ruffled shirt was even worse, but the teenager himself was very handsome. He actually bore more of a resemblance to my brother Alex than to me, but even that was merely superficial, as I had assumed. He had dark eyes and brows, strong features, broader than mine, and thick black hair. Had he allowed himself to become a man, he would have been gorgeous. He was one of those guys you knew would get better with age. The awkward duckling would have become a swan. It was quite a compliment to be compared to him, but the similarities were fleeting.

"He had a nice face," I said gently, smiling at Lucien as I returned the picture.

"Yes, he did."

I cleared my throat. "But I'm not him, no matter how much you might like that."

He furrowed his brows. "No, I know."

"I just want you to be sure you see me and not him."

He nodded. "I do."

"Okay." I squeezed his shoulder.

Lucien turned sideways then and put his arm around me, clutching my waist. I was going to say something, but Cord did it for me, appearing out of thin air.

"Move your hand," he warned coldly.

Lucien stepped back. "I apologize, Inspector. I didn't mean anything by it."

Cord nodded, but he took hold of my wrist and drew me close, turning me into his larger frame. I put a hand on his abdomen and leaned my head into his shoulder.

He rubbed his chin in my hair as Lucien excused himself.

"You scared him," I whispered, inhaling deeply, drinking in the smell of soap and a trace of rain and musk.

"I don't give a fuck," he grumbled. "He should never think that touching you is okay."

"This possessive side of you is kind of hot," I teased. "But with me, you never have to worry."

"I know," he said softly, his voice husky.

Looking up at him, I saw his jaw muscles flex. "So, what did you have to go over with the chief?"

"I just wanted to make sure he vetted everyone who was going to be working with him for the next couple of days. There is other crime going on, even in this tiny little burb, so he's bringing in some outside help."

"I see."

"So, have you seen any good art?"

"Nothing I feel the need to take home."

"I'll walk around with you."

I took his hand and led the way, accepting a glass of champagne now that he was there. "First one of the night, you know."

"'Cause you didn't want to get tipsy without me?"

"That's right."

"But now it's okay?"

"Yeah," I said, shrugging, "because you'll look out for me."

"Yes, I will," Cord growled, taking a step forward so I had to tilt my head back to see his face. His gaze was locked on mine, and the intensity of the look made me squirm. "Always."

"That a promise?" I asked, smiling crazily up at him. I put my hand through one of the belt loops of his jeans and gently tugged him forward.

"Yes, it is."

He put his arms around me then, one on the small of my back above my tailbone and the other around my shoulders. He pressed me gently to him, and I put my hands on his chest. We stayed like that in our cocoon of two for a few minutes until he walked me backward and put me up against an exposed-brick wall.

"You're shitty at protecting Breckin and Celia," I accused him.

"True," he admitted, taking a deep breath and then dropping his mouth to my ear. I felt him wedge his leg between mine, and his breath on my skin caused goose bumps over every square inch of my body. "But I don't care."

"Cord," I said, and then I looked up.

He bent and kissed me until I was vibrating under him, clutching at his dress shirt, trying to get closer to him.

"We need to go."

"Yes," I said, rubbing against him.

"Stop, or you'll get attacked in the car."

"The car sounds good," I husked, gazing up at him.

"You drive me nuts when you look at me like that."

"Like what?"

"All vulnerable and sweet."

Me? I was going to say something, but he walked away then, and as he had my hand, I went with him. He laced my fingers with his and led me through the crowd, past everyone else and out into the night. There was a car there parked next to the curb, right in front.

"Get in."

"Where did you get this?"

"I borrowed it from the impound yard, courtesy of the chief."

"Isn't that bad?"

He glared at me. "Get in the car."

I opened the door and slipped into the passenger seat, then waited until he got in. Once he did, he didn't immediately start the car.

"You okay?"

"Yeah," he answered flatly.

But he wasn't. Something was wrong. The silence became oppressive after a few minutes, and I turned to look at him. He reached for me then and put his hand on the side of my face, and I climbed over the emergency brake and fell into his arms. His mouth was hot on mine, and I kissed him and kissed him until I was out of breath. When I pulled back suddenly to look at him, he told me we had to go. He started the car as I rolled off him and stared out the window.

"Why did you do that?"

"I wanted to," I answered, turning.

"And what else?"

"You looked like you needed me."

"I always need you," he said as he took my hand, laced his fingers with mine, and held tight.

When he pulled up to a motel, I understood. "I thought you were taking me somewhere romantic," I teased him.

"This'll be romantic," he grumbled at me as he turned to stare into my eyes.

"I thought everything was filled up because of the cheese festival or whatever."

"Not the by-the-night places."

I started laughing.

"What?"

"Your idea of romance is a little twisted, Nolan."

"Do you care?"

"No," I replied honestly. I unlocked the door and opened it.

He got out fast and came around the car, and when he stepped in front of me, I reached up and slid my arms around his neck.

"What's wrong?"

"I want this to be over," he said with a catch in his voice. "I want to go home, and I want you to fall in love with me. I'm frantic for my life to start and terrified that it won't."

"It will," I promised before I drew him close and kissed him.

I thrust my tongue inside his mouth. I was thorough, forceful, all hunger and heat as I tasted him, dragging a ragged moan deep from the man's chest.

He wanted me. It was there in the way he dug his fingers into my ass, wrapping my legs around his hips, and the way he coiled his arms tight around my back.

"Tracy." He cried my name as I writhed in his hold.

He was so mine; all I had to do was say the words. No matter what he said, whatever protest he could come up with, the truth was here between us, and it was surrender. I would stop running from him, he would stop hiding from me, and we would truly begin. I couldn't remember ever wanting anything, or anyone, more.

I was vaguely aware of moving inside from outside, carried and clutched tight to his chest, the jingle of keys and locks clicking beside me before I was put on my feet. When he tried to pull away, I caught his face in my hands and pulled him back down to me. He pressed his lips to the side of my neck and opened them on my skin. My knees barely held me up.

"I'm sorry it took me so long to tell you the truth," he croaked out, unbuttoning his overcoat and then letting me slide it off his shoulders.

"I'm sorry I didn't really see you," I soothed him, draping the garment over a chair beside the small desk.

"But you do now."

"I do," I assured him. I unzipped my jacket and dropped it onto the seat of the same chair.

"Maybe we should talk about—"

"No," I insisted, chuckling as I toed off my shoes before going to work on my belt. "I don't wanna talk. Take off your clothes."

He raised one eyebrow as he stared down at me. "I'm not that easy."

"The hell you're not," I teased, leaning close and kissing his throat, chin, along his jawline, and finally his ear, flicking my tongue over his lobe.

"Oh God." He groaned like he was dying.

"Strip now," I commanded, tugging on his bottom lip, nibbling, trying to get him moving.

"Tracy," he moaned, and the sound, ragged and full of ache, broke through my carnal haze.

I stopped unbuttoning my shirt and leaned back to look up into his face. "What's the matter?"

"I just—you have no idea how much I...." He bent and kissed me.

I was lost in it, the slowness and the build, but I cleared my head because this was important. He was important. Taking hold of his face, stilling him, I stared up into his eyes. "Tell me what you're thinking."

He looked pained.

"Please, Cord."

"It's fast," he said simply, his voice was husky and low. "This is fast."

"Yes."

He furrowed his thick brows, and I traced over one of them with my thumb.

The man was adorable.

"Stop worrying," I said.

"I can't help it. I only have you by default."

"What're you talking about?"

"If Breckin hadn't messed up, where would I be?"

"Seducing me at a Christmas party?" I suggested.

"Shit," he grumbled miserably as he dropped his head forward onto my shoulder.

After sliding a hand behind his neck and holding him there, I whispered into his ear, "Listen, I didn't know why Breckin cheated on me at the time. It made no sense. But now I understand. He needed something I couldn't give him."

"What?"

"Excitement."

He lifted his head to scowl at me. "Do you even know what you're talking about?"

I nodded. "Breckin likes diversity. He likes the thrill of newness. I got old, and so he went on the prowl for something fresh. I have no doubt there would have been another after Sean. There would have been a whole string of people."

"You can't know—"

"I think Breckin likes the idea of being monogamous, but it's not his natural state."

His gaze searched mine.

"And it wasn't yours either."

A quick nod from him.

"But that's changed, yeah?"

"Yes," he said, swallowing hard.

"And you want to come home to me every night, don't you?"

"More than you know," he ground out.

"No more running around for you."

He shook his head.

"Gonna settle down with me," I murmured.

His lunge made me laugh as he wrapped his arms, corded with thick muscle, around me, crushing me against him. "I'm keeping you, Trace. You need to get it right in your head."

I already had. Fast had never scared me, only indecision.

When I eased back, he was smiling lazily, the laugh lines in the corner of his eyes crinkling in half, and all of it, just him, drunk with me, was simply too much to resist. I kissed under his impossibly square, sharp jaw. "Don't be scared anymore."

"Okay," he said, resigned, as I leaned back, finished unbuttoning my shirt and slid it off, then put it on the seat of the chair where my leather jacket was as well.

He yanked off his tie and shirt, dropping them on the floor.

"Gimme all that," I directed, pointing.

"Really? We're calling off the seduction to tidy up?"

"If you're not still hot for me after I pick up your clothes, we're doomed, Nolan."

Moving quickly, he grabbed his discarded button-down oxford and draped it over the back of the chair, on top of his coat, before turning on me.

I snorted out a laugh before he pounced on me.

"You're a slob," I protested as he wrestled me into his arms, carried me to the bed, and fell down with me on top of him.

"Yeah, so what?" he teased, wiggling under me.

I grabbed his hands, pinned him to the mattress, and straddled his hips.

"You're gonna be taking care of me from now on, right?" he said.

"Doesn't make me your damn maid," I said, trying not to laugh.

"Manservant?"

"No," I insisted.

He huffed out a breath.

"What?"

"I don't wanna… play."

I bent and kissed his collarbone. "Why not?"

He moved fast and rolled me to my back, covering my body with his a moment later. "Your eyes are so dark and wet."

I quivered under him. "I had no idea you were like this—could be like this."

"You've turned me into a sap."

His disgust made me laugh as he bent to kiss me.

"It's not funny," he groused softly.

"No," I agreed as he sealed his lips over mine.

The kiss was hard and slow, and I took my time because all I really wanted was to taste him. He closed his eyes, and I kissed his throat and his jaw before returning to his mouth. He moved his hands over my chest and down across my stomach to the snap on my jeans. He was not gentle and tugged the snap open roughly. I dug my fingers into his shoulders to bring him close, and he smiled down at me before covering me with his big, hard body, crushing me gently under him.

"I'm lucky you finally saw me," he whispered against my mouth.

"Why?" I asked, threading my fingers through his hair, savoring the silky feel.

"Because I was fuckin' miserable without you," he confessed, obviously not happy about coming clean.

"Talk to me from now on, huh?"

He grunted, and I couldn't help smiling as he covered my throat with hot kisses and then moved slowly downward.

"Cord," I pressed him.

"I swear," he assured me, and with that I felt him relax in my arms.

His easy grin flushed me with heat, his contentment obvious. He got up just long enough to strip out of his Dockers, and I did the same with my low-rise jeans, though he grabbed the cuffs and yanked them down and off.

"They're on the floor," he announced evilly before he tossed a small tube onto the bed beside me. "Should I fold them?"

"Try not to be such a wiseass."

He shrugged, and I get a trace of a very wicked grin.

"Always come prepared with the lube, do you?"

"For you? Yeah."

I was laughing as he flipped me over on my stomach but stopped instantly when he pressed his hard, muscular chest along my back. He felt too good, too hot.

"You want me?" he checked.

"Oh yes."

"You know, I had no idea your voice could sound like that."

"Like what?" I asked as I heard the pop-top snap open.

"Like sex," he rumbled before sliding his lubed middle finger deep inside my ass.

"Cord," I rasped, bucking under him.

"I was gonna take my time, but I want you too much," he said, adding another finger and gently scissoring me open.

"Yes," I whimpered, writhing as he wrapped his left hand around my throat and tipped my head back, curling his fingers into my mouth.

"So you have to take me in."

"I want to see you."

When he rubbed his chest over my back, I realized I was slick with sweat that fast, flushing hot and cold as he pressed against my entrance.

"Please, Cord."

"Trace," he moaned, his breath rough in my ear before he rolled me to my back and lifted my calves to his shoulders.

As he pushed forward, just the slight stretch burning, sucking all the air from my body, I begged him to hurry.

"I want promises first."

I understood. I couldn't hold back. I had to trust him completely. Maybe it wasn't fair, but it was how it had to be. And I knew him, knew Cord Nolan.

"Love."

Damn. I already was that. "It's not fair."

"I know."

I was going to explode if I couldn't have him. "Fuck me!" He slid a fraction further, and I wanted him deeper, harder, faster, and my frustration erupted in a snarl of craving need.

"Say it!" he growled back.

"You belong to me now, Cord," I croaked out. "You're mine."

"Yours," he echoed and then thrust home.

The breach took my breath away as I flung out my arms and fisted the blanket in my hands, twisting it tight as he slid almost free and then hammered back inside, over and over, in and out, the press and retreat annihilating any thought but him. There was only Cord, the focus of my world.

He changed his grip, milking my cock with one hand, stroking, squeezing, tugging, keeping the other on my hip, holding tight, lifting me into a position of absolute submission.

He was so big, so strong, and being in his hands, under his power, held, dominated, was something I'd only ever dreamed of.

"I'm gonna come," I cried.

"Now," he commanded. "Because you feel so fuckin' good, I can't... now!"

My muscles all clamped down around the long, hard, hot length of him, and I yelled his name as I came hard, spurting over my own abdomen.

He pounded me through my orgasm and the aftershocks, keeping his hands anchored on my hips when he pulsed deep within my body, filling me, my name bouncing off the walls.

I loved the kissing and licking over my throat as he stayed buried inside me, his dick still rock hard as he stroked over my ribs.

"We're never gonna be apart," he explained softly, gently.

I lifted my gaze to his. "No?"

"No," he said confidently before he suddenly smiled. "Look at your beautiful dark eyes," he whispered, leaning down to me to seal his lips over mine.

I started shaking then, and he eased from my still-clasping channel, careful with me. After falling down onto the bed, he opened his arms wide. "Come here, honey."

"When you decide on something, there's no halfway, huh?"

"Nope," he said, patting his chest. "I wanna hold you."

I lifted up and then dropped into his waiting embrace and coiled around him, holding on as tight as I could. He rubbed his chin in my hair as he wrapped me in his strong arms.

"Don't fall asleep."

"No," I said even as my eyes drifted closed, the man's warmth irresistible. I found it impossible not to snuggle up into his shoulder.

"Are you listening to me?"

I was. I so was.

CHAPTER

Thirteen

I WAS dying of thirst, so I got up, dressed, and went in search of a vending machine to get us both some water. I only found snack machines, though, so I came back, prepared to drink out of the faucet in the bathroom. Hand on the doorknob, I prepared to go back inside.

"Wait."

Whirling around, heart in my throat, I was surprised to not be facing a mad man with a gun, but instead a very ordinary-looking guy with a ball cap pulled low across his eyes. He had a barn coat on over a hoodie, and what looked like painter pants and heavy work boots. There was nothing even vaguely threatening about him except that he was there.

"Sorry?" I asked, taking a step back toward the door.

It was then he withdrew a gun. "No, you can't go back in there. He said there's a cop with you, yeah? I'll go back to prison for this if I run into a cop."

I stopped moving and waited.

"All I'm supposed to do here is make sure you don't go back in."

"What if I hadn't come out?"

"Then I was supposed to knock soft until someone answered."

"And if the cop had answered instead of me?"

"I was supposed to shoot him."

My stomach clenched tight just thinking about Cord hurt.

"But really," he said quickly, catching his breath, "I don't wanna shoot anybody. I will, but I don't want to."

I nodded.

"I just gotta give you the phone in my pocket, tell you what number to dial, and then we go for a quick walk."

I nodded.

"Come away from the door."

I could have yelled. If I did, Cord would wake up, grab his gun, and fly out the door to save me. The stranger who really didn't want to fire his weapon would, in fact, shoot the man I was planning a future with. I wasn't ready to roll the dice on my happily ever after, the one where I got to eat dinner every night with Cord Nolan.

"Tell me what you want me to do."

"Just follow me."

"Okay," I agreed quickly.

We walked together through the open-air corridor between the doors and the parked cars until we reached the dumpster. It was there that he passed me a tiny flip-top phone. He recited a number, and I punched it into the display.

"Do you want me to put it on speaker?" I asked the man.

He shook his head. "No. I know where I'm supposed to take you already."

The message on the phone said "dialing" as I pressed it to my ear. It only rang once.

"Hello? Tracy?" It was a woman's voice.

"Yeah, who's this?"

"Celia."

"Oh, okay, are you all right?"

"Yes. Is Cord with you?"

"No," I answered, "not at the moment."

"Good. You need to come to Auto Haus Garage right now."

"Why?"

"I don't know, but he says you have to, or he's going to hurt me."

And suddenly what was happening started sinking in. "Oh shit."

She whimpered softly.

"Where are you?"

"I'm here, at the garage waiting for you."

"But not alone."

"No."

I was so cold, inside and out, scared for the first time, but not for myself. Not even for Celia. I was terrified for Cord. If anything happened to me, he would never forgive himself, and the idea of that made my heart hurt.

"Tracy?"

"Celia," I said softly. "Are you hurt?"

"Not yet," she answered, the catch in her voice making it wobble.

"Okay." My throat was dry, and I couldn't stop shaking.

"But he will, Tracy. He said he will hurt me if you don't come now."

"Who?"

"Please. Come now."

"Celia, if I go wake up Cord, he—"

"No. Tracy… he… I have a baby."

I knew she did. "Okay. I'm coming right now."

"Just you, no Cord."

"Got it."

"The man with you, just do what he says."

"I will."

"He says nothing will happen to me if you follow directions."

"Okay," I said, after taking a breath. "So he's right there talking to you?"

"Yes, he is, and I've been told to hang up. I'll see you soon."

The line went dead, and I had a moment to imagine how terrified she must be. I turned to the man beside me, placing the phone in his outstretched hand. "So I guess I'm coming with you."

"No trouble? You're not gonna fight?"

I shook my head. "I promise."

He nodded and put his hand around my bicep and shoved his other hand, the one holding the gun, into his coat pocket. "Good."

It was late, so there was no one at all on the road. Added to that was the temperature, right above freezing, and no one was out who didn't need to be. So there was no one out to witness us walking side by side out the front of the motel's parking lot.

Once on the sidewalk, we took a right, walked a half a mile down the road, and then took a left at the first stoplight. I could see the auto-body shop as soon as we made the turn.

"He told me to take you around to the back," the guy said as we closed in on the auto repair shop.

"Okay."

"And so you know, he promised he had no plans to hurt either you or the woman."

But that was lies. Hurt, torture, maybe not. Kill, yes. "He who?"

"Lucien Ritter."

I WAS an idiot. If I'd listened to clues, I would have figured it out. The man was a chemistry teacher; he could have figured out how to mix up a batch of C4. And Cord had said that the chief was starting to vet people to help them with surveillance, he didn't say there were people already on the job. Lucien had lied to me… if only I had been listening closer. But Cord had all my attention, as I had his. It was why we were both caught off guard.

As I'd walked away from Cord instead of toward him, the action had felt both stupid and wrong. The only thing that kept me moving was my concern for Celia. I was freezing after just minutes outside, and trying to calculate how long it would take Cord to realize I wasn't in bed with him was problematic. Hopefully he'd miss me sooner rather than later. But if I was about to be shot in the head, time wasn't on my side.

When we reached the garage, we went around to the back, and I saw that the door was open. As we got close, Lucien stepped out from the shadows.

"Why are you doing this?" I asked him softly.

"I think you know," he said calmly before he turned, lifted the gun he was holding, and shot the guy who had brought me there in the head.

"Lucien!" I yelled. I turned to the fallen man but was stopped by both Lucien's order and the high-pitched scream from inside.

"He's dead," he snarled at me. "And the way I shot him—with the blowback—you shouldn't have gotten anything on you."

His concern was that I didn't have any blood on me?

"Who," I gasped, pointing at the fallen man, "is this?"

"No one," he told me. "He's nothing."

I stared at him, at Lucien, mouth open, not stunned or surprised, but simply unsure who he was. This was not the same man I'd spoken to over lunch; he was completely altered in both thought and deed. The man I'd met would hurt no one.

The scream from inside repeated.

"You better get in there," Lucien said calmly, the murder weapon trained on me. "I think Celia thinks I killed you."

"And if I say no?"

"That's not an option for you," he replied simply.

Exhaling sharply, I took a good look at him. The man did not look like himself. His pupils were fully dilated, and he was sweating.

"After you," I said softly.

"Oh no," he sighed, gesturing toward the door with the gun. I knew what it was; I had seen a Glock up close—both my brother's and Cord's. "You first."

He waited silently for me to make my decision. As soon as I stepped through the door, I saw Celia on the other side of the shop bay standing beside a Volkswagen Bug. Rushing to her side, I cupped her face in my hands.

"Are you all right?"

"Yes," she whimpered, and I saw clearly that she had been crying. I was surprised when she brushed my hands away and lunged at me, grabbing me tight.

"It's okay," I promised. "You're gonna be okay."

She nodded frantically. "I thought I heard a shot—I thought he killed you."

"You did hear a shot."

She clutched tighter, the information scary, I knew because it was for me as well.

After a moment I turned to face Lucien, nudging Celia behind me. "What's going on?" I asked him.

"I think you know," he repeated, still holding the gun on me, lifted now to chest level.

"I don't."

He huffed out a breath. "About six months ago, I started looking for Breckin."

"Why?"

"Because it was finally time."

"I don't understand," I prodded him. "Help me understand."

"He took Turi away from me."

And that fast, everything made sense. "You blamed Breckin."

"Of course," he said flatly. "It was his fault, after all."

Celia slid her hands over my back and grasped my jacket.

"Why did it take you so long?"

"What do you mean?"

It was imperative that I keep him talking—the longer the better. I needed to give Cord time to wake up and find me. "I mean," I said, clearing my throat, "why did it take so long for you to go after Breckin?"

"To exact my revenge, you mean."

"Yes."

"I tried for so long to let it go, to get over it, to be okay."

"But you just couldn't."

"That's right. It was like the first thing I thought about in the morning and the last before I went to bed. It was always there, in the back of my head, playing like a movie on an endless loop," he said, his breath catching. "It was like being slowly suffocated, and no amount of trying to forget about it, trying to be normal, helped."

"So finally you gave in."

"Yes," he confirmed. "I've been watching Breckin for six months."

I nodded. "You killed Tim Stanson?"

"Yes. He told me he was going to tell Breckin that I came to ask him questions. He said it was the right thing to do."

I stayed quiet.

"But he was wrong obviously. He could have just promised to keep his mouth shut, but he wanted to argue with me instead." He was so calm that it was chilling. "Foolish."

"And so what?" I asked, drawing out more of the story. "You saw me and Breckin together?"

"Yes," he said, smiling suddenly. "And I was jealous, of course, because, really, he replaced Turi with you."

That was hard to hear even though, in retrospect, with my new knowledge, I was certain that it was probably true. The reason Breckin had responded to me the way he had was because I reminded him of his first love, his dead lover. Everything clicked into place.

"But I was going to walk away. I was. Tim was collateral damage of looking for him, of course, but Breckin... I was going to forgive."

I understood what had happened next.

"He looked so happy, and so did you...."

And I had been. Deluded, but happy, and I was glad I had been woken up. I just wished it had not happened as it had. I wished Breckin had just told me the whole thing: that I had made him remember someone from his past. That he wasn't in love with me, but instead with someone who looked like me.

"But then he cheated," he rasped, inhaling sharply. "And I didn't understand. It made no sense to me. I mean, Breckin's gay."

"He's not," I clarified. "He's bi, and as such, he loves women too."

"No."

"Yes," I insisted. "You can't make him something he's not. He was as attracted to Celia as he was to me. Just because you're not bi doesn't make that true for him."

"But he loved Turi."

"I suspect you're the one who loved Turi," I said flatly. "I can't speak for Breckin."

He shook his head. "Whatever the case, he killed Turi, and now I'm going to kill what he loves—you and his child."

"But—"

"Shut up!" he roared, striding toward us, gun raised, ready to kill me.

"Didn't Turi kill himself?" I asked because I needed to give Cord more time to find me. I knew he was looking; I had been gone too long. He would have woken and called out for me and when I didn't answer, he would have gotten up. When he tried to call me and found my phone still there in the room with him that would have tipped him off that something was really wrong. He was a cop—he had a cop's instincts. I prayed I was right.

"I told you the story," he snarled at me, unhinged that fast. "Breckin left him behind, and Turi lost hope."

"No. Turi lost hope before Breckin left town. He killed himself because Breckin told him he wasn't taking him with him. That's what you told me."

"Yes, but—"

"So isn't it actually your fault?" I asked him. "I mean, if Turi knew you loved him, why wouldn't he have lived for you?"

"No. It was Breckin—Breckin and Turi's parents who didn't give a fuck about him."

It hit me then. "You killed Turi's parents."

He nodded. "They had no brakes when they hit that patch of ice."

Jesus.

"All I wanted was to live my happily ever after with Turi, but Breckin took that from me, and now I'll take from him. He's been living on borrowed time."

"Why can't you just walk away?" I asked him.

"Because Breckin needs to be punished," he explained as though it was logical. "He can't just go on having a happy life. I mean, I know he doesn't get to have you anymore. It's obvious you're in love with the policeman, but why does he get to have a baby? Why does he get to have a practice? Why does he never have to pay for Turi?"

"Because it was Turi's choice," I maintained, imploring him to listen to reason. "Breckin has made mistakes, but do you truly believe that was one of them?"

"I do," he confirmed, sounding apologetic. "I was happy when Turi was alive. I was different. It's like how you were happy before he cheated on you, but now you're not."

"I am very happy with how things turned out," I said honestly, thinking of Cord. "And if I can be happy, so can you, Lucien." And it would have been true before Tim Stanson. But maybe years from now, when he got out of prison…. "There can be a new life for you. I'm sure of it."

"I tried," he said tiredly. "I did. But there's nothing left, Tracy, and I'm sorry about that."

"Why are you sorry?"

"Because I wish I had met you before Breckin did."

I smiled at him. "But you would have only seen Turi in me too. Cord's the only one who just sees me."

"I hope he can forgive me."

"Please," I pleaded with him, wondering where the hell Cord was at the same time. "Don't hurt me. Don't hurt Celia."

"No one walks away," he assured me, suddenly yelling. "Breckin needs to pay for Turi! He destroyed him! He destroyed me!"

"Turi took his own life," I argued quietly, trying to lower his volume by speaking softly. "He made the choice, no one else."

"He was only eighteen! What the fuck did he know about the rest of his life? He had no idea he could ever get over Breckin Alcott."

"You were his friend. Why didn't you tell him you were there for him?"

"I couldn't!"

"Because you were scared he'd reject you."

"He wanted Breckin!" he screamed at me. "Breckin was his shot!"

"Turi needed to be his own shot." Trying to speak softly was hard because I was terrified. My voice kept coming out as a raspy whisper.

He took a deep, settling breath as he lifted the gun. "You're right. Logically I know that, but my heart will never agree," he said calmly. "So let's see how Breckin likes losing his love and his baby."

"Freeze!"

Oh thank God.

"Drop the weapon!"

The relief was so overwhelming that for a moment, I thought I was going to do a face-plant on the floor.

I heard the shot, like a pop, and stood there, frozen, before I heard another shot, and Lucien screamed as he went down.

Standing there, as the man was buried under three policemen, I was startled when Cord suddenly appeared in front of me, holstered his gun, and ran his hands frantically over me.

"Honey, are you hurt? He shot at you point-blank."

But I wasn't hurt, and when Cord grabbed me and hugged me, almost too tight, squeezing the breath out of me, I had enough presence of mind to ask him to check on Celia.

He manhandled her, spinning her in his hands, checking everywhere, and when she smiled at me before she fainted, I knew we were both okay.

"So he missed," I said to the man I loved as he held Celia in his arms.

"Yes," he agreed, and then his mouth dropped open.

"What?"

He reached out and touched the collar of my leather jacket. When I turned my head, I noticed when he pulled on it that right above a riveted snap was a perfectly round hole.

"Motherfucker," I groaned, turning my gaze back on his face. "This is my favorite jacket."

The muscles in Cord's jaw clenched.

"Awww c'mon, that was funny," I teased him as Lucien was dragged to his feet. "Give me a kiss."

He looked like he wanted to punch me out.

I puckered up. "Please, baby."

He didn't move.

"Because I'm not Breckin Alcott's love. I'm yours."

I got one for that.

THE CHIEF and two of his deputies met me, Cord, and Celia at the hospital. I was fine, but we had to make sure she was okay. Plus the fact that the woman did not want to let go of my hand. She was certain I had saved her life. And even though I knew it was crap, she assured everyone who asked that I was a hero.

Breckin and his family arrived, and I was pleased to see him go right to Celia. I was an afterthought, and I found that fitting. When he finally checked on me, all he got for his trouble was Cord in his face, so he retreated quickly. I watched my savior fume as he paced in front of me, me sitting in one chair, my feet on another.

"Why don't you come hold my hand," I suggested.

"I should go over there and explain to Breckin's family that he cheated on you, and that's why they have a grandchild on the way."

I grunted.

"He's a piece of shit, and because of him, you were almost fuckin' killed!"

"That's one way to look at it," I agreed.

He pivoted to face me.

I shrugged. "Another is that Breckin cheated, showing me the kind of man he really is, and because of that I finally realized that the right guy was here the whole time."

Moving quickly, he took my face in his hands and kissed me, long and hard. I wrapped my hands around his wrists, and when he finally eased back, my eyes drifted open, and I smiled at him.

"You freaking out yet?" he questioned me.

"About us?"

"No," he said irritably, squinting. "Why would you be freaking out about that?"

Giving him something new to worry about was not a good idea. "I wouldn't be."

"Then why would you—"

"What were you going to ask?"

"Well, I was thinking that almost getting shot might have given you a slight scare."

I chuckled because his voice could not have been dripping with any more sarcasm if he tried. "No, not me, I'm a rock."

"Is that right," he said drolly.

"I am," I insisted, noticing how focused on me he was. "I swear."

He didn't seem convinced.

"I promise."

"Okay, fine. But after this, after we talk to the police, and after I talk to my captain again, you're going back to the motel. I'll go get our stuff from the Alcotts. We're not going back there."

"That sounds good," I consented, leaning forward.

He drew me close, and the solid strength of the man grounded me. I was working really hard not to lose it, but as my adrenaline waned, I started to shake. What I wanted to do was sit in his lap, but I burrowed against him instead.

As Cord mandated, I didn't go back to the Alcott house. Three hours later, he drove me to the motel, and even though I was barely coherent,

Cord put me in the shower. He brought me a large bottle of water, and I hydrated some more—I had drunk what seemed like a gallon at the hospital—before I collapsed in bed. I fell asleep with my head in Cord's lap as he talked on the phone.

I woke up because my phone was buzzing. I answered it blindly.

"Hello?"

"You are fine?"

Dimah. "Yeah. I should be home tomorrow, so I'll be at work the day after. What's today?"

"It is Thursday, but don't worry; you will be back when you're ready."

Something occurred to me even as fuzzy as I was. "How'd you know I was fine?"

"Danya told me."

I coughed. "You sent him here to watch over me?"

"*Da*. He and Vassi are both there."

"I haven't seen them."

"I should hope not."

"Well, you know, they kind of suck at their jobs," I told him, sitting up in bed, not happy to realize I was the only one in it. "I almost died tonight."

"No, you did not. Danya said that your inspector had everything under control."

"Oh, did he?"

"He said he found you with no difficulty. Danya stayed with him, Vassi trailed after you."

"He shot at me, you know. Lucien, the guy who was trying to kill me," I explained. "He shot at me."

"Vassi said he was poor shot."

I growled at him. "Tell Vassi I'm gonna kick his ass when I see him."

The low chuckle made me smile in spite of myself. "I will, *dorogoi*, I certainly will."

Clearing my throat, I finally got up the guts to ask, after so many years of friendship between us, what the Russian term meant.

"What?" he asked me.

"*Dorogoi.* What is that?"

"Dear," he said flatly. "It means dear."

"So," I hedged. "You like me a lot."

"*Da.*"

And that was all I needed to push further into his life. "We should hang out more once I get home. Like, you should come over, and we'll have dinner, and you can meet Cord. All right?"

"I would like that."

"It's long overdue."

"Agreed."

"First Saturday when I get home."

"I will hold you to this," he said hoarsely.

"You won't have to; I'll make sure it happens."

"Good."

And it would be.

WHEN THE door opened two hours later, Cord walked in with pepperoni pizza, a six-pack of Pepsi, and peach cobbler. If I hadn't been in love with him before, that would have sealed the deal.

"I'm gonna have Dimah over for dinner when we get home," I announced as we both sat down at the table.

"That sounds great," he said, grinning before he leaned sideways and kissed me.

I wanted that to keep going, but his stomach growled, so I pulled away. "Food first, then more fooling around," I announced.

"Definitely."

"Hey, what time is it?" I asked while we were both shoving pizza into our mouths.

He muttered something I missed over the chewing.

"One more time, Nolan."

"It's three in the afternoon."

"Oh shit, I lost a whole day."

"You were up until seven in the morning, so you needed the sleep," he informed me, reaching out to touch my cheek. "You were wiped out."

We ate more, and finally I asked him what was going to happen to Lucien.

"Well, first off, he'll be extradited back to California, and second he'll be evaluated to see if he's fit to stand trial or if he's too much of a whack job."

"What do you think?"

"I think he's good to go," he apprised me, passing me another napkin before placing two more slices of pizza on my paper plate. "I don't think there's any problem with his reasoning. He knows what he did and why. He killed Tim Stanson to cover his ass. That right there tells me he was very much aware of what he was doing. Mark my words, they are gonna lock Lucien Ritter up for the rest of his life."

My eyes flicked to his. "But if they don't, they'll tell me before they let him out, right?"

"Baby, if they let him out, you don't have to worry. I'll be right there with you."

I nodded.

"You trust me?"

"Absolutely."

He looked quite pleased. "Good."

"Do you know the name of the man who Lucien shot?"

"I do. His name's Michael Ivory, and he was a handyman here in town. Nice guy, from what everyone's told me. He just had some gambling debts that Lucien had been good enough to pay off for him in exchange for a favor to be named later."

"And tonight he called it in."

"Yes."

"Poor guy."

"Yes and no," Cord reasoned. "I mean, baby, come on."

"What?"

"No matter what someone does for you, you don't let them put a gun in your hand and agree to kidnap someone. This is not *The Godfather*, yeah? This is real life."

There was that.

"He had other choices besides doing exactly what Lucien Ritter asked of him."

"Yes."

"Running, going to the police," he said, listing them for me. "I mean, really, there are lots of alternatives to perpetrating a federal crime if you're a rational human being."

"Maybe he felt like he had no choice."

"I promise you, there is always a choice."

I was too tired to be logical. "Okay."

"Okay, Cord, you're right? Or okay, Cord, I'll do anything if you just shut the fuck up?"

"Both?" I smiled at him. "Somewhere between the two?"

"I'll take it," he soothed me.

"So," I began, "when can we leave?"

"Tomorrow morning. I already have the tickets."

I got up and tackle-hugged him, falling down into his lap.

"God," he groaned, and I felt a tremble run through his long, muscular frame. "Please don't let this change. Please like me this much when we get home."

But he didn't have to worry.

CHAPTER

Fourteen

CORD MOVED in with me, and his name went on the deed of my little house in Noe Valley. My bungalow that fit in with the other eclectic homes in the area, was, Cord promised, just what he'd always been looking for. So he happily took on the responsibility of the remaining twenty-six-year mortgage with me. I'd been paying on the loan for the house for four years on my own; it was nice to have help. At the same time he left the San Francisco Police Department and became the lead investigator for Stone Markham Wainwright. He had his own office and staff, and even Alex had to agree that life looked pretty good from the 26th floor. He told my father all about it at Sunday dinner. My dad loved having Cord there, I loved having Beth there, and Alex worked really hard at warming up to her. When Evan flew out the following weekend, I had to explain everything to him, which almost made me homicidal.

"Who's Lucien again?" he asked for the fifth time.

I rolled my head on the back of the couch and looked at Cord for help as he proceeded to choke on his beer.

"You should make flash cards," Alex singsonged under his breath. "He's a visual learner."

I took a breath and started again.

"So, are you guys gonna get married?" Evan asked my dad and Beth out of the blue.

Then it was her turn to choke.

Alex gently patted her back.

But it wasn't my father who was next: it was me. Cord came home a week before Christmas and got down on one knee. I almost tripped over him. I was making spaghetti for me, him, and Dimah a month after he moved in, and I needed mushrooms from the refrigerator. When I turned, Cord was there, on the floor, and I walked right into him.

"Cord, what are you—"

He held up the small black velvet box, and I went mute. "I want everything with you. A house, babies—all of it. So marry me, okay?"

All I could do was stare at him.

"Please, love."

And I loved him, there was no doubt, but did I trust him? The man had been the biggest manwhore in the history of ever. Could I trust him to be true?

"You know I'm good for the happily ever after, yeah? I'm your guy."

It was the little things that told me I could place my faith in him. The way he always had to stand close to me, in my space. How he tracked me with his eyes whenever we were out, and when I glanced up and met his stare, it was always heated and possessive. Mostly his hand in mine, all the time, walking, sitting, driving, whatever it was—he had to touch me, and that spoke of his need for me, to have me with him, close by, never beyond his reach.

He deserved my trust, and I would give it to him, along with my vow to love him and marry him and stand at his side. Forever.

"Trace?" he asked, his voice pitched low, worried, I was certain, over my silence.

"Yes," I said and put out my hand. He slid the heavy platinum band with a channel-set two-carat diamond onto my ring finger.

"And we're partners, fifty-fifty. I don't expect you to do more with the kids than me or more with the house. That's not what this is, and that's not who we are. We're the same, and I love that about us."

I did too. "I love you," I said as I tilted his head back for my kiss.

His deep, contented sigh was very sweet. "I love you back."

More words were unnecessary.

THE SPRING wedding, in March, was small and intimate. We tied the knot in my dad's backyard in Sausalito, overlooking the bay. Cord wore a brown tuxedo that made my tongue stick to the roof of my mouth, and I wore my black one.

"You're gorgeous," he husked when I was standing beside him in front of the minister.

All I could do was smile. No words were happening besides vows and "I do." Everything had happened so fast, and while I was happy to ride the whirlwind, it caught up with me while I stood there looking into the eyes of the man I loved.

"Just hold my hand," he whispered, leaning forward, his breath warm on the side of my face. "Don't let go."

I didn't ever plan to.

The reception followed immediately, and I was touched at how beautiful the house looked with all of Matt's thoughtful touches. There were branches in clear glass vases with floating candles on top, small white lights strung in every tree as well as decorative lanterns as centerpieces on each picnic table. There was a canopy of lights over the outdoor dance floor, and between the breeze outside, the flowing white-wine sangria, the small acoustic band, and my father's amazing food, it was wonderful. Everyone loved it, and I was so happy, Evan said I was glowing.

I'd been watching my brother the DEA agent meet Dimah, and it had been fun. They'd circled each other like sharks, but at the same time, having me in common drove them closer. Later I teased Alex about it as he and I sat quietly together out by the pool.

"Maybe Dimah does have a brother," he conceded.

"You're being recorded," I informed him.

"Shut up."

I chuckled, and he turned to meet my gaze.

"I'm sorry Cord's folks didn't show up."

"Yeah," I agreed.

"They love him, they just don't do the gay part," Alex said, explaining what I already knew. "He's their only child, so I'm sure they'll come around eventually."

"I hope so."

"But meanwhile he has us—our family. Now his."

"Yep."

He sighed deeply. "Fuck, I'm so glad this worked out."

"What do you mean?"

"Well, you and Cord, of course."

"I got that, but what're you talking about?"

"I'm just happy, is all."

I turned in my chair, wanting to see his face. "Speak."

He sighed deeply. "Look, I can't say for sure when it was that he first starting loving you, but I will say that it's been years. He carried it around, but he kept it to himself, and the absolute restraint he showed while you were with Breckin was really something. I couldn't have done it. I would have had to come clean."

"He knew I never would have believed him."

"Because you didn't trust him."

"No, I didn't."

"But now you do?"

"Yeah, now I do."

His smile was huge. "I'm glad the part of you that always wanted him finally kicked in."

I snorted. "I'm not sure that was it."

He reached out and tousled my hair. "But so you know, you should never concern yourself with wondering if he adores you or worships you or thinks about you or whatever, because there isn't a guy who could love you more than he does. You take up so much space in his head, and I have seen him carry that shit around, and now it's time for you to feel that same way about him."

"I do," I promised, staring at my brother, who I never thought would be talking to me like he was in that moment. "I love him and I'll take care of him, I swear."

"Good. You're my brother and he's my best friend, so this has to work or I'll be in a world of shit."

It was all about him, as usual. "Of course."

"Excellent," he said, looking very pleased with himself.

"Ask you a question?"

He grunted.

"How come you were okay with me and Cord being together?"

"I don't get what you mean. I just told you that he's my best friend and you're my—"

"No, I get that, but he was a dog, right? Why would you ever even trust him with me?"

"I didn't at first," he confessed. "When he first noticed you, I told him to forget it. I would have put a bullet in him myself if he got anywhere near you."

I couldn't keep from chuckling. "Oh yeah?"

His gaze locked with mine, and his tone was flat, serious. "Yeah."

"So what changed?"

He shrugged. "Cord did. He got serious. He became how he was with just me, with everyone. He went from being a manwhore to a stand-up guy."

"Explain."

"Well, like, I always knew he was dependable and loyal and all that, but no one else ever saw it—least of all you. He fucked around, was a big flake, and nobody trusted him."

I nodded.

"But then he turned it around. It was time to grow up, so he did."

Cord's transformation had been lost on me. I had completely missed it.

"And when I saw him making an effort to be a better guy, him wanting you became an okay thing."

"You could trust him with your brother."

"Yeah."

"Okay," I sighed. "I was just wondering, is all."

"You thought I wasn't protective."

"I just wondered."

"Well, I am," he apprised. "And you know better."

He was right, I really did.

SIX MONTHS later, we were still getting along, my stomach still flipped over when I saw him at the end of the day, and he still held my hand when we walked anywhere together. I was crossing the street with Cord on a

Saturday afternoon before we met Dimah for dinner out at a new place he wanted to try when he explained that my brother was coming along as well. Alex missed him, and I could understand that.

"I stole his best friend," I said, snickering.

Cord glared at me.

"What? It's true."

"Be nice."

"I invited Matt and Eric too," I informed my husband. He stopped moving suddenly in the middle of the sidewalk, looking absolutely sick. It was like he couldn't think of anything worse than spending time with my friends.

"Cord?" I was defensive.

It seemed like he was on the verge of puking.

Instantly I was upset. "Since when don't you like Matt and Eric?" I asked him pointedly, concerned that I had missed his apparent dislike of two of the most important people in my life. How did my husband not like my best friend?

I had thought we were all getting along amazingly well. Even better, we didn't have to go out clubbing anymore. Everyone, including Ira and Courtney as well as her friends, liked coming over to our place for dinner and game night. A lot of times the games were forgotten, and we all ended up just lounging around our house, talking, drinking, and cementing what I felt certain would be lifelong friendships. It was different with Cord. We didn't have *my* friends and *his* friends. We had *our* friends, and that was even better. Plus, I got to add my brother and my business partner permanently to the mix.

The most interesting thing about having Dimah in my friend circle was how well the DEA agent and the importer/exporter got along. The first time Alex told me that he and Dimah were hitting the bars together, alone, I nearly passed out.

"Why're you surprised?" Cord asked me. "I can't be his wingman anymore, so he needs a new one. Hot Russian guy with the killer accent is an excellent choice as a substitute."

I had stared at him like he had gone right out of his mind.

"What?"

"You think Dimah is hot?"

He squinted at me. "It's not a question of do I or don't I. Empirically speaking, he's gorgeous."

"What happened to 'Dimah's a bad guy, and none of us should go anywhere near him'?"

"I was wrong about him, and so was Alex. We know that now."

I had taken crap for years, and I was just supposed to let it go? How was that fair?

"It's not like we're wrong often."

The things you learned when you weren't even trying were astounding. But to find out that the mere suggestion that I had invited two of my oldest friends out to dinner with us that evening was upsetting him left me stunned.

"Cord, why—"

"Did you replace the couch?"

I was lost. "I'm sorry?"

"I remember you told me you came home and found Breckin fucking Sean Granger on the couch," he said, his gaze locked on mine. "Did you ever replace it?"

Was he serious? "That's what you're upset about?"

He nodded.

"Not our friends?"

He shook his head.

My smile was uncontrollable. "What precisely led you from thinking about Matt and Eric to the couch?"

"It just"—he coughed—"popped into my head, and I actually didn't even hear what else you were talking about."

I chuckled. "I see. Well, you'll be relieved to know that I replaced the couch the day after that happened. I got the one we have now from Ikea."

His relief was apparent. I was grabbed and kissed and hugged and finally tucked up against his side as we walked together up Telegraph Avenue in Berkeley toward Moe's Books. I was looking for a gift for Beth for her birthday, and she had shared a fondness for Elizabethan poets, so I was going to poke around and see what I could find.

"So," he began slowly, "I saw Breckin's wedding invitation on our refrigerator. Are we actually going to that?"

"Oh no, I just wanted to remember to call and congratulate him."

"And did you?"

"I didn't, but I don't have to now, because I ran into him last week when I was picking up Thai food from that place you like. He was coming out of the Italian restaurant across the street."

"You didn't tell me."

I shrugged. "It wasn't important. We talked for maybe ten minutes."

He arched an eyebrow and waited.

"What?"

"There's a reason you didn't tell me. I know you."

I sighed deeply, and his eyes widened almost comically.

"Are you kidding me?"

My groan was loud as I started walking away from him. He caught up easily and swung me around to face him. "He was with somebody else?"

I let my head fall back on my shoulders.

"Holy shit, Trace. Man or woman?"

"Man," I said to the sky, refusing to meet his gaze.

"So he's getting married in a month, he's got an infant son, and he's already sleeping around on Celia."

I made a disgusted noise in the back of my throat. It had been so embarrassing. Breckin had grabbed my arm and dragged me halfway down the street explaining that he and Celia had an understanding. He was allowed to sleep with men but no women. His bride-to-be was apparently quite accommodating.

"So what did you say?" Cord grilled me.

"I said we weren't going to the wedding."

"Did he hit on you?"

"No," I said, almost with a straight face, tipping my head forward. "He complimented me on my ring and asked how long we'd been married."

"He knew you were married to me?"

"Yes, dear."

"And did you tell him that it's already been six months?" He growled, taking my chin in his hand, making sure I was steadily meeting his gaze.

"Yes, I did."

His grunt was adorable. "I know he asked how it was going with me."

What Breckin Alcott had actually inquired about was how serious it was between me and Cord Nolan. I had explained about our plans to move into a bigger house since Cord had one of the senior partners at his firm beginning to work on an adoption for us.

"So it's serious, then," Breckin had concluded.

And it was. It had been from the start and would continue to be so, 'til death do us part. I was never giving Cord up, and amazingly, thankfully, he felt the same way about me. I thought I had been in love before, but it turned out I had no idea about anything until the day I finally opened my eyes to the possibility of me and him.

"What did you say?" Cord pried, his voice hoarse. He was fiercely territorial, and I had found that I loved how possessive he was.

My attention grabbed by his anxious tone, I took hold of Cord's Henley and tugged the man close. "I told him I love you and that we fuck like bunnies whenever we get a chance."

His smile was huge before he kissed me. "Yeah? You love me?"

"You know I do."

He was so smug. "Yeah, I know. And the bunny part was a nice touch."

Only he would think so, and that was why we worked. He got me and I got him. It was all we needed.

Change of Heart Series from MARY CALMES

http://www.dreamspinnerpress.com

A Matter of Time Series from MARY CALMES

http://www.dreamspinnerpress.com

Also by MARY CALMES

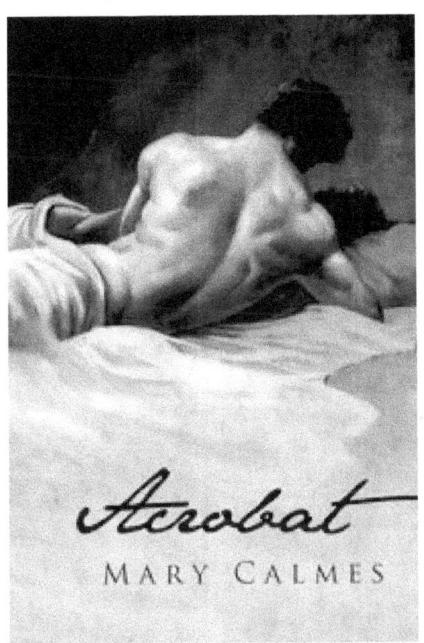

http://www.dreamspinnerpress.com

Also by MARY CALMES

http://www.dreamspinnerpress.com

The Warder Series by MARY CALMES

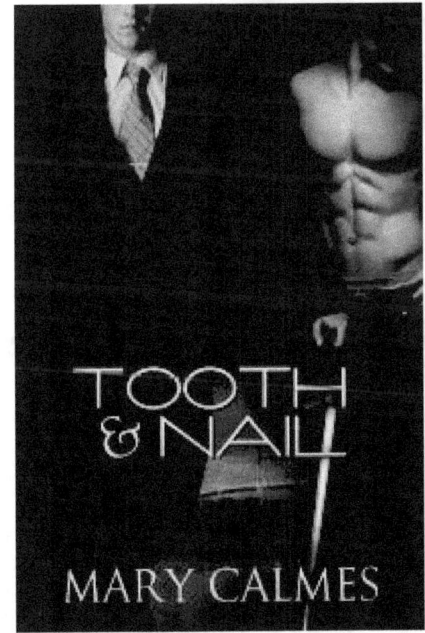

http://www.dreamspinnerpress.com

The Warder Series by MARY CALMES

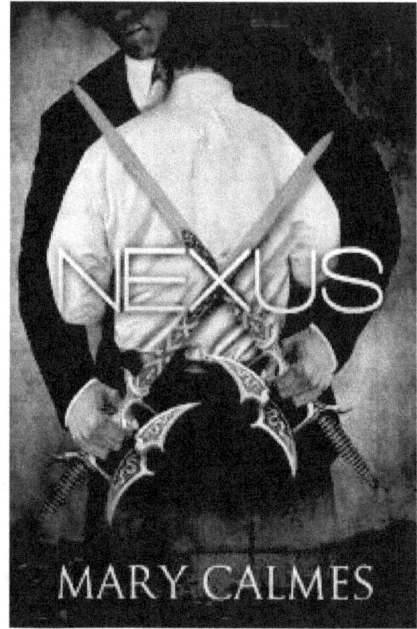

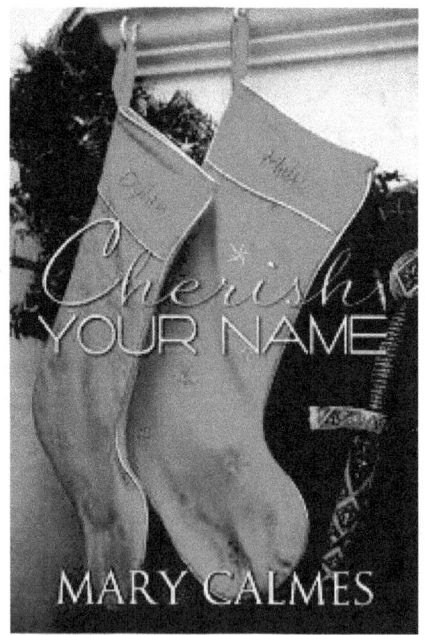

http://www.dreamspinnerpress.com

Also by MARY CALMES

http://www.dreamspinnerpress.com

Also by MARY CALMES

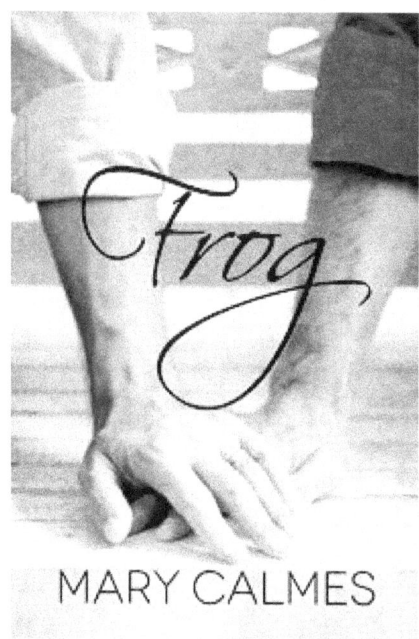

http://www.dreamspinnerpress.com

Also by MARY CALMES

http://www.dreamspinnerpress.com

www.ingramcontent.com/pod-product-compliance
Lightning Source LLC
Chambersburg PA
CBHW070105260626
47160CB00004B/1329